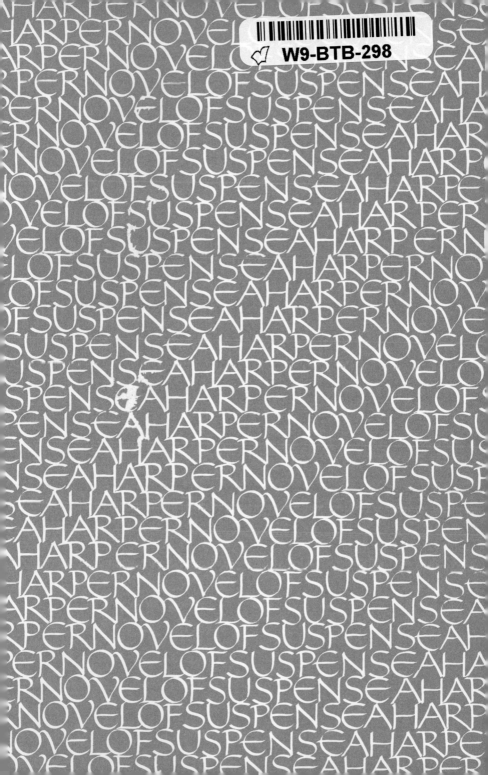

PAPER CHASE

Books by Lesley Egan

PAPER
CHASE

by Lesley Egan

1817

HARPER & ROW, PUBLISHERS

NEW YORK, EVANSTON, SAN FRANCISCO, LONDON

A JOAN KAHN–HARPER NOVEL OF SUSPENSE

FIRST EDITION

STANDARD BOOK NUMBER: 06-011158-5

LIBRARY OF CONGRESS CATALOG CARD NUMBER: 72-76244

BUTTERCUP: Things are seldom what they seem,
Skim milk masquerades as cream;
Highlows pass as patent leathers;
Jackdaws strut in peacock's feathers.

CAPTAIN   Very true,
(puzzled):   So they do.

—Gilbert and Sullivan,
H.M.S. Pinafore

And though she be but little, she is fierce.
—*A Midsummer Night's Dream*
(Act 3, scene 2)

1

JESSE WAS just about to take off early at five-thirty of this gray Friday, when Miss Williams bustled in with the Gorman will. He sat down to check it over and five minutes later buzzed her back in. "Miss Williams," said Jesse gently—she would probably faint if he ever called her Margaret—"you've left out an entire paragraph on the first page of this."

"Oh, *dear!*" said Miss Williams, looking ready to burst into tears. "I *have?* Oh, *dear,* what a nuisance. I'm terribly sorry, Mr. Falkenstein—"

"Yes, well, it'll have to be recopied. Mr. Gorman's coming in on Monday to sign it." Recopied, of course, in triplicate. But Jesse regarded Miss Williams in some surprise; as a legal secretary she had drawbacks, but she was a remarkably efficient typist. He'd never known her to make such a careless mistake.

"Oh, dear," said Miss Williams. Her long earnest face, innocent of all cosmetic but very pale pink lipstick, wore a distressed look. "Of all the annoying—I'll just have to come back this evening, I can't possibly Saturday, and—"

"You fussing about this Felton thing?" asked Jesse. "Really needn't—it'll come out O.K., if we have to bring suit. Told you that. No reason to fuss."

"Oh, *heavens,*" said Miss Williams, simply casting her eyes to heaven. *"That."* Four days ago, a drunken neighbor had smashed his car into Miss Williams' in front of her apartment house, and it seemed he'd had three accidents and three citations for drunk driving within the last two weeks, his insurance and license had been revoked, and the garage's estimate for repair on the car ran to eleven hundred bucks. "I'm not really, Mr. Falkenstein. It's just terrible, really I feel sorry for Mr. Felton, it's just since his wife died he's taken to drinking, but of course I couldn't afford—and eleven hundred, and all the payments still to—"

"Man owns a business," said Jesse. "We'll get the money, don't fuss. But this will, now—"

"Oh, how very annoying," said Miss Williams vexedly. She bit her lip. Jesse reflected idly that she wouldn't be at all bad-looking, smartened up a bit. Her dark hair in unfashionably tight curls, her pale-blue eyes unaccented, at the moment she looked rather like an earnest pony. "I can't imagine how I came to do such a thing. And the *first* page. I'll have to come back this evening, that's all. I *am* sorry, Mr. Falkenstein. I'll just run home and fix Mama's dinner and come right back. I couldn't possibly tomorrow, Sally's got to have her booster shot, and then the florist—all the flowers for Sunday at the— And I promised I'd pick up the programs, that dreadful printer—the last minute, and—"

"Well, doesn't matter as long as it's copied by Monday," said Jesse.

"Yes, of course. I'll come back tonight and do it," said Miss Williams, looking as nearly cross as he'd ever seen her.

He went out and punched the button for the elevator. Someday, he thought, he'd really have to gird up his loins and fire Miss Williams. Get a really trained legal secretary. Business had picked up a little over the last few months. Downstairs, he got into the Ford in the lot and started home. The sky looked threatening: this winter had been wet.

It had, in fact, started to rain by the time he got to the house

2

on Rockledge Road. He slid the Ford in beside Nell's car, shut the garage, and came in the back door to a succulent smell of pot roast.

"*More* rain," said Nell as he kissed her. "Yes, I'm fine. Only getting more enormous every day. Just like a hippo." The baby was due in April.

"You look fine to me," said Jesse. His lovely Nell, come to think also pretty unfashionable, her long brown hair never cut and in its usual big chignon—but his beautiful Nell even so. Athelstane the monster was sitting hopefully beside the stove where she was stirring something. They hadn't, of course, discovered that Athelstane was a mastiff until after they'd acquired him; and they'd bought this house chiefly because of the chain-link fence round the back yard.

"And Fran called—they've just got back."

"Oh, good. Where?"

"Well, her apartment, until they find a house. She's mad to start hunting." Nell laughed. "I will say for Fran, she doesn't do things by halves."

Jesse grinned, building himself a bourbon and water. Miss Frances Falkenstein, at length taking the bull by the horns last month, had finally annexed Sergeant Andrew Clock; they'd been married three weeks ago and set off for a honeymoon in Hawaii. Clock had said he couldn't possibly take off that long, and Fran had told him firmly he hadn't had a real vacation in years, he wasn't all that important to the Homicide office at headquarters. Fran usually got her way in the end.

"They're coming to dinner Sunday, and your father. And, Jesse, *what* do you suppose Edgar gave them?" asked Nell in awe. "That old—reprobate!"

Jesse grinned at the thought of their shrewd old maestro Edgar Walters. "What?"

"A service for twelve in *sterling*! What it must have cost— Well, I know he's got the money, but— Fran said she scolded him like anything, but he just said—"

"Can guess what he said. Said he tends these days to give people presents they can hock in case of necessity." Jesse laughed.

"Exactly. But of all the extravagances—"

"Um. He can afford it. I wish," said Jesse plaintively, "I had more guts."

"What for?"

"Enough to fire Miss Williams. Poor girl, sole support of a widowed mother, but—*A fool is not aware of his folly.* I wonder who Sally is. And May. Well, no more dithery than usual, I suppose, but—"

"Poor woman," said Nell. "Are you going to get the money to pay for her car?"

"Maybe with a little trouble. Man's good for it—we'll get it eventually."

He went to the office on Saturday morning to look over the statements on that damage suit; the court calendars being full, that probably wouldn't get to court until next month. Mr. William Gorman's will was neatly on his desk, recopied in triplicate, this time correctly. Miss Williams had done her overtime.

And on Sunday Fran and Clock turned up beaming at the Falkensteins' and Falkenstein senior, Fran moaning about five pounds gained and Clock telling her fondly she'd been too skinny anyway. And Hawaii had been fine, except for all the exotic rum drinks pressed on you, but it was good to be back. "The daily grind," he said, accepting a drink from Jesse. "The thankless job I picked. I wonder if the boys got that heist man."

"I had to fall for a cop," said Fran.

"Beauty and the beast," said Jesse, and Clock said with a grin, "More truth than poetry." He certainly couldn't claim any beauty prizes, Clock, with his Neanderthal jaw and heavy shoulders, and slim, small, svelte Fran could have doubled as a model instead of editor on that fashion magazine. But one good man, Clock; Fran would be safe with him.

"You can't imagine," said Fran luxuriously, "what bliss it is to have *no job*. Just the housework. But I'm starting right out house hunting on Monday." The Falkensteins regarded the Clocks benevolently: good to see them settled down together.

"And I also wonder," said Clock, "whether I win my bet with Pete. I haven't been seeing any papers. Has that psycho killed anybody yet?"

"What—oh, the Masked Monster," said Jesse. "Don't blame me for the name—what the media started calling him. I don't think so."

"Lay a bet he will," grunted Clock. "As I said to Pete. Robbery's baby right now, but I'll just bet that eventually he'll kill one of those women and land it right in my lap. And of all the shapeless cases to work— Well, I needn't borrow trouble." The Masked Monster had been around for a couple of months, and victimized a dozen women in that time: all women living alone, regularly or temporarily. His M.O. was depressingly simple: ring the doorbell, hold a gun on them. In every case he had forced the woman to drive his car to some isolated spot where he had beaten all of them severely, raped three of them, and then shoved them out of the car somewhere in downtown L.A. A couple of them had been injured seriously; one was still in the hospital.

The girls talked houses and furniture. Even as Jesse had before him, Clock said he vetoed only one area: the Valley. "Don't be silly, darling," said Fran. "Not so far away from Jesse and Nell. Somewhere around here, because of baby-sitting."

"What?" said Clock. Women jumped so.

"Baby-sitting. Us for Nell and Jesse, and of course later on—"

"My God," said Clock, "talk about being forehanded."

"She looks so frivolous," said Falkenstein senior. "Surprises you sometimes. Head screwed on tight, Andrew."

"I'm finding out," said Clock. "Same like the rest of the

family." And of course he hadn't had a family in years, and maybe he was enjoying the feeling.

Clock walked into Parker Center that Monday morning, a little late, with the grateful feeling of coming home. He had been wedded to his job before ever he met Fran. He surveyed the Homicide office as he came in, and it felt fine to be back—the office looking just as usual; he might never have been away. Petrovsky was on the phone, taking notes. Keene and Dale were typing reports, and Mantella just starting out the door. Homicide busy as usual.

"Andrew—good to have you back!" Petrovsky put the phone down, beaming at him. "But you ought to've brought home a better tan from the islands."

"In January? Be your age. So what've we got on hand?" Clock went into his office and sat down at his desk with a sigh of content. And he growled about the never-ending thankless job, but he'd be lost without it: it was his job. Mantella and Joe Lopez came in with Petrovsky, echoing his welcome.

"The usual slate," said Lopez. "Unidentified body in an alley off First. A mugger hitting a little too hard—senior citizen killed over in MacArthur Park. A suicide Johnny doesn't like—"

"Not one damn bit I don't," said Mantella. "Ordinary respectable young woman, three kids, everybody who knew her said it was impossible, she hadn't any reason, she'd never have done such a thing."

"But what evidence have you got?"

Mantella shurgged. "Nil. It's Boyd Street—a backwater—everybody away at work mostly. All the near neighbors. I think the husband did it, but there's nothing to say so."

"Note?" asked Clock.

"Oh, for God's—" Mantella said something pungent in Italian.

"In a kind of way, a note," said Petrovsky. "Across the mirror in the bedroom, in lipstick. Just *I can't go on.* Anybody could have—"

"Well, I'll be damned," said Clock. "That's a funny one, all right."

"There is also," said Lopez, "an A.P.B. out from Denver on this Gerald Eboe. On the run from a murder-first charge. He used to live in L.A. and probably has pals here. And that heist man pulled another last night—"

"The same boy we were looking for? You haven't—"

"Oh, a little progress," said Petrovsky. "We know who he is now. He pulled another three nights after you left us—we know it was him because Ballistics told us it was the same gun that killed Cameron at that liquor store. He didn't kill anybody on that job but he took a shot at the clerk when the clerk went for a gun, and the slugs matched. Then last week he pulled another and left us some nice latents on the cash register."

"One Henry Nadinger—six months out of Quentin," said Lopez. "There's an A.P.B. out on him. And then there is Reba Schultz."

"So tell me about Reba." Clock lit a cigarette.

Petrovsky leaned back with his eyes shut, smoking lazily. His round snub-nosed face looked obscurely angry. "Seventeen," he said. "Apartment on Virgil. Father a mailman. Mother works part time in a dress shop. And everybody says Reba a nice girl, well-raised, family goes to church, et cetera, et cetera. So Mama comes home from work last Saturday and finds Reba's slashed her wrists. She left a note—a nice genuine note, handwriting identified. She's pregnant, and the note says she's just too ashamed to live, and it was last November, some boys she didn't know dragged her into a car on her way home from school and raped her, only she didn't know that then because they forced her to take some pills and she was out. When she came to they let her out of the car and she was ashamed to tell anybody. Then. Only when she found out she was—"

"As Jesse would say, *The instruction of fools is folly*," said Clock. "What a— And I suppose she didn't give us anything useful like a description of said boys, or the car? Even a charge of accessory before—"

"Just one thing," said Petrovsky. "She put down that she didn't know the boys but she'd seen them around school and she thought one of them was named Jim."

"Oh, for God's sake," said Clock. "Well, we usually end up doing it the hard way, boys. Anything new gone down?"

"I was just going out to look at it," said Mantella. "And I don't know how but that son of Satan we'd like to get. Or those. The playful prankster tossing rocks off freeway overpasses. He just did it again, onto the Harbor Freeway. One woman killed instantly, the rock smashed through her windshield, and the car crashed into two others."

"Son of Satan is about right," said Clock. "I'll come with you on that." And of course there'd be nothing in the way of leads. There wasn't anything to say, on the half dozen such cases they'd had the last year, that it was the same X throwing rocks onto the freeways. A series of somebodies it could be, probably j.d.'s having the wanton fun.

He grumbled as they went down to the elevator; but he was glad to be back.

When Jesse got to the office on Monday morning at nine o'clock, to his surprise it was locked and empty. Miss Williams always arrived at eight-thirty on the dot, and had the mail opened and sorted by the time he came in. This morning he had Gorman coming in to sign the will, and a new client at ten-thirty; he'd be in court most of the afternoon with the continued Reynolds suit. He was annoyed, gathering up the mail from the basket on the door; really Miss Williams was getting more inefficient by the week, and he'd have to summon up the guts to fire her. Sole support of widowed parent be damned.

He was looking through the mail when the phone rang out

on her desk ten minutes later. He pushed the office button and picked it up. "Falkenstein."

"Oh, Mr. Falkenstein, I'm just as terribly sorry as I can be," said Miss Williams breathlessly, "but I can't come in this morning— It's an *extremely urgent* matter or I wouldn't dream of— But I simply *must* tell her and— I'll come in just as soon as I possibly can, it shouldn't take more than an hour. I'm terribly sorry—"

Jesse summoned resolution. "You know you're supposed to put in a full day's work. What I'm paying you for."

"I *know*, Mr. Falkenstein—" She sounded almost tearful. "I'm so terribly sorry, but I've got to—it's just terribly *important*—or of course I wouldn't—but I'll be in as soon as I *can*. It can't take more than an hour, I had to look up the address, it's West— I'll be there as soon as I can, Mr. Falkenstein! I don't ever take time off, do I, I'm never ill, and it's just part of the morning— I'm *sorry*, but I'll be in just as soon as I've done it." She breathed at him heavily for a moment and hung up.

"Women!" said Jesse. He was more annoyed at Miss Williams than he'd ever felt in the nearly nine years she'd been his secretary. Hanging out the new shingle, back then, he hadn't had much backlog and couldn't afford the salary a really trained legal secretary could demand, even that year of grace. But now —he'd got used to the woman, he supposed, putting up with her. An efficient typist at least. And possibly sorry for her. She tried, did Miss Williams. These days things were a bit different: he had a regular roster of clients, and the steady income from the legal guardianship of Harry Nielsen, since Mrs. Nielsen's death— That case had been a funny one, all right, involving him in the detective work again, which didn't appeal to him—and even with the house payments, and an ever pressing need to think about a new car, he could afford a more efficient secretary, and he ought to harden his heart and fire Miss Williams.

Only when it came to the point, with her anxious china-blue eyes on him and her breathless voice apologizing for something,

9

he wondered just where else Miss Williams could get hired. At what. Well, she tried her best, she muddled through things somehow, and oddly enough besides being the efficient typist she kept an excellent set of files. But he really should—

And it didn't make for such a good image for the new client, Falkenstein alone in a rather shabby office. Jesse swore. When the new client arrived at ten-thirty (no sign of Miss Williams yet) he told him casually that his secretary was home with flu, took notes himself. A rather complicated will, that was. There was no sign of Miss Williams up to noon when he left, forced to lock the office—and he wondered how many phone calls, and possible new clients, would go unanswered.

He was in court until four, and only went back to the office to see Miss Williams. By then he had worked himself up to the proper state of annoyance to feel quite capable of firing the woman without a qualm.

But as he rode up in the elevator, conscience reminded him that she was quite right about that, at least: in all the time he'd employed her he couldn't remember that she'd ever been out of the office for illness. She was punctual and willing, heaven knew: and the efficient typist.

She was also not there. The office was still locked. Jesse swore, his annoyance rising all over again. He went in. No sign that she'd ever been here today, her desk in the outer office tidy and unburdened. Jesse looked in the office directory, found her home phone number, and dialed. He was quite prepared to fire her over the phone, firmly turning a deaf ear to the voice of his conscience.

On the seventh buzz of the phone, he remembered that her mother was an invalid in a wheelchair—heart attack, stroke?—and being a little deaf never attempted to answer the phone.

Well. So said old Jeshu ben Shirah, *Answer not before thou hast heard the cause.*

Jesse went home and told Nell he would really have to get rid of that idiotic woman. "No, she didn't give any reason—just it was extremely urgent. Dithering at me. And she never showed at all. Damn it, it's just too much. I've put up with her, but—"

"But, Jesse, that's funny," said Nell. "She never came to the office all day? I know she dithers, poor thing, but she's never done that before, has she? Even when you've complained about her, you've always said at least she's conscientious. I wonder what—"

"That I've got to say," admitted Jesse. "It *is* funny. But I'm not curious enough to go see her and ask why. Doubtless be offered an involved explanation in the morning. Maybe Sally needed another booster shot." He finished his predinner drink, which he had needed.

"Who's Sally?"

"No idea."

He was to find out. At eight-thirty the phone rang, and he went down the hall to answer it, pursued by Athelstane, who was deeply curious about the mysterious voices inside. With Athelstane sitting on his feet and leaning his hundred and sixty-five pounds on him, he said, "Falkenstein."

"Oh, Mr. Falkenstein, this is Mrs. Hulby. You don't know me but I'm a neighbor of Mrs. Williams, Mrs. Hortense Williams— her daughter Margaret is your—and Mrs. Williams asked me to call you. She's worried, you see, and—well, did you ask Margaret to stay and do some overtime work? She always calls when she stays over—or comes home first to get Mrs. Williams' dinner —but she hasn't, and we—"

"What?" Jesse was startled. "You mean she hasn't been home today, Mrs.—"

"Why, of course not, she went off to work at the usual time. And she always lets her mother know if she has to stay overtime, and she hasn't called, and Mrs. Williams called me and we both—"

"Be damned," said Jesse. "Look, funny is no word. I'll come

round—I think I'd better talk to Mrs. Williams. Be there in twenty minutes." He collected his jacket and went to tell Nell.

"But that's—" said Nell. "Miss *Williams*? Vanishing? Dithery horse-faced Miss Williams? It's impossible, Jesse. There'll be some ordinary explanation."

"And I'd like to know just what," said Jesse.

Miss Williams and her widowed parent lived on Berendo Street, an old section of it near downtown. It was a small apartment house, perhaps sixteen units, two-storied: a narrow driveway down to a row of garages in back. The drive was empty: only one parking slot left in front.

The Williams apartment was upstairs, in front. When he shoved the bell push a buzzer sounded angrily and a dog barked sharply once, a rasping tenor bark. In thirty seconds the door opened.

"Mr. Falkenstein? I'm Mrs. Hulby." A plain middle-aged woman, graying hair, glasses. "Come in—this is Mrs. Williams. You *didn't* keep Margaret overtime? But—"

The dog barked again and the fat old woman in the wheelchair said, "You be quiet, Sally. But where *is* she, Mr. Falkenstein? We just can't understand—"

Jesse looked at Sally. Sally was a barrel-chested bowlegged black-and-tan Peke. She regarded Jesse with hostility and came to smell his shoes suspiciously.

"She didn't," said Jesse baldly, "come to work at all. Called and said she had something extremely urgent to do—said she'd probably be in in about an hour. She wasn't. Never showed up."

"Not at all? But what on earth— Oh, my heavens," gasped Mrs. Hulby, "what can have happened to her? Margaret of all people—so reliable, so—"

"Mrs. Williams? She tell you she wasn't coming right to the office? Tell you why?"

Mrs. Williams was in her seventies, heavy and white-haired; metal-rimmed glasses, obviously false teeth; her pale-blue eyes looked frightened. Slowly she shook her head. "She never said

12

a thing, Mr. Falkenstein. She just went off at the regular time, like always. She washed the breakfast dishes and got dressed for work and kissed me good-bye and— What? Well, I don't know, now I think back she seemed a mite worried, but I don't— Well, Margaret worries over a lot of little things, and of course she was upset about her car. That man Felton—all that money. She doesn't like the car the garage loaned her to drive—it's got what they call, I don't know, where you don't have to shift gears— I never drove a car, I couldn't say—but Margaret says it makes a car use a lot more gas, and she doesn't like it. But *where*—"

"Mr. Felton," said Mrs. Hulby, and clicked her tongue. "I guess you've got to feel sorry for him, but it's just awful, him going right off the rails like that—drinking—since his wife died. Always been quiet tenants, and now— But where *is* Margaret, Mr. Falkenstein? Where'd she *go*?"

"Good question," said Jesse. "She didn't say anything at all to you?" Mrs. Williams shook her head again. "But would she have?"

Mrs. Williams went on shaking her head numbly. "I'm not so well these days, don't get around so spry, like you see, Mr. Falkenstein. Margaret's a good girl, looking after me the way she does. A good girl. I daresay she'd've liked to get married, have her own home and family, but somehow she never had the chance. But she never complains—Margaret's a good dutiful girl. She thinks the world of you, you know—she looks up to you."

"She does?" Jesse was surprised.

"Oh, yes. And of course your being such good friends with that police officer too— Margaret was just so pleased about your sister getting married to him. She— But where *is* she? Where's she gone?"

"I think maybe," said Jesse, "we'd better ask the police to have a look." Because this was very funny: he didn't know anything about Margaret Williams' private life, but he could make an accurate guess, the kind you could set a clock by: the orderly routine exactly followed. He found the phone; he called Missing Persons downtown. The women watched him with frightened eyes, supplied information docilely. Margaret Williams, thirty-eight, five-five, a hundred and thirty, brown and blue, no marks: a plain beige shirtmaker dress, tan stockings, black pumps, beige camel hair coat, black felt hat, black patent handbag. They didn't know the plate number or the make of the loaner she'd been driving: get that from the garage tomorrow.

And that was all they could tell him. She'd left at the usual time and hadn't said a word about taking time off to do something "extremely urgent."

Which was very funny indeed.

Sally condescended to having her head patted after long examination of Jesse's shoes. He bestowed the pat as a polite gesture: he might have known Miss Williams would keep a silly little animal like a Peke.

He went home and told Nell it was funny. "Now where the hell is she? A dreep like Margaret Williams—"

Nell was sitting up in bed reading, with the monster ensconced on Jesse's side making whuffling noises in his sleep. "That is all very peculiar indeed, Jesse," said Nell. "Miss *Williams.* What on earth can have happened to her?"

"No remotest guess," said Jesse, unbuttoning his shirt. "I'll be interested to hear what she has to say tomorrow morning—if she shows up."

"Something extremely urgent," said Nell meditatively. "You know, I think it's more than funny, Jesse. I think something must have happened to her. Because she is conscientious. I mean—"

"Female intuition," said Jesse, yawning. "Wait and see."

He was never operating on all cylinders first thing in the morning, and was just out of bed, summoning the strength to shave and dress, when the phone rang and Nell called, "It's Andrew."

"Hell," said Jesse, and went down the hall in his pajamas. "So what do you want?" It was just ten past eight.

"You," said Clock. "I seem to recall your secretary's a Miss Margaret Williams? Thirtyish, medium size, dowdy dresser?"

"Yes—what the hell about her? She—"

"She's just," said Clock, "turned up dead. Apparently mugged as she came home last night, in the drive of the place where she lived. Purse rifled, bang on the head with the blunt instrument. We just got the call, I'm about to go look at it. If you'd—"

"What?" said Jesse, coming fully awake. "Mugged? But, Andrew— Well, I'd better be the one to break the news. Wait for me—I'll be there."

2

BY THE TIME Jesse got to the apartment house on Berendo, there was a little crowd and confusion. The body had been found by the first tenant leaving for work, Brenda Lightner; she had, said the uniformed patrolmen, gone to pieces and been taken to their apartment by her father. Five other tenants had appeared since and been asked to wait for the detectives. Four of them were standing meekly by looking shocked and a fifth man was protesting loudly that he'd be docked if he was late, he was sorry for the poor woman but he hadn't known her.

Clock and Petrovsky were contemplating the scene; Clock gave Jesse a rundown tersely. "But my God, Andrew, what happened to her? She—"

"Kind of thing happens these days. Mugger waiting for people coming home late. Funny it should be your secretary."

"It's funnier than that," said Jesse. "She pulled a vanishing act yesterday," and he told them about that. "Can't begin to get it across to you just how funny that was, Andrew. For Miss Williams. The set routine, year in, year out. That kind. If she'd all of a sudden started wearing scarlet lipstick and calling me dearie, couldn't have surprised me more. Where the hell did she go, and why?"

"I'll be damned," said Clock. "But it needn't have one thing to do with this, Jesse. This looks—ordinary. The mugger, period." They looked at the scene: the scene showing the silent traces of wanton violence.

The loaner car the garage had given Miss Williams was a two-year-old white Chevy four-door. It was halfway down the driveway, just opposite the apartment front. The uniformed men would know better than to touch the car; Clock peered in the driver's window. "Hand brake on, ignition off, keys in, lights off," he reported. "X attracted her attention, maybe he was in the drive and she had to stop." The passenger's door was open and the pathetic corpse of Miss Williams was sprawled untidily on that side of the car, half on the drive, partly on the brownish lawn in front of the apartment. It was again a very dark overcast day, dawn had come reluctant, and after four hours' cessation it had started to rain again, thinly; not surprising that nobody had spotted her until the Lightner girl left the apartment. She was prone and ungainly there, in her sodden camel hair coat: and obvious even to a layman was the violent dent in the dowdy black felt hat, at the back of the skull.

Jesse felt pity and a curious guilt. "Poor damn woman. She dithered, but she tried, Andrew. Did her best. And I don't suppose she had over ten bucks on her."

"The muggings get done for peanuts," said Petrovsky sadly.

The black patent handbag lay beside her, open: a handkerchief, a comb, and an old-fashioned double-sided coin purse spilled out of it. That was also open and empty except for a few coins.

"Damn it," said Jesse. "Suppose I'd better break the news to her mother. And what's going to become of her?" He looked up; a lab truck was turning in the drive. "And listen—I left here about nine-thirty last night, so it was after that."

"Thanks very much, that may be helpful," said Clock. He was standing there smoking, he and Petrovsky just looking. Now he said suddenly, "There are a couple of things I might wonder about, Pete."

"Oh, so am I," said Petrovsky. "X forced her to stop? By jumping out in front of the car? She still intended to drive on to the garage at the back, why'd she cut the lights and ignition and set the brake?"

"The passenger's side," said Clock. "He attacked her from the driver's side, getting that door open, and she scrambled away from him out the other door?"

"If you ask an opinion," said Jesse, "I'd say ninety-nine out of a hundred women driving alone at night'd keep the doors locked."

"And I'd agree with you," said Clock.

"I still say, what the hell happened to her yesterday? Because—"

Clock dropped his cigarette and stepped on it. "Pete, if the lab team's feeling zealous you can point out that that's my litter, not X's. Turn 'em loose—the works—and see if any of these neighbors know anything. I'd better help break the bad news."

A few more people were coming out on front porches along the block now, seeing some excitement going on. Inside the apartment's front door they found Mrs. Hulby and another middle-aged woman talking excitedly with a bald old man in an open door labeled *Manager.* "Oh, Mr. Falkenstein!" exclaimed Mrs. Hulby. "Is it *so*—it's Margaret Williams—*murdered* out there? My heavens! My husband came back and told me, a corpse"—evidently Hulby one of the waiting tenants "—but Mrs. Wolfe here saw the Lightners come in and Brenda was crying and saying—"

"It's Margaret Williams," said Jesse. He introduced Clock. The apartment manager was a John Shackleton. "You didn't hear from her after I left last night, or Mrs. Williams?"

They were all looking horrified, astonished, and inevitably excited at being involved in something out of the ordinary. "No —but my heavens," said Mrs. Hulby, "what's that poor woman going to do? She's just got the state pension, and she can't do much for herself. Oh, the Lord forgive me, I was feeling an-

18

noyed at Margaret last night, just going off like that— I had to help Mrs. Williams get to bed, and I looked in not an hour ago to get her up and dressed, and give her breakfast— Oh, I'd better come with you. Not that I relish the job, but that poor woman, she hadn't another relation in the world, and only the state—"

Jesse wasn't looking forward to it either; and damn it, he had to be in court at ten. Upstairs, he pushed the bell. Mrs. Hulby called, "It's me, Mrs. Williams—" and Sally uttered her sharp belligerent bark. After a wait the door opened, slowly, to show them the fat old woman in the wheelchair. "Oh, you poor dear, it's just terrible but we've got to tell you— This is a police officer, dear, and it seems—"

Sally dismissed Jesse with a recognizing sniff and started going over Clock's shoes carefully.

They were quiet and gentle, but evidently not enough; when it penetrated Mrs. Williams' mind what they were telling her, she turned greenish white and began to gasp for breath. "Margaret—Margaret's *dead*? You're—saying—" She slumped in the wheelchair.

"Oh, hell and damnation," said Clock. "That ambulance should be here— Maybe a heart attack or—" He took hold of her wrist, feeling for a pulse, and Sally promptly fastened her jaws in his left ankle. "Here, you little bastard, let go—"

The first ambulance was there then, the one called to take the body, and those attendants came on the double to deal with Mrs. Williams instead. They said possibly a stroke. Jesse had pulled Sally off Clock and when they started to get the old woman onto a stretcher, Sally attacked gamely, surprising the attendants. "For God's sake, it thinks it's a bloodhound," said one of them, and yanked her off his leg by the scruff of the neck, to drop her a second later, his hand streaming with blood.

"That dog's dangerous," said Mrs. Hulby. "I always said so. Oh, dear, I suppose she ought to have somebody with her—but they're just neighbors, I've got my breakfast dishes—"

Jesse said, "I'll be checking on her, Mrs. Hulby. Guess you've done all that could be expected." He had hold of Sally again; apparently Sally approved of him, remembering that the old woman had accepted him as friend last night. "And what the hell do we do with the dog? Er—Mrs. Hulby—"

"Oh, no," she said. "I don't like that dog and what's more she don't like me. That's a vicious dog, ask me."

"For God's sake," said Jesse.

"Don't look at me," said Clock. "She was your secretary."

"I've got to be in court at ten, damn it— Look, Andrew, you'll be in touch, let me know what shows up." He looked at his watch, putting Sally down. "What the hell am I going to do with you?" he asked her.

Sally studied the question and trotted away out of the room. When she came back she was carrying a leather leash. She dropped it at Jesse's feet.

"I will be damned. I never thought your kind had any brains." He fastened the leash to her collar and started downstairs. The lab men were busy taking photographs; there were quite a few people out now, staring, talking; Petrovsky talking to the little crowd of tenants, the uniformed men still there. The first ambulance had gone, another was just stopping at the curb.

Sally hopped into the Ford and Jesse started for home. "I only hope to God the monster doesn't make one mouthful of you. And what's to become of you eventually—" He caught the light at Third and Western, and as he sat there waiting for the green, suddenly all hell broke loose in the closed Ford. Jesse jumped and turned. In the lane beside him was a station wagon with two enormous Great Danes in the back. Sally was telling them at the top of her voice just what mayhem she'd commit if she could get at them.

It was twenty past nine when he got home. He looked in the back door. Nell was measuring flour into a sifter, and turned looking surprised. "What are you doing—what's *that*?"

"Miss Williams'," said Jesse economically. "Mother had a sei-

zure— carted off to hospital. This is Sally. Sally, this is a friend
—a *nice* lady. Nobody to bite. See? We're all on the same side.
Just take it easy with her, she won't bite you—maybe." He
handed Nell the leash and fled.

"For heaven's sake!" said Nell. Sally was investigating her
shoes with an air of deep suspicion.

By the time the lab team had gone, the second ambulance
with the body, the truck arriving to tow the Chevy in, and
Petrovsky came to join Clock in the Williams apartment, Clock
was looking a little dazed.

"Turn up anything interesting? There were just a couple of
things that make it look—maybe—not just the ordinary mugging."

"Ordinary," said Clock. "Ordinary woman, Jesse says to me.
The dreep Miss Williams. Now I'm wondering—whether it has
anything to do with the homicide or not—just where the hell
she was yesterday too. Some funny things here, Pete. Look." He
gestured. In this living room, otherwise an ordinary room for an
apartment of this vintage—old furniture, uninspired cheap
seascape on one wall, old-fashioned damask drapes—if the room
was neat and clean, were two walls of bookshelves. They were
neatly but solidly filled with books, about half and half hard
cover and paperback. Petrovsky walked over and looked at
titles.

"Oh," he said. "I can't read these things myself but I know a
few names. And all in alphabetical order, very nice. All the
mystery novels."

Clock steered him down a short cross hall to the second bedroom at the rear; the bathroom was between the two bedrooms.
The room was about fifteen by thirteen, and it contained more
bookshelves on two walls. Minimal space was left for a virginal
single studio couch made up as a bed, a three-drawer chest;
there was a walk-in closet. The shelves were filled with more
books, mostly more detective novels on the first shelves they

looked at. Along one bottom shelf were neatly ranged larger volumes: bound magazines. Clock pulled out one at random and opened the cover. An entire year's issues of *Master Detective.* "I'll be darned," said Petrovsky. "Never read any of that stuff either. The pulps."

There was a tall metal file case in one corner. Next to the chest of drawers was a student desk—about the only size that could be crammed in here. A straight chair was fitted neatly into the kneehole. Clock flicked open the top drawer. There was a loose sheaf of dime-store typewriter paper, maybe a hundred sheets. The top one read, in a very businesslike hand, KILLER AT LARGE, *by Margaret Williams.*

"For God's sake," said Petrovsky. "Ambitious to be a lady novelist, was she?"

Clock looked at the file case speculatively. "I suppose it'd be a waste of time to dust this place. Damn it, it looks like a run-of-the-mill mugging, Pete. God knows we get them, day in, day out. So who she was isn't important—what she'd been doing. Is it?"

Petrovsky said thoughtfully, "Looks. Sure. Just a couple of little things—maybe not important. I don't know, Andrew. That brother-in-law of yours sometimes sees things, and he said it was wild, her just taking off without asking. Where did she go and why, I wonder."

Clock went over and tried the top section of the file case. It was locked; but Petrovsky had her keys. The third one Clock tried fitted the lock. He opened the top drawer. It was fitted out with the usual alphabetized separators. Filed between them were letters and carbons of letters. The first few Clock picked out at random were signed by names he recognized vaguely: writers of mystery novels. The carbons all seemed to be copies of letters Miss Williams had written. Clock rummaged further and presently said in naked astonishment, "I will be damned!"

"Something?" asked Petrovsky interestedly.

Wordlessly Clock handed it to him. A letter on stiff bond

paper. The letterhead said *Federal Bureau of Investigation, Washington, D.C.* The letter was a neat production from an electric typewriter, addressed to Miss Margaret Williams at that address, and read: *Dear Miss Williams: Please accept my gratitude and that of my entire department for the quick wit and courage which enabled you to recognize the fugitive Raymond Wiles so readily and to act upon your knowledge. Such willingness to accept responsibility as a good citizen is most gratifying to those of us professionally engaged in investigative work. My congratulations and thanks.* The letter was signed *J. Edgar Hoover.*

"My God," said Petrovsky. "And look at this," he added a minute later, bending to peer at bookshelves. "Not the fiction here, this whole section. The true-crime stuff, old trials, history of criminal investigation. Even the textbooks—"

"What?" said Clock inattentively. He was still rummaging in the file case.

"She was a police buff," said Petrovsky, sounding surprised and amused at once. "Look at this—latest textbooks on fingerprinting and ballistics, yet. Handguns. That book of Jack Webb's. *The Art of Detection.* I'll be—"

Clock turned. "That you can say. With a vengeance, it seems." He had a couple of papers in his hand; he held out a blue-tinted half sheet. "Know anything about this outfit?"

"Mystery Writers, Incorporated. Nope. Suppose some association of pro writers." The sheet was a receipt for one year's dues, twenty bucks, made out to Margaret Williams. "That's funny. If she hadn't had anything published yet—"

"This is also funny," said Clock. He handed over the other sheet. It was another letter: the letterhead, in overlarge print, said ALEC TOOMEY, an address in Bel Air. The letter was without salutation, and had been scrawled, apparently in some passion, untidily in large writing. *I hope to hell you're satisfied, you damn old-maid meddler! Can't produce anything yourself*

so you have to tear down anybody who's had any success!
——— *you!* There was no signature.

"And what do you suppose that's all about?" said Petrovsky. "A plain mugging, Andrew? Falkenstein saying an ordinary dreep of a woman? And all this—"

"Well, he seems to've been wrong there," said Clock. "Seems she was a little more—complex a female than she looked on the surface, doesn't it? And damn it, is that important? A mugging? I think we ask the doctor and the lab to do some careful looking on this one, Pete."

"So do I. With everything else we've got on hand, maybe a real mystery now."

Clock called Jesse's office at five o'clock. "Some interesting things have showed. You busy?"

"Not for the next hour. And I'm sorry as hell, Andrew, but I'm going to have to borrow your bride."

"What?"

"Well, Nell doesn't type. I've tried three employment agencies and none of 'em can promise me a girl the rest of the week. And I've got four wills, a partnership contract, and at least ten letters that have to be got out by Friday. I called the apartment but Fran's out somewhere—"

"House hunting," said Clock. "Listen, she'll be furious, Jesse. She's on the nest-building kick."

"I can't help that," said Jesse, sounding annoyed. "The damn work's got to be done. When I think how I complained about that woman—What's turned up?"

"Tell you when I see you. Did you check the receiving hospital?"

"Soon as I got out of court. Mrs. Williams has had another stroke. Still unconscious, and the doctor doesn't hold out any hope that she can be questioned soon—or understand enough to answer questions ever. Time will tell, he said."

"Oh, hell. But you said she didn't know where the Williams

woman had gone yesterday anyway. Well, nothing says for certain that is important, but—you didn't tell me about Robert Felton and the accident to her car."

"What's that got to do with it?"

"I don't know that it's got anything to do with it," said Clock. "Look, I'll get hold of Fran—meet you at your place and we'll take the girls out to dinner. You're going to be damn surprised at some of what I've got to tell you."

"I am?"

"Ordinary dowd of a female, my foot," said Clock. "I'll see you."

Jesse looked up another employment agency in the yellow pages and phoned. Oh, a legal secretary, said the contralto he talked to. Well, she couldn't call to mind that they had an applicant on the books, but if he'd hold on— Yes, there was one. A Miss Susan Mills. What was the salary? The address?

Feeling more hopeful, and illogically missing Miss Williams, Jesse locked the office and headed home. It was still raining, a thin drizzle.

"You could have taken the creature to a boarding kennel," said Nell.

"Wasn't time to look one up. Besides, can't leave her at a place like that the rest of her life. Doesn't look as if Mrs. Williams'll be able to take care of a dog again. Why, she been a nuisance? I did wonder if the monster would make one mouthful of her. And we're going out to dinner with Fran and Andrew."

"What? For heaven's sake," said Nell, "I'll have to get dressed — So you can just feed that pair and see for yourself." She started out of the kitchen. "That creature. Five hours ago I was thinking toy dogs have delicate stomachs so I went out and got some ground round for her. It's in the refrigerator."

"Oh?" said Jesse. He went to look for the monster and Sally. Athelstane was sitting behind Jesse's armchair and Sally was on the couch. Athelstane came to welcome Jesse ecstatically, followed him back to the kitchen, and watched while Jesse heaped a large bowl with kibbled meal and chunks of stewing beef. The ground round, a minute portion, went into a small bowl; Jesse went to fetch Sally.

Athelstane was gobbling his dinner in the service porch. Sally smelled the ground round and sniffed audibly. She went over to Athelstane and barked at him. He backed off and Sally began to eat kibble and stewing beef. The monster slunk in to Jesse and complained.

Jesse shook his head and went to find a clean shirt. "Always thought those fool lapdogs were brainless," he said.

"So did I," said Nell. "Evidently we were wrong about Pekes, at least." She backed up to him and he zipped up her smartest maternity suit, the navy knit.

When the doorbell chimed and he went to let Clock and Fran in, Athelstane was behind the armchair again and Sally was on the couch licking her hairy chops. When she looked in his direction Athelstane retreated further behind the chair.

"I suppose," said Jesse doubtfully, "it's safe to leave them loose together?"

They went to Frascati's and Clock did most of the talking. "Well, I will be damned," said Jesse over coffee. "Come to think, her mother said something—about her looking up to me, I gather because I'm brother-in-law to an upstanding L.A.P.D. man. Police buff, our Margaret? The collection of detective novels, true crime—true police pulps. I'll be eternally—"

"Separate compartments," said Nell. "Don't people, sometimes? She wanted to write mystery fiction—tried to. Was your secretary meanwhile just for the eating money."

"But the funniest damn thing there," said Clock, "if you forget the letter from J. Edgar, was the letter from the chief of the Phoenix force. I can't make head or tail of that—I brought it along to show you."

26

Jesse held out his hand.

The letterhead, *City of Phoenix Police Department.* The date, early this month. Miss Margaret Williams, the address on Berendo Street. *Dear Miss Williams: I appreciate your letter of 12/25, calling my attention to "Crimefighters West." All you say in regard to fictional license and the public image of law enforcement is quite true, and on surface facts it would appear that there may be a case for a libel charge. In any case, my thanks for the carbon copies of your letters in regard to this matter, to Ace-Ames Productions, the board of directors of Weinstraub Corporation, and Messrs Toomey, Anderson, Selig, and Reilly. I have called the attention of our Mayor to this matter and will certainly keep you informed as to any appropriate action which may be decided upon. Sincerely yours.*

"What the hell?" said Jesse blankly.

"Just what I said. Your dowdy dreep of a secretary, the dithery Miss Williams," said Clock, "getting letters from J. Edgar and writing to police chiefs. And there was that letter from one Alec Toomey—at least on his stationery. Not exactly a threatening letter, but Mr. Toomey didn't like your Miss Williams. And—"

"That's a TV program, isn't it?" said Fran. She was bent over the letter with Nell. " 'Crimefighters West'? I've never looked at it, but it's Wednesday, I think, prime time."

"It is. I have. Once," said Nell, wrinkling her nose.

"So what about it?" asked Clock.

"The only thing I remember about it," said Nell, "—Jesse was out somewhere and I was just turning around to see what was on—the only thing I remember is that it seemed—old-fashioned."

"A TV show?" said Clock and Jesse together.

"Well, unrealistic, do I mean? It's a crime show—supposed to be police in action, you know. And one of the clues was a cigarette stub, and the supposed cops didn't even think to have the lab run a saliva test. I mean, even I know that much."

27

"Oh," said Jesse. He handed the letter back to Clock. "All very surprising and unexpected indeed, but do I infer you're having second thoughts on the plain mugging as our Margaret came home? From wherever she'd been?"

"I don't know," said Clock, looking annoyed. "Wait to see what the lab turns up—what the autopsy says. But one thing, Jesse—your dowdy mousy little Miss Williams was something more than you ever thought she was, in private life. And after I'd talked to Brenda Lightner—and then that Felton. Toomey — Well, it seems there were people who didn't like her. Actively didn't like her. There are people I want to talk to, in her address book."

"People," said Fran dreamily, "are funny. Surprising. You thought she was such an ordinary woman, Jesse—and look what shows up on her. Trying to write mysteries. Spotting a fugitive for the F.B.I. You really never do know about people. . . . Did you say that agency's sending you a new one?"

"Hope so."

"So do I. That place on Pinehurst would do—French colonial, and the rooms a good size. I want Andrew to see it. I don't feel much like coming in to do your typing, Jesse."

"Well, hope you won't have to."

The Falkensteins spent Tuesday night trying to convince Sally that their bed was not intended to be shared with a dog —even a dog that size. Sally was not disposed to pay attention. She spent the night curled in a ball on top of the electric blanket, and after cleaning up the ground round for breakfast, bounced out to join Athelstane in the back yard. When the meter reader came up the drive she threatened him with instant bloody mayhem, and the meter being inside the fence, Nell had to hold her while he accomplished his mission.

"It's the little ones you got to watch out for," said the meter reader nervously, backing out the gate. Athelstane was down at the end of the yard under the birch tree.

28

And there was the heist man, and Reba Schultz—though that would be a minor charge if they could identify those boys—if it would be gratifying to catch up to them—and the mugger in MacArthur Park—not a single lead there—and Mantella's questionable suicide which wasn't legally questionable. Homicide, Central Division, was usually busy, if not with the mysteries, which came along seldom. The probable j.d.s throwing rocks onto freeways—

"It just suddenly occurs to me," said Clock at eleven-thirty on Wednesday morning. "L.A. has another first to its credit, Pete."

"We have? What?"

"A new method of homicide. Throwing rocks onto freeways." Four people had died of the new method in the last year, cars traveling at a fair clip on freeways and the sudden rocks through windshields and canvas tops creating the crises. "Dubious distinction," said Clock.

The Masked Monster hadn't struck a new victim for nearly two weeks. Robbery's job; maybe eventually he'd kill, and make it Clock's job.

The various A.P.B.s had turned up nothing so far.

But just as Clock was thinking about lunch, the inside phone rang and he picked it up. "Homicide, Clock."

"A report I will send you up, Sergeant," said Dr. Van Vogt. "All nice and formal. But all the years I make the autopsies, too many, and all the worst of humanity we see, not?—it is the strangest thing ever I see. I say you will want to know at once. This corpse—a woman—yesterday she is brought in. Mugged?"

"Yes?" said Clock.

"To her I just now get," said Van Vogt. A place like L.A., bodies did pile up—mostly accidental homicides, suicides, the autopsies usually mandatory. "I have not yet done the autopsy. But I look at the corpse, and there is something in her mouth. Part way down the throat. A gag? I don't know, Sergeant, if or no. But I take it out. I look—there is naturally saliva, mucus—

29

but what is wadded up inside her mouth, down the throat, it is part of the cover of a periodical."

"A— What?" said Clock.

"A magazine. It is mutilated, and the saliva—but I have recovered it, I have it under glass perhaps for the laboratory. It is part of the cover of a magazine called *Master Detective*, a current issue, Sergeant."

Clock held the phone away and stared at it. "Now what the hell!" he said incredulously.

3

"SO THAT'S pretty definite," said Clock, relaying that to Petrovsky. "Not the mugging, with the random victim. But what a damn queer thing. A magazine cover—used as a gag? She wasn't tied up—"

"But set up to look like a mugging," said Petrovsky. "Wasn't it? Which just brings up more questions. A deliberate kill—a private, personal kill?"

Clock lit a cigarette pensively. "Well, by some of what we heard yesterday, there were people who didn't like her. Yes. Jesse's mousy secretary something else in private life. And I have a hunch we may come across a couple more—we still don't know what's behind that Phoenix bit. A TV show? That's wild. But by what the Lightner girl said—and Felton—"

"Yeah, and what's funny is that it doesn't seem she meddled, interfered out of any bossiness. And Felton—well, his own fault. But where there was Brenda, there could be others like that." They both thought about Brenda, and Robert Felton, talked to yesterday. Clock had passed that on to Jesse last night too. . . .

Brenda was eighteen, just out of high school last June and working her first job as a file clerk in a big office. She looked like a nice girl, pretty and auburn-haired: a very young eighteen.

She'd stopped crying by the time they talked to her, and her father wanted to stay, but he didn't know anything; after they'd talked to him a few minutes he left a little reluctantly. He was an accountant at Robinson's. And what Brenda had to tell them came out artlessly.

"It was just such a shock, finding her. Like that. Poor Miss Williams. Oh, well, we've lived here since my mother died when I was twelve, of course we know most of the other tenants, not awfully well, but most of them have been here ages too. But Miss Williams—I guess you could say I owed her a lot, just lately, and that was another reason I was upset."

"How's that, Miss Lightner?"

"Well"—she was twisting her hands together—"it's Daddy really. You see, with Mother being—being gone, he's—I guess you'd call it overprotective. He worries about me, and who I go on dates with, like that. I mean, a lot more than he might if there weren't just the two of us, you see? I *know* that, naturally, and lots of times he's made a fuss about some boy I dated for no reason at all, his hair was too long or he didn't wear ties— silly. You know? And he really raised a fuss about Dan Purcell. He lives just down the street, I just met him a couple of months ago, he seemed all right—he's awfully good-looking." She blushed a little. "And Daddy made a fuss. We argued some. I thought he was just being—the mother hen, you know."

"Your father disapproved of this Purcell? Why?" They were giving her time.

"Well, that's just it—I wouldn't listen to him because I thought he was being unfair. But, well—you see, there's a laundry room in the basement, and some machines— Not all the tenants use it, take the laundry out to a laundromat instead because it's cheaper, but I do sometimes, and a couple of weeks ago I was there when Miss Williams came in. She was nice, you know. Friendly, and about the only older woman I knew—well, not *older* exactly, sort of in between, not really old at all but older than me. Anyway, I'd had an argument with Daddy and

I—sort of blew off steam at her. About Dan. And she said some things that—well, made me think. Maybe not so different from what Daddy'd said, but you know, I—listened to her, because — About being careful who you picked up with, and all, and being sure about your friends. She said, in a city, anybody might be—well, anything, and—

"Well, it made me think. And I went and asked Mrs. Wolfe, and Mr. Shackleton—they've lived here for years and know everybody—and my goodness, they said Dan's been in jail for robbery! Just last year."

"So?"

"So I didn't want any more to do with him," said Brenda. "I told him so, next time he asked for a date. Yes, I told him why. He was mad, but— You see, I guess I listened to Miss Williams because she hadn't any—personal interest. In me."

When they went back to the office, Clock had asked R. and I. for Purcell's pedigree. He was only twenty-two but he had a j.d. record for petty theft and grand theft auto, an adult record of one charge, robbery from the person with violence, a one-to-three in Folsom. He'd done a year and was just off parole now.

Conceivably, they were thinking now, Purcell might have been sufficiently smitten with Brenda to have resented the interfering Miss Williams. Would ingenuous Brenda have mentioned her name? Probably. And he had a record of using violence. At any rate, there was Purcell.

There was also Robert Felton. They'd heard about him and Miss Williams' car from other tenants. Shackleton the manager said, shaking his head, "Awful pity to see a man go to pieces like that. They were steady tenants for nearly fifteen years, Sergeant. Quiet people. Mrs. Felton a nice lady. They didn't have a family, just the two of 'em, and I guess it was more than just her dying—she had cancer and she suffered a lot, poor lady. He just couldn't stand it, he said to me 'twasn't fair, she never did anything to deserve— And it was then he commenced to drink, see. After he'd been to see her at the hospital. And he's been worse since she died, acourse. That was a couple o' months back. He seemed to have the sense, up to a month or so ago, to stay home to get drunk—but like you know, last few weeks he'd go out in his car, drunk as a lord, and he had those accidents."

Felton had, of course, done more than ruin his own life with the drink; he'd brought money troubles on himself, inevitably. He owned a hardware store out on Vermont, a store solvent up to a couple of months ago. But he still owed the hospital; and the bite for a drunk driving charge in L.A. these days was five hundred bucks. The store was now mortgaged to pay his fines and bail, and he'd damaged two other cars besides Margaret Williams'.

When they'd talked to him yesterday, at his apartment, he'd been slightly drunk and belligerent. "Goddamn old maid," he said thickly. "Why the hell she had to leave her damn car practically across the drive? Nobody coulda helped hittin' it! Wasn't my fault, and I'd only had a couple— That damn woman, another pile o' money and that damn lawyer—"

Felton you could feel a little sorry for: not much. He was in his sixties, and everybody said it was obvious he'd never been a drinker before. The two clerks at his store said he'd always put in a full day there, six days a week; since Mrs. Felton's death he hadn't been in at all except to pocket the receipts and pay salaries.

But there was Felton. Petrovsky asked now, "Resenting her enough maybe, half drunk, to lie in wait for her?"

"But what about the magazine cover? That is the damndest queer— There are people we haven't talked to. Who may have known something about what she'd been doing lately. And I wonder a little harder where she was on Monday." She'd had an address book. . . . Yes, considering what Jesse had said—the efficient typist and file keeper—Clock thought that Miss Williams had been a much more organized and rational woman than she looked on the surface.

That letter from the Chief over in Phoenix had mentioned

carbons of letters to other people: Toomey, Anderson, Selig, Reilly; Ace-Ames Productions; and Weinstraub Corporation, would that be the big beer company? No such carbons in Miss Williams' files. Her own copies?

Mrs. Hulby had said vaguely the Williamses didn't entertain at all, had few people come to see them. She supposed Margaret had friends her own age she went to see; could recall seeing only one, a woman Margaret had introduced her to once, Wayland or some such name, maybe they'd go out together sometimes. There was a Martha Weglund in the address book.

Clock stared out to the communal detectives' office past his door without really seeing it. Mantella's suicide had been officially written off as suicide at an inquest this morning. A couple of new bodies had turned up and Mantella and Lopez were on those. They'd had a tip from a usually reliable pigeon that that Nadinger was renting a room over on Temple; Dale was staked out there. Keene and Lindner were typing reports.

Homicide didn't often get the mystery. The puzzle. But this looked like being one.

Clock sat up, removing his mind firmly from Fran, where it had as usual strayed, and told Sergeant Pitman on the desk to get him the lab. He got Winter.

"Have you got anything on that car—the Chevy towed in yesterday?"

"We've got nothing to do down here but Homicide's work. I'll check—I think Woods and Hartner are still on it." And after a hiatus Woods came on.

"We haven't finished dusting it, no. Tell you a few things. It was pretty clean. Nothing in the glove compartment but maps and Kleenex. It'd been washed fairly recently, and vacuumed."

"Have you dusted the wheel and dash?"

"Yep, first thing. Nil," said Woods. "The wheel's got only the vaguest smudges on it, I think the hand brake was wiped, and ditto the push buttons."

"Oh, you don't say," said Clock. "You don't say." That made

35

it definite. He thought back to the corpse. The handbag. There had been a pair of black cloth gloves in the bag; she hadn't been wearing them. "So now we know. Anything else in the car?"

"Just two things. Well, three. A pair of flat-heeled shoes on the floor in front, passenger's side. And a magazine on the floor in back." Well, thought Clock, didn't a lot of women change their shoes to drive? Ask Fran.

"What's the magazine?"

"Copy of the February issue of *Master Detective*," said Woods, "and about three-quarters of its front cover is missing."

Clock uttered a regrettable word.

But he thought Jesse would be interested in all this.

"For the thoughts of mortal men are miserable, and our devices are but uncertain," said Jesse bitterly to old Mr. Walters. "I criticized that woman, Edgar, I laughed at her—dithery Miss Williams—I've been saying for five years I'd have to fire her. Calling down judgment, my God. I tell you, I'd give a year of life to have her back. The efficient typist. My God, all this paper work piling up—"

The legal secretary the agency had promised him had turned up at nine-thirty. Miss Susan Mills. She was a blonde about twenty-five, very smartly dressed, and she had looked at Jesse and the office, asked about the salary and hours, in that order. And then she had said, "Oh, I couldn't possibly take on a one-girl office, Mr. Falkenstein, I wouldn't consider it. Too confining." And she had walked out five minutes after she'd walked in.

"Turned up her nose at you, hey?" said old Mr. Walters. He'd showed up about noon, with the inevitable bottle tucked in his breast pocket, and listened with interest to Jesse's tale of woe. But he was, their old maestro, much more interested in Miss Williams' sudden surprising end than Jesse's troubles. "If that isn't the funniest damn thing—and it couldn't have been just the random thing, now that Andrew's turned up all this funny background on her. I wonder if he's found out anything else."

"All very funny, and I'm with you there, but it's more immediate to get this damn paper work done. Yes, Miss Williams something more than I ever thought—and her dog, come to think. That's been a revelation. A *Peke.* I thought all these lapdogs—"

"Pekes not lapdogs," said the old man, adding a little bourbon to his drink. "Definitely no. Most of 'em seem to think they're police dogs. And stubborn as all hell they can be. Betty had one once. Lum Soo or some such silly name. Not a silly dog though. Brainy—and when that prowler broke in one night, that dog like to killed him, he was bleeding like a stuck pig when the cops carted him off. They call 'em lion dogs, y' know."

"I didn't know," said Jesse gloomily. "And Fran's off looking at houses, and Nell can't type. That other agency's supposed to call back by three—I hope to God they turn up somebody."

"*I* want to know more about this rigmarole," said the old man. He got his wish the next minute: Clock called and offered to meet them for lunch.

"All this might suggest something to you, I don't know. Well, I'm curious enough, I put in a call to the Chief over in Phoenix, but he's out on a search party—they've had a teen-age girl abducted— Expected back by four or so, they'll have him call me."

"Now that," said old Mr. Walters, his eyes glistening, "is the queerest damn clue I guess any detective ever came across, Andrew. The cover off the new *Master Detective!*"

"Most of it's queer," said Clock exasperatedly. "Your mousy Miss Williams—trying to write mystery stories. Spotting a wanted man for J. Edgar. Reading that kind of magazine."

Their old maestro laughed, finishing his sandwich and casually adding bourbon to his glass. He was undoubtedly a deplorable old fellow, fat, untidy, moustached Edgar Walters with cigar ashes on his vest and the perennial bottle in his pocket, but for all he was eighty-three nobody could consider him senile. "Never looked at any of those, Andrew? You'd be surprised. Those boys very hot on your side, boy, nothing but praise for the cops—law 'n' order. And you find some pretty good writing in them too, mostly. I guess it'd be the public relations department those writers'd deal with—any big force—so you wouldn't know. They run photos out of police files and all, nice straight reporting—good guys against bad guys."

"Is that so?" said Clock.

"And the best of 'em—*Official Detective, Master Detective, True Detective*—they'll run the interesting articles on important things. The narcotics, and parole systems, and sex crimes. Interesting stuff."

"Well, live and learn," said Clock, waving away the bottle.

"But all that—the magazine cover, and no prints on the wheel or brake—that makes it definite, hey? The personal, deliberate thing. A real mystery."

"Personal, yes. Deliberate—not if it was Felton. As it may well have been."

"Well, I think it's a little more complicated," said Mr. Walters stubbornly. "Seeing you've found out there were at least three people who had some reason to dislike the girl, you'll likely find more. And you know, whoever gets murdered usually has something to do with why, and I think it might be important to find out just where she was all day Monday."

"And just how the hell can we do that? I'd like to know, sure, but there's no possible way to trace her back—"

The old man poked Jesse. "We can try. Jesse, what exactly did she say when she phoned you Monday morning?"

Jesse sat up and finished his coffee. "Not much to suggest any leads. Said it was an extremely urgent matter. She had to tell. Presumably, tell somebody something. And it shouldn't take over an hour. Oh, and she'd had to look up the address, it was West—"

"West what?"

38

"That's all she said, she broke off there. Dithering."

"And she might've meant West Something Street, or West-wood, or West L.A., or whatever. Unprofitable," said Clock. "I've got to get back to work."

"And I hope to hell that agency—" Jesse started to slide out of the booth too. Mr. Walters regarded both of them disapprovingly and said young men were all pessimists these days.

Petrovsky chased down Martha Weglund by three o'clock. The address he had was that of an apartment in Hollywood, where the manageress told him Miss Weglund worked at a place down in Commerce. It turned out to be a big plastics manufacturer where Martha Weglund was general manager of the office.

She looked at his badge and said, "Oh, about Margaret. But I don't know what I could tell you—"

"Detective Petrovsky." He'd got used to the surprised looks; maybe people expected any Petrovsky to be the tall dark cossack type. She nodded and said they could talk in the employees' lounge, it'd be empty now, and led him down to a big square room with old comfortable furniture, a Coke machine, a cigarette machine. She looked like a sensible woman, about Miss Williams' age, sturdy medium-sized figure, dark hair, horn-rimmed glasses, not much makeup. And she offered him no How terribles or Isn't it awfuls.

"I couldn't believe it. Margaret, killed like that. And poor Mrs. Williams— I went to the hospital last night, she's still in a coma and the doctor isn't very hopeful." She shook her head. "But when it seems it was just a random criminal—"

"Well, maybe it wasn't, Miss Weglund. We just like to be thorough."

She looked startled. "You mean—"

"Well, if you'd just tell me—"

She was cooperative, if slightly bewildered at his interest. He got a lot of chaff, letting her talk, and maybe a few useful bits and pieces. Williams and Weglund had been at college together, U.C.L.A. "They say opposites attract but that was really on the surface, you know. Margaret—she was always a little shy, and she got flustered easily, but she had quite a good brain and she was a very efficient organizer, you know. Oh, it was for years she'd been interested in that—the police, police work. She'd always read mysteries, but mostly, the last years what they call the police-procedural ones. She listened to the police calls and —" They had spotted the little radio with the marine and police bands in her room. "Margaret—people underestimated her, you know," said Martha Weglund thoughtfully, "because she sounded so—lightweight and dithering. She wasn't like that at all, in herself. . . . Well, that dog. I suppose that's a good example." She lit a cigarette for herself before Petrovsky could reach for matches.

"The Peke?"

"That's right. It was Mrs. Enright's dog. Sally Enright. She was at college with us too. And she'd just got the dog, it was just a puppy, last year, when she was killed in an accident. Mr. Enright didn't want the dog, he gave it to Margaret. And Margaret said, Pekes, people always gave them outlandish names like Yum-Yum or Pitty Sing, it was silly—and she just named the dog for Sally. I suppose some people'd be shocked, but it was typical of Margaret."

"You don't say," said Petrovsky.

"She sounded silly sometimes. She wasn't," said Martha Weglund.

"Could you tell me anything about a letter from J. Edgar Hoover we found in—"

"Oh, that!" Miss Weglund smiled. "She was so very proud of herself over that. Yes, I can. She used to read all the true-detective magazines, you know—she said they were interesting. And you know—or maybe you don't—a couple of them usually run the police photographs of wanted men, off some F.B.I. list—"

40

"Ten Most Wanted?"

"Something like that. With descriptions and so on. And Margaret used to study them religiously— Well, I don't suppose it'd happen in a blue moon, any ordinary citizen having the luck to actually spot one of them, but she did. It was in a market, down on Vermont. This man's official photo had been in one of those magazines just that month, and Margaret recognized him, I guess he wasn't in disguise or anything. And she kept her head —you mightn't expect her to, but she did. I heard all about it, of course. The man was just shopping, with a cart, and so Margaret slipped out right away and called the police from a pay phone. Told them what it was, and they got a patrol car there by the time the man came out. I said how had she dared, it mightn't have been the right one at all, but she just said she was positive, and it was. The magazine paid her a hundred dollars reward, just imagine."

"Well," said Petrovsky. Little Miss Williams something more than she had looked, all right.

"She was good at organizing. Well, we both belong to the Southern California Professional Women's Club, and she was on the committee in charge of the reception this year. Last Sunday. But you aren't interested in that, excuse me. Whatever I—"

"We might be. What happened last Sunday?"

"What? Well, it was just the annual reception for the incoming president. A—party. We invited husbands and guests and there's a guest speaker and entertainment. May Foster was head of the committee, Margaret arranged for the flowers and corsages. It—"

"She was there?"

"Well, of course she was there. It was the usual jam, and the speaker wasn't very interesting, but—"

"Was that the last time you saw her?"

Her eyes saddened. "Yes, it was."

"Did she seem worried or—well, worried about anything?"

"Worried? What do you— Well, she'd been annoyed about her car, of course. That drunk ramming into it, and turning out to have no insurance. But she'd said Mr. Falkenstein—her employer, you know—had assured her they'd get the money to pay the repair bill."

"Did she tell you anything about her plans for the next day —Monday?"

"No, why would she? Just an ordinary workday."

"Ever mention a Brenda Lightner to you?" She shook her head. "Dan Purcell?"

"No. She wanted—so much—to write that kind of thing," she said irrelevantly. "She'd been trying for years. She never said much about it, but I knew. We'd go out to dinner together sometimes—break the monotony, you know?—and now and then I could tell she'd had something rejected again, she'd be so—determined to be cheerful. She even joined that club, whatever they call it—"

"Mystery Writers Incorporated?"

She nodded. "It's for professional writers, but they have what they call a nonvoting membership, which means people who haven't had anything published yet. She used to attend every meeting she could. Not, funnily enough, that she thought much of any of the people in the local group."

"Oh?" said Petrovsky.

"Well, most of the people in the local group aren't novelists, they're TV writers or screenwriters. Margaret—"

"Oh. Miss Weglund, would you happen to know anything about why Miss Williams happened to write a letter to the Chief of Police in Phoenix?"

She looked at him. "That. Oh, that was quite a thing, Mr. Petrovsky. Yes, I can tell you—"

"That goddamned meddling bitchy old maid!" said Alec Toomey. "Interfering! And just why the hell, in the first place —just because old maids have to meddle! And the hell of it was,

42

she was nobody. Nobody!" He hadn't asked Clock to sit down; he hadn't sat down himself. He hadn't asked Clock what the police interest was in Margaret Williams; the name had triggered his temper.

Clock had found Alec Toomey by the simple expedient of trying the Bel Air address on his stationery. It was a new, probably expensive apartment—a deeply carpeted long living room with a view toward the hills, violently modern furniture, a built-in bar at one end.

Toomey was thirtyish, balding, hawk-nosed, very nattily dressed in expensive sports clothes. He said bitterly, "Not that I'll ever *understand* it! She's *nobody*. This—this nothing of a little flat-chested old maid—trying, my God, to write detective novels—joining MWI to meet the real big pros—and, by God, having the gall to criticize writers like Jerry Selig and Rudy Anderson—and *me!*—and I'll never *understand* it, but stirring up all this goddamned mess— A nobody like that! Offer you a drink?" he asked abruptly.

"No thanks," said Clock. "We assumed you weren't loving her, Mr. Toomey. By your letter to her."

"What? Excuse me, I'll have a drink," said Toomey. "Letter? Oh, my God, I let her know how we feel about the goddamned mess. Wouldn't I? That series was worth a hundred grand a year to me, my friend, and I don't pretend I'm not damn sore about it. *Is* worth, I hope, I hope—if Jay can settle it with the sponsor. And how she *did* it, this nobody from nowhere, this little bitch —" He splashed whiskey into a glass, and ice rattled.

"You're not making sense, Mr. Toomey. What did Miss Williams do to you?"

Toomey swallowed Scotch, set the glass down on the bar, and looked at him. "You said you're a cop. Is that it? That letter I wrote her? She sicked you onto me?"

"Not exactly. What did she—"

"Then how come? By God, I wish somebody'd explain it to *me*," said Toomey angrily. "Everything hotsy-totsy, big sponsor, prime time, all the publicity, big names—well, one big name, Ray Dawson—and all of a sudden, boom. Canceled. My God, what that means in this business—Dawson under contract, kicking up a fuss—the producer—a hundred grand a year to me. And the other writers on it."

"Mr. Toomey—"

"Can I explain it to you, my God? Her meddling—why, who knows? We figured out, the letters— And this guy lands on Jay like a ton of bricks— What? Jay, Jay, the producer, Jay Wilmot. And *he*'s under contract to Ace-Ames— My God—this bloated old goat Reinhardt, with what he says is a P.R. man but, my God, like no P.R. man *I* ever knew—the *sponsor*, see? My God." He drank.

"I don't see. What are you—"

" 'Crimefighters West.' " Toomey laughed. "Sounds good. My God, the pilot cost— Another cop series, they're big these days with the viewers. So you get a format, get the scripts out, make a pilot, find a sponsor. Which represents the hell of a lot of work, if you don't know it, over about a year's time. In this business. Webb's got the L.A.P.D. sewed up, and there's that other big name on the Frisco P.D. series. O.K., we say, why not Phoenix? We dream up a format, sign the name, make the pilot. And we get Weinstraub for sponsor—big deal." He added more Scotch to his glass. "It's been running the whole season, my God. And now it all goes boom—and we've got all next season's episodes on film! Jesus H. Christ." He drank.

"Why?" asked Clock.

"Why? I should know why? Look, friend, what in hell's name I or Jerry or Rudy know about the fuzz? Who the hell cares? The series about the fuzz in action is big with the viewers right now —so write up the fuzz as good guys, the Sherlock bit with clues and gimmicks, it goes over. The noble boys in blue. I'm not Jack Webb, friend, or is Jerry or Rudy or— So do I know what the hassle's all about? All of a sudden, boom, canceled. The sponsor raising hell. That fat old bastard bleating about public images

— All I know is, if it doesn't get settled and we get back on the air, it's a hundred grand a year down the drain for me. All on account of that strictly-nothing little bitch meddling—"

"In your business."

"In my—" This wasn't the first drink Toomey had had today; his tongue slurred. "What the hell, the damn sponsor all fussed up, him and his square P.R. man—Beverly Hilton at forty bucks a night—"

The other agency sent a girl over at two o'clock. A Mrs. Angela Keller, slim and dark and shrewd-looking; probably older than she looked. Jesse asked her questions and found himself answering some.

"Oh," she said. "Just—well, I wouldn't consider it, a one-girl office, Mr. Falkenstein. Not for the salary."

Jesse wondered if he ought to start looking around for a partner. He went on dialing the apartment on Edgemont Avenue, and at three forty-five Fran answered.

"For heaven's sake, Jesse. I've got better things to do than—"

"*Man is born to labor,* so it says in Job. Damn it, the typing's got to get done, Fran."

"The papers talking about all this unemployment, I should think there'd be scads of efficient—"

"Don't seem to be. They all want a nice big office with half a dozen secretaries and stenos to be congenial with. And the electric typewriter is Greek to me. Family feeling I've got to plead. Yes, I've called two more agencies, got the double-talk. Old Testament says obedient woman worth more than rubies."

"I think you've got that quote wrong."

"And to think how I complained about our Margaret. *Mea culpa.* Eventually I hope to get a new secretary, but meanwhile—"

"Oh, all right. I'll come in. Andrew will not approve you monopolizing—"

"Desperate cases demand desperate remedies."

"I'll come in," said Fran crossly.

When she did, of course she got absorbed in the job (both Falkensteins had been raised in the tradition of anything-worth-doing-is-worth-doing-well) and when Jesse left at five-thirty she said she'd just finish up this will, if he'd call Andrew and explain where she was. He left her typing energetically and went home. It had stopped raining during the morning, but was starting to drizzle again.

"We'll have to do something about Sally, you know," said Nell. "Athelstane's getting a neurosis."

"Just treating her polite because she's a female," said Jesse.

"Because he's afraid of her. Be realistic, Jesse. You know what a softie he is. You've said yourself, kind to welcome any burglar with open paws. And Sally—a *toy* dog they call them, honestly! There was a peddler came by with a Seeing Eye dog, and if I hadn't had the screen door locked— She is a terror. She stole Athelstane's lunch and he brooded all afternoon. Out under the birch tree. Didn't Miss Williams have any bosom friends who might want Sally as a keepsake?"

"Well, we can ask Andrew." Jesse was making himself a drink.

"And I do wonder if it *can* be twins. I'm getting more enormous every—"

"Borrowing trouble." Jesse wandered into the living room. Athelstane came to welcome him with slurping tongue as he sat down; and Sally bustled over, barked at Athelstane, and climbed into Jesse's lap. Athelstane retreated, looking aggrieved.

"Listen," said Clock on the phone at seven-fifteen, "the idea was that Fran should stop being a career woman. Nine to five."

"My apologies. The paper work has to get done, and Nell doesn't type."

"Well, you'd better find a new secretary quick. And this TV

thing turns out to be quite a— Ramifications you can say. Involving money. Which is sometimes a factor in homicide. I've heard what the Chief over in Phoenix has to tell us. And Mr. Toomey. I've got an appointment to talk to a chairman of the board of Weinstraub, Incorporated, at the Beverly Hilton at eight o'clock. You like to come along and hear about the hornet's nest Margaret stirred up?"

"The beer company. I don't like beer," said Jesse. "A hornet's nest?"

"Well, it could be quite a something. Meet you in the lobby."

4

"I'm AFRAID I don't understand what the interest of the police is in a private business matter—" Mr. Bernard Reinhardt looked from Clock to Jesse perplexedly. "That is, Los Angeles police. Of course, anything we can do to oblige you, gentlemen—" He had let them in himself, to this plush suite high up in the Beverly Hilton, and added now, "This is Mr. Schwab. Sergeant—er —Clock? And Officer—" He looked at Jesse's lank height doubtfully.

"No," said Jesse laconically. "Lawyer, Mr. Reinhardt. Representing Miss Margaret Williams." Which he was, in a sense.

"Who?" Reinhardt looked even more at a loss, but Schwab nodded shortly once, and offered a hand to both Clock and Jesse. He was short and plump and dark, with shrewd dark eyes. Reinhardt was sixtyish, with a comfortable paunch, a thin showing of white hair. "In fact, I'm at a loss to know how the L.A. police—you *are?*—know anything about the matter—"

"It might tie up to a case we're working, sir," said Clock. "That's all I can say at the moment, but we'd be obliged if you'd give us the whole background."

"Do sit down. Can we offer you a drink? Er—Nat?"

Schwab was smiling faintly. "Private business matter now, maybe. Very damn public it probably will be. I suppose we don't ask what case or how. Well, no harm, Mr. Reinhardt. Nothing we need to apologize for. You said Williams—oh, yes."

"From the beginning," said Clock. "I gather this is something to do with the beer company—Weinstraub? And a TV—"

"I am chairman of the board of directors, yes," said Reinhardt. "Representing Weinstraub. Mr. Schwab is with Leopold and Kravitz—"

"Advertising management," said Schwab. "We handle a good many accounts. Big accounts. I'm assigned to Weinstraub. It was me got them involved with the series, you see. 'Crimefighters West.' "

"Now let's be fair, Nat. I passed on it. Wouldn't I? We both saw the pilot and three or four episodes already taped. We both passed on it. I have never," said Reinhardt agitatedly, "been so shocked in my life, we've never had such a thing happen, and I can only thank God you stipulated in the contract—" He sat back in his chair and wiped his forehead. "I'll say this. When Nat proposed this series as our new TV material I was pleased at the idea. A good many of us have been concerned with the current terrible problems, the crime rate, our young people, all these attacks on police—quite aside from the fact that this type of series is enjoying some popularity. I was glad to see Weinstraub sponsoring a series to promote the public image of our police. I liked the show—we both did—the idea of it being laid in Phoenix, a beautiful and interesting city, we felt it would go over. We liked it." And that sounded sincere; Jesse thought this was a plain and honest man.

"And I'll add this," said Schwab. "Hoary old joke about businessmen watching TV programs just to enjoy their own commercials—just a joke. We're all busy men. I hadn't watched the show at all."

"Neither had I," said Reinhardt.

"So it came as a little bolt from the blue when we got the letters of protest. Not many people take the trouble to write letters about that kind of thing, of course, and there weren't many. I don't know if the producer got any, or what kind. The ones we saw came to Weinstraub as the sponsor—the main office in Milwaukee. My outfit's based in New York. The one that triggered this off went direct to Mr. Reinhardt—not by name, just Chairman of the Board—marked Personal, and his secretary—"

"Well, actually the letter was opened by her secretary, but when she saw it, she thought the specific charges were grave enough to call to my attention. As they were," said Reinhardt. "Then I started an inquiry about any other complaints and eventually turned up a handful. But—"

"Letter from Miss Williams?" asked Jesse.

Schwab nodded shortly and produced a photostat from his inside pocket. "Of all of them, it was the most detailed and precise. Lists all the—relevant telecasts and details. Mr. Reinhardt contacted me, and of course we wanted to look into it."

"When was this?" asked Clock.

"Middle of last month. Everything stopped for the holidays, of course. We didn't get any satisfactory answers out of the producer—it's being actually filmed by Ace-Ames Productions, I should say has been filmed, they make a whole season's episodes before the thing is actually telecast, you know—we couldn't get any answers by phone. We landed out here to look into the matter three weeks back, and—well, there's been a row," said Schwab frankly. "A first-class A-number-one row, gentlemen. With reason. The series has been canceled, at least temporarily. We always stipulate in a contract that sponsorship may be withdrawn at any time. . . . Sure you won't have a drink?"

"I'll take you up," said Jesse, and Clock nodded shortly. One letter from Miss Williams . . . empire tottering, you could say, a prime-time telecast sponsored by as big an outfit as Weinstraub.

"I'll get them, you go on, Nat." Reinhardt got up.

"You needn't bother to read that in detail, Mr. Falkenstein," went on Schwab. "Most of the complaints about 'Crimefighters' don't mean much. I don't know who this woman is, but evidently she's familiar with actual police work. That kind of thing couldn't matter less, either to the sponsor or to us—that this fictional series purporting to show police in action isn't authentic in detail. I don't know what she's talking about, this Voiceprinter thing—and I wasn't aware that police used computers —but that doesn't matter. The general public doesn't know about such things either. What set us off were the specific charges. Cases where some really serious allegation— Well, about then we had, rather Mr. Reinhardt had, the letter from the city attorney of Phoenix—"

"Oh," said Jesse, accepting a glass from Reinhardt.

"Oh, my," said Schwab. "By then, of course, we had insisted that the producer run off these actual episodes for us. Mr. Reinhardt went straight up in the air and I wasn't far behind." He finished his own drink. "My God. There was one episode showing a plainclothes officer making a date with a prostitute— episode with another officer shown associating socially with a known criminal—another officer beating up a suspect without provocation—an officer drunk on duty—"

"For God's sake," said Clock. "Any modern city force— Oh, I see."

"Yes," said Schwab. "Not that either of us would have passed such obvious implications anyway, even when it's a purely fictional—just a TV program—but it's specifically laid in a real city and supposed to show a real police force in action. You can see all the ramifications. Well, in short, there was a row."

"And what's the situation now?" asked Clock.

"The series is canceled, as I said. We've been discussing with the producer and director, looking at the episodes already filmed for next season. A couple of them are objectionable. Unless we can come to some firm agreement, to abide by certain rules and regulations, I'll have to recommend to Mr. Reinhardt that Weinstraub withdraw all sponsorship."

"Excuse me," said Jesse interestedly. "That looks likely? So where does it leave the producer and everybody connected with it?"

Schwab's smile widened sardonically. "In a little mess, Mr. Falkenstein. With a name star under contract to be paid through at least another season, about twenty-five expensive episodes on video tape minus a sponsor, and at a conservative estimate in the hole about a quarter of a million on salaries and sets and equipment and so on. And after the publicity breaks, Weinstraub backing out, I doubt if any other sponsor who could afford the prime time would touch 'Crimefighters West.' "

"Oh, ouch," said Jesse.

"Of course it's hardly the sole material owned by Ace-Ames. They're not likely to go bankrupt over 'Crimefighters.' But they'll drop quite a bundle, and everybody's feeling damned annoyed."

"I can imagine," said Clock. "But how the hell did any producer let that kind of thing slip by in a script? I should think anybody'd know—"

Schwab shrugged again. "Pay your money and take your choice. I'd have thought so too, Sergeant. That anybody would know that most city police forces these days have very high standards, the rules and regulations. But a couple of the writers on this series are fairly young, and maybe they'd swallowed some of the irresponsible smears, I don't know. The director said he'd asked the producer to tone down a couple of those scenes, had an argument with him when he refused. I don't know the ins and outs. And now—"

"Excuse me," said Jesse. "Letters of complaint? How many?"

"Oh, Lord, I couldn't tell you offhand. Not many—people don't take the trouble. The ones who did, on this, were from the kind of people who might be expected to. Just offhand, I remember a retired police officer, a sheriff somewhere in Montana. I suppose the people involved somehow with law enforcement. I couldn't guess how many altogether."

52

"But you picked this one to photostat. Why?"

"Yes. As I told you, it contained the briefest and most relevant précis of the various charges. We—"

Jesse passed it to Clock. "Our remarkably efficient organizer Margaret," he said hollowly. "To think I ever complained about that woman as a ditherer and a fool! *Whom the Lord loveth*— Mr. Schwab, do you have any idea how many of these photostats are floating around?"

"Not a clue—why? We've been discussing this thing back and forth with a number of people—the writers, producer, director, the management at Ace-Ames—and I wanted everybody concerned to be fully informed about the specific issues. That was the most convenient— Why? I'm blessed if I can understand what the L.A.P.D.'s interest—"

"Very simple, Mr. Schwab," said Clock. "Miss Margaret Williams was murdered last Monday night. Apparently as she returned home, in front of her apartment. And you had broadcast God knows how many photostats of her letter—containing her address—among these people, who could reason that she pulled the trigger on your TV epic."

Schwab stared at him. Reinhardt uttered a faint moan and closed his eyes.

"Awesome," said Jesse. "That's the word I've been trying to think of. Awesome. Our Margaret. Of course other people had their two cents' worth in, but she pulled the trigger. And all the time sitting there eight hours a day answering my office phone and typing up the wills and keeping my files in order. And my thinking of her as the flustered female mouse. *The way of man is froward and strange,* all right."

"Yes, when you think," said Clock, "what the result was—my God. Talk about throwing a stone into a pond. Action and reaction. I will be damned." He laughed. "I'd heard Phoenix's side of it this afternoon—talked with the Chief. He'd never heard of the fool show till he got her letter—which was, by the way, an afterthought, can we say? Because she hadn't made carbons of the other letter to send him, had to send her own. He said he hardly ever watches the idiot box, didn't know there was a series on supposed to be about his own force. When he did, he watched it. He was annoyed, of course. The one he picked up evidently didn't show any drunken detectives or third-degree stuff, but it was, he said, the damndest fairy tale he ever saw. They were chasing a murderer, and when they got a tip where he was living, the captain of detectives said he hadn't enough men for a twenty-four-hour stakeout. I ask you, he said. On a city force. You'd think anybody— But it is a fact, of course, that the pro hoods know more about us than the respectable citizens. Anyway, he said the libel threat was just talk, they didn't think it was worth the time to follow it up. By then they'd heard from Schwab that the series would probably go off."

"I still cannot get over it," said Jesse. "My God, Andrew. When it rained she used to bring her lunch in a paper bag and eat it in her car. I've seen her."

"Poring over the current *Master Detective,*" said Clock.

"Stone in a pond— A prime-time TV show sponsored by Weinstraub. My God," said Jesse.

"And do you think it's likely that any of these—how many people—connected with 'Crimefighters' took note of her address, marked her as the trigger, and were mad enough about the whole thing to lie in wait for her?"

"I don't know. Heard you say often enough that the motive in a homicide can be anything or nothing, it depends who has it. That writer you saw—"

"Dashed off a nasty note to her, yes. And that's all? And it just could be that one of them did," said Clock. "And—even as per the fictional captain—I have only just so many men, and bodies don't come singular in central L.A. What a job to question every — And would we get anything? Asking for alibis or whatever?"

"No clues in the car—at the scene? Not a single button or ballpoint pen or—"

"You've been reading detective novels. I'll keep you posted," said Clock, and swung away to his Pontiac.

Jesse needed cigarettes; he stopped at a drugstore on the way home, and on impulse along with the cigarettes bought a copy of *Official Detective.*

And Clock had intended, after looking at overnight reports and organizing what routine there was on hand to be done, to brief a couple of men on all that and at least chase down and question those writers, the producer and director. But if a police officer's work like woman's is never done, it is also always getting interrupted by the new urgent things to do. On Thursday morning he came into the office to find a new report.

The night watch had been turned out at 1 A.M. to hunt for a missing baby-sitter, over on Loma Drive. The parents had arrived home to find the baby asleep and Michelle Stover missing —TV on, back door forced, evidence of a struggle in the living room. The girl was described as sixteen, blond, medium-sized. They hadn't located her up to the time the watch changed.

Clock swore. Not his business yet but he could have an educated guess it would turn out to be. And the boys had no sooner begun to drift in than a call came to Homicide from a black-and-white. Body found by some kids, on a school playground. Belmont High School—that was only a block or so from Loma Drive. Having a premonition, Clock sent Mantella to look at it.

He was telling Petrovsky, Lopez, and Keene about the TV development when Mantella called in. "It's her," he said. "The Stover girl. By the description of her clothes and so on. Looks as if she was raped. Beaten up anyway. Probably last night. Do you want the works?"

"Might as well do it according to Hoyle," said Clock resignedly. He went out with the lab team to take a look himself, and came back to call R. and I. Irrelevantly thinking of "Crimefighters," he said, "You've got some computers down there. Suppose you put one to work. The deviates with rape and/or violence pedigrees"—that would amount to a lot of names, of course—"and any recent Peeping Toms down here." That would amount to a lot more. They usually did it the hard way.

In fact, he reflected, still thinking about "Crimefighters," these days any city cop hardly had the time to make dates with prostitutes, or get drunk, even if he had the inclination.

Jesse, having at least temporarily solved his paper work problem, was concerned about Miss Williams and intrigued by the mystery she'd bequeathed them. That bit about no man being an island, he thought vaguely, sitting down beside the client in Justice Botts' court at ten o'clock, was all wrong. People were. People rubbing elbows, judging others by surfaces, and each individual as remote from another as the farthest-flung South Sea shore in the vast Pacific.

He wished he had really known Margaret Williams before she died. She'd been an interesting and unusual woman, by what they now knew about her; and a courageous one, you could say. All the ambition and secret dedication kept apart; doing the routine job eight hours a day as efficiently as she could. And egotist Falkenstein never suspecting what she was really like at all. He had the sudden curious thought that, while Miss Williams hadn't deliberately acquired a dog, she had been like the dog she kept. Like Sally. They both looked so lightweight and frivolous and shallow, but both of them something very much more. . . . And something would have to be decided about Sally, who had slept with them again last night, and only by force been prevented from stealing Athelstane's breakfast.

He got the interlocutory granted, spent ten minutes listening to the client's gratitude, and called Fran at the office to ask if there'd been any phone calls.

"From one of the agencies. You have a potential new secretary coming in at two o'clock. Thank God. When I've finished your paper work I'm leaving. I want to find a house and start buying furniture."

"On a cop's salary, don't forget."

"Well, I've got some savings. I was just enjoying having no job."

"Patience," said Jesse. "I'll be back to see the potential new one. No appointments? O.K."

It was eleven-thirty. He had got the name and address from that receipt in her files: secretary of this MWI, one Roland Henry, address in Westwood. In fact, when he got there, an expensive-looking rambling Spanish house probably with the outsize swimming pool in the rear, on a quiet street. TV? he wondered. Anybody connected with TV seemed to think in terms of big money.

Henry was a little surprise to him. He answered the door himself—no white-jacketed houseboy, no maid. Of course, these days— But as the door opened, a bell suddenly rang in Jesse's head and he remembered the name. Of course he knew Henry. Nell liked him too, she'd handed that book to Jesse a while ago, the only thing of Henry's he had read. Maybe he also wrote scripts, but that had been a collection of unusual, offbeat tales—humorous science fiction, imaginative, dry, with a wry sense of humor.

Henry was in his forties, with thin dark hair, deep lines in his face, a cynical mouth. He looked at Jesse's card and said, "Am I being sued or has somebody left me a million bucks?"

"Neither. Want to ask some questions. Also like to say that thing of yours—short story, 'Home on the Range'—beautiful. Hilarious. And God knows, more truth than poetry."

Henry threw his head back and laughed. "The twentieth century's a damned unpleasant one, Mr. Falkenstein. Have to use a sense of humor on it or we'd all go crazy together. Come in. What can I do for you?"

"Some questions." Jesse followed him into a big light living room with unpretentious furniture, and for a wonder no built-in bar. "About Margaret Williams."

57

"Oh?" Henry sat down opposite him. "What about her? She's an odd one."

"Was," said Jesse.

"What?"

"She got murdered last Monday night."

"The Williams woman?" said Henry incredulously. "Murdered? Well, for God's sake! What happened to her?"

"We aren't sure. Yet. But it looks like a personal motive. Not just at random, if you take me."

"I'll be damned. That sounds impossible. That— Well." Henry shook his head. "I didn't know her, exactly. None of us did. At all, personally. You coming here, I take it you know—"

"A nonvoting—read unpublished—member of this MWI. Yes. We've heard that she got to most of your meetings. As a spectator, as it were, or did she—er—mingle?"

Henry got out a cigarette and looked at it. "Who's we?"

"Me and the police."

"Oh. You her lawyer?"

"She was my secretary."

"Be damned. I don't think I ever heard what her job was. Well, she wasn't the ordinary kind of member like that we get. Probably a hundred or so on that list, across the country—little people, people ambitious to write, eager to boast they're our members—some of 'em make it and get into print. With this and that. Not many of them get to meetings. We meet bimonthly. Usually have a guest speaker, some aspect of the job — The meeting in December, for instance, we had Lew Spencer, he's a producer—"

"Know the name. Suspense stuff."

"—on scripting, that sort of thing. You'd have expected one like the Williams woman to sit back and listen all quiet, you know." Henry grinned. "She didn't. She asked questions and she hadn't any hesitation in expressing opinions. More power to — You said murdered? I'll be—"

"What kind of opinions? Cross anybody in your bunch? Serious?"

"For God's sake, you're not trying to pin it on one of us?" Henry laughed. "That's senseless. But—if you want to know, it was such a surprise to everybody. This nonentity, this little nobody, speaking up. I got a kick out of it," he added thoughtfully. "Which is neither here nor there."

Jesse grinned. *"There is one who is wise for many, but for himself is a fool.* I gather you don't like stuffed shirts, Mr. Henry."

"Oh, you see things, don't you? What's that?"

"Old Rabbi Jeshu ben Shirah."

"Yes. Well, what the hell is it but a little facility with words? Very little great literature getting produced these days. I do a script when I'm commissioned—for the money. Very nice thing, money. I like it. But I don't set myself up as a great writer. By any standards. All the ragtag and bobtail getting published —and scripting the ephemeral series for TV. Some of 'em let it go to their heads."

"I can see where they might."

"Used," said Henry, lighting the cigarette at last, "to being approached with the proper respect. The Williams woman didn't."

"Damn it," said Jesse wistfully. "I wish I'd known her. Really."

"I thought you said—"

"All the while thinking she was the empty-headed dithering female, when—"

"Oh," said Henry. "Like that? Well, she'd get flustered, but she stuck to her guns. I got a kick out of it, because once or twice she flustered the hell out of somebody else, see. Rich Tower, for instance, raking it in hand over fist with that paperback series getting onto TV last year—the big man, big name— She really savaged him at the December meeting. And of course she was quite right," said Henry.

"Over what?"

"You read Tower? Oh. Well, he writes that Ace Bowman series—he's been at it for twenty years. The hard-boiled private eye. Of course it's completely unrealistic, way out of date. If we're talking off the record, Tower annoys me, you know. Look, people pick up the paperbacks to read on the plane, pass away time in the doctor's waiting room. They finish it, toss it away, and forget it. Hardly deathless prose, Mr. Falkenstein. But there are some like Tower, famous author because he gets printed in hundred-thousand editions, taking himself so seriously."

"Always fatal," agreed Jesse. "Our Margaret clobbered him? How?"

"After the meeting. He was holding forth on contriving plots —a handful of hangers-on listening all respectful, you know. She just interrupted him—it was a little like a Peke sashaying up to a Saint Bernard—and told him if he knew anything about crime in real life, or police work in general, he'd know his silly complicated plots were about as implausible as plots could get. Which," said Henry, "they are, of course."

Jesse laughed. "Reaction?"

"Tower's? He went red and walked away. . . . You aren't seriously thinking," said Henry, "that— Murdered? That's wild. How?"

Jesse told him absently. "Been a pleasure meeting you, Mr. Henry." He got up. "So I'll present you with the one wild card we've turned up on it. It was set up to look like an ordinary random mugging—blunt instrument, purse rifled—but it wasn't. In her mouth, possibly as a gag, most of the front cover of the current *Master Detective.*"

Henry stared at him. He said reverently, "But what an utterly magnificent clue. *What* a—"

R. and I. dispatched a list of names and addresses up to Homicide by nine-thirty. Of course the computers saved a lot of time.

As a rule this sort of anonymous thing, the baby-sitter abducted and raped and killed, posed a lot of leg work. They turned up the m.o.s, the sex deviates out of records, found them and leaned on them, and if they were lucky sooner or later got a confession, or solid evidence from the lab linking up one of them. Once in a long while they got a luckier break.

In the first batch of names the computer turned up was one Jonathan Noonan. He had accumulated a lot of little counts as a j.d.—the significant counts: stealing feminine underwear off clotheslines, Peeping Tom—seven counts of that over four years; and four months back, attempted rape. That had been reduced to attempted assault and he was on probation. Clock muttered about softheaded judges.

But more to the point was the fact that Noonan lived, or had lived four months ago, on Columbia Avenue, two blocks from Loma Drive.

Clock sent Dale over to pick him up, if he was there. The stakeout at the room on Temple, for that Nadinger, had been called off: Nadinger hadn't shown, may have smelled cop, may have run. Dale called back half an hour later. Noonan still lived there, with an older brother who had done a little time for burglary, and his divorced mother, who was a lush. Noonan wasn't there now, presumably would be sometime. And fortunately, of course, he had turned into an adult just five months back on his eighteenth birthday, so they had printed him on the assault charge.

Just once in a long while they got very lucky and cleaned up one like this in a hurry. Clock left Dale there to pick Noonan up when he showed; at three-thirty Dale brought him in.

Whoever had broken in the back door and abducted Michelle Stover to beat and (probably) rape her in the schoolyard had sustained some scratches from her nails, some bloodstains on his clothes; and he had dropped, just inside the forced back door, a snickersnee of a switchblade knife with a blade eleven inches long, and some nice clear latents on it.

Jonathan Noonan had some scratches on his face. Dale and

Keene went away to see if the lab could match the prints; Clock and Petrovsky questioned Noonan.

"I don't know nothing about it," said Noonan, who was an overweight, outsize kid in dirty jeans and T-shirt, with a bad case of acne and greasy blond hair. "I ain't done nothing."

They didn't waste much time talking to him. The lab made the latents on the knife within half an hour. They checked with Noonan's prints on file.

"So happy day," said Clock tiredly. "We clean this up fast. Pete, you can book him in. And we might as well give the D.A. all the ammunition available—tell the jail to send his clothes to the lab."

"Sure," said Petrovsky. "Come on. Up."

"I didn't do nothing," said Noonan sullenly.

Clock stretched and for the first time since eight o'clock thought about Margaret Williams.

Fran had finished all but a couple of letters and departed before the potential new secretary showed up at two o'clock. "I'm doing a special recipe for Andrew. That tome of a cookbook Nell found is definitely useful. Your new girl can carry on from here."

And that was a fat chance, thought Jesse, looking at the clock.

Ten minutes after Fran had left, she wandered in. "Oh, is this where they said to come? Mr. Forkensteen?" She was about twenty, thin and platinum blond and bucktoothed, in a plaid skirt barely covering her thighs and a turtleneck sweater.

"Falkenstein. Miss—"

"Dawn," she said. "Dawn Kingsley. I can take dictation if it isn't too fast, and I do typing at forty words a minute."

Jesse looked at her helplessly. "I'm afraid—it's a trained legal secretary I—"

"Oh," she said. "I was afraid I wouldn't do. I'm sorry." She trailed out sadly.

Jesse went home, to find Sally briskly on guard at the gate of

62

the chain-link fence, her tail raised like a banner, her rasping tenor bark alerting Nell to his arrival.

Athelstane was lurking behind Jesse's armchair in the living room.

"Yes," said Jesse, eyeing Sally. "Resemblances, all right. You *look* so harmless and silly, don't you? By God, I wish I'd known that girl. Quite a girl, Sally. Under the surface."

"Is that you, darling?" called Nell from the bedroom.

5

JESSE CALLED their old maestro after dinner to pour all that at him. "Really I can't get over it—"

"And I'm havin' some afterthoughts too," said old Mr. Walters. "Damn it, Jesse, the times I dropped into your office, tag along to lunch, and sat there watchin' her type or something— uninteresting horse-faced old maid. Never exchanged one unnecessary word with her. And all the while— Well, people kind of like icebergs, sometimes, hey? Nine-tenths submerged. Quite a female, and nobody halfway suspecting it."

"Something Andrew said Petrovsky heard from the Weglund woman—people underestimated Margaret. That's sure as hell. But all this—"

"This 'Crimefighters' thing, yes. D'you know, Jesse, I wonder if she realized what she'd done there. The—the magnitude, you can say, of what she triggered off. Sure, I wouldn't doubt that sooner or later the advertising outfit, or this Reinhardt or somebody, 'd have spotted the TV epics maligning the cops, and blown the whistle—and other people wrote letters to the company. But in the general excitement, everybody seems to have overlooked Margaret Williams as the—um—catalyst. Reinhardt didn't remember her name. Schwab did, barely, because he'd had the letter photostated. As the clearest précis—so anybody who saw one of those photostats might've connected her, sure. But I'd have a guess, in all the excitement and argument nobody bothered to contact Miss Williams 'n' tell her what was going on. Why should anybody? It wasn't any of her business. And were you thinking of 'Crimefighters' as a motive for murder?"

"It could be."

"I wonder," said the old man. "It was after the fact, y' know."

"What—oh."

"Cat was out of the bag. Sponsor making a fuss—canceling the show. Damage was done. Damn whose fault it was."

"Yes, I see that."

"I tell you, Jesse, if 'Crimefighters' sparked off the murder, it was somebody in that bunch just takin' a childish, spiteful revenge—that'd do him or nobody any good. If there's a character like that among 'em, have a closer look at him. Otherwise—"

"See that too."

"I just wish we knew where she'd been Monday. Tell you one thing occurred to me. This extremely urgent matter—it must have come up awful quick, Jesse. The day before, even just that morning. Because say she knew about it—whatever it was—Friday, Saturday, she'd have tended to it then, wouldn't she? Where was she on Sunday—home?"

"There was an affair of some sort Sunday night, this club she belonged to—"

"Remember, sure. Well, there you are. It's all up in the air—but this Weglund woman, probably the closest friend she had, she was at that party too, I seem to recall. And she didn't mention any extremely urgent matter to the Weglund woman." The old man was silent and then said, "It's a funny rigmarole. Do some more thinking on it. Any good to talk to other people at the party? Where was it?"

"No idea, we can ask Weglund."

"It's the magazine cover worries the hell out of me, y' know. Seems no rhyme or reason to it."

"Say it again. No immediate ideas?"

"I think I'd like to know a little bit more about that party," said the old man.

Jesse heaved Athelstane off his feet.

Clock kissed Fran good-bye at seven-thirty Friday morning. "You helping out Jesse today?"

"Not except under pressure. I hope to goodness he finds a new one soon. I'm going out looking at houses with that real estate woman. And I want you to see the one on Pinehurst, darling—"

"It's all right with me if you like it. How much is it?" asked Clock, belatedly cautious.

"Thirty-two thousand, but—"

"Don't remind me. Civil servant always gets a break, good risk, and the banks are out of their minds, with cops getting ambushed and assaulted—"

"Don't remind *me*, Andrew."

"Well, don't fuss. It hasn't happened to me yet."

Clock hadn't had a family in a long time. It felt just fine, acquiring the ready-made one along with Fran.

He got to the office at eight sharp, and again today he meant to follow up some of those TV people, the ones, say, who stood to lose the most on that silly series. There was paper work to do on that Stover-Noonan thing yesterday, and time to waste in court for the arraignment sometime next week. They were still hunting for Nadinger. The A.P.B. on Gerald Eboe, on the run from Denver, hadn't turned him up. Clock was wondering too if it was worth the time to bring in Dan Purcell and question him on Williams—the thought had struck him that Purcell lived in the same neighborhood, could easily have ambushed her there.

A new body overnight, again no mystery except as to who he'd been, but more paper work. Elderly man found dead, of probable natural causes, on a bench at the corner of Third and Alvarado.

Petrovsky, Dale, Lopez, Mantella had drifted in; Clock went into the detective office and had just said Petrovsky's name when Sergeant Pitman out at the switchboard said tersely, "Right, sit on it, somebody'll be down. New body, Sergeant. That was the black-and-white. Seventeenth and Figueroa."

"Hell," said Clock; but it was Homicide's job to deal with the bodies. "All right. Pete, you come with me. Johnny, you and Joe try to chase down some of these TV people, will you? The badge ought to get you in, even the studios." As a rule, easier to get an interview with the President than into the studios, any studios.

They took Clock's Pontiac and went to look at the new body. And a vague presentiment was at the back of Clock's mind already; when he took a look at the terrain, and the body, he did some swearing.

There were two squad cars sitting on it now, holding the people away: this wasn't normally an exactly deserted intersection, and the usual little crowd had collected. One of the uniformed men said to Clock, "I suppose a dozen people spotted her, weren't sure, didn't investigate, but finally somebody took a closer look and reported it."

Which figured. The body was in the street, Seventeenth Street, up against the curb, huddled in the gutter. Rather obviously it had been shoved out of a car stopped briefly there. Clock and Petrovsky squatted over it.

At least it had stopped raining.

The body was that of a woman; the glimpse they had of a half-hidden face, at her clothes, not a young woman or an old one. In her forties, fifties. She'd been a little plump; she was wearing a black cloth coat, a fairly good one by the feel, and low-heeled pumps, tan stockings, a dress of some sort. No hat. She'd had bleached silver-blond hair, tousled now. And she looked as if she'd sustained a beating, by the bruises visible on her face.

"God give me strength," said Clock, and stood up. "I suspect I've won my bet with you, Pete."

"The Masked Monster," said Petrovsky. "I haven't seen all the details on that, but just at an offhand glance, maybe so."

"I said he'd end up killing somebody, that damn psycho. You stay here and start the routine—the lab truck'll be along. I'll have to see Hellenthal, see what he's got on that."

Back at the office, he told Pitman to connect him to Robbery. He asked for Lieutenant Hellenthal and drummed on his desk for a few minutes, waiting.

"So what do you want, Andrew? We're busy—"

"So are we, damn it. I think your Masked Monster—my God, what a handle—has just graduated into my jurisdiction, Adam. Body just found. I want your opinion—and your files on him."

"Now, you don't tell me," said Hellenthal. "Well, it was always possible, of course. And while it's been technically robbery and abduction, he did rape a couple of them, and Vice has been sitting in on it too—Kaiser. We've collected the hell of a lot of bits and pieces, but it doesn't add up to much. R. and I.'s done us no good at all. You sure this is one of his jobs?"

"No, that's why I want to see your files on him. It just looks damn suspicious, by what I've seen about him."

"Well, we're supposed to cooperate. I'll get hold of Kaiser. My office in ten minutes."

"First job, last November twelfth," said Hellenthal briskly, opening the bulging manila folder. "We didn't spot it for the same joker until the third job, when the details began to add up. Now, of course, we know. And you'd think we ought to have a fairly good description of him, out of thirteen women, but we haven't. In all but four cases he forced them to drive his own car. He—"

"Why not those four?" asked Clock.

"Because they didn't know how to drive," said Hellenthal amusedly. "The first one like that—oh, the statements are all in here, names don't matter—said he seemed a little surprised when she told him that. Then he marched her into the bedroom and used her own stockings—clean stockings out of a drawer—to tie her up and gag her. Put her in the trunk of his car, drove her somewhere, and beat her up. She couldn't even say where —some isolated spot. We could guess. The women who drove knew where they went, of course. Favorite spot is up Mulholland Drive, you know how isolated that is at night. Two of them he took to Barnsdall Park in Hollywood, also isolated."

Lieutenant Kaiser of Vice, an older man than the other two, gray-haired and tired-looking, said, "We can mark out a pattern of sorts, Clock. From thirteen cases. They were all middle-aged, roughly speaking. Youngest forty-five, oldest fifty-nine. All of them were women in good circumstances, living in nice places —nine single houses, four apartments. He cases the women, at least superficially, to know they'll be alone. Because seven of them have husbands visibly living with them."

"Why weren't they home when he came ringing the door-bell?"

"That's it," said Hellenthal. "Two of them out of town on business. Two more at lodge meetings. The others were working overtime. And all he had to do to find there were no husbands at home was to tiptoe round the house looking in windows. Even simpler, at the apartments, notice the husband's car gone from its slot. You know these new apartment houses, mere garage space underneath with no doors. In the case of the apartment-livers, none of those women had her own car."

"Oh. Any kind of area to the pattern?"

Hellenthal shrugged. "Very generally, Hollywood. Which takes in a lot of area, don't tell me. Addresses all the way from Mount Olympus"—that was a new and very exclusive residential area up in the Hollywood hills—"to Los Feliz Boulevard. One in West L.A., another one around the Silver Lake area. But there's a pattern, all right. All these women are upper middle class, substantial incomes, between those ages, and they all tell us much the same things about him—what they do tell us."

"So, give."

"We got the least, of course, from the four he tied up. It was dark in every case, and even the ones who put on a porch light when they answered the door can't say much, except that he's quick and cool—so they were all startled, shocked, confused. Naturally. He's definitely middle-sized, not a big fellow, and most of them say, tentatively, young or youngish, by the way he moves. He wears a black ski mask covering his entire head, and of course that would distort his voice. In six cases—some women have a little sense—there was a locked screen door, and before those women could unfreeze at sight of the gun, and scream, he slashed the screen with a knife and came right in."

"No make on the gun."

"What could you expect? He doesn't give 'em much time— Demands any money they've got and—here's a funny twist— he cleans out the handbag but makes 'em carry it along."

"Why, for—"

"Well, Adam's got an offbeat idea about it," said Kaiser. "You never know what a psycho'll do. Beating them up, raping them, and then—but Adam says it could be he wants them identified right off. As more of his handiwork."

"The m.o. would tell us that— Oh," said Clock. "Yes. Which he might not clearly see. Yes. I suppose that makes sense of a sort."

"Well, the nuts. You don't know. Now, the women who were forced to drive his car, of course, tell us something about it. And that tells us for pretty sure he's got access to at least two cars. Nothing like a complete description, naturally. None of them ever got a look at a license plate, and it was after dark. But most cars are labeled inside, on the dash or somewhere, and he does something about that. First description." Hellenthal shuffled papers. "Put together from statements from six of 'em. Medi-

70

um-sized car, sedan, either two- or four-door, uncertain. Light color but not white. Inside, bench seat in front, adhesive tape pasted across lower middle of dashboard—presumably across the car's label there. Dash lights green, stick shift, upholstery either dark blue or green, possibly gray. Not a new car—five, six years old or even more. Second description— All this stuff came in dribbles, just a little from each victim, you know. From three other women we get an entirely different picture, obviously a second car. Most of those women tried to keep their heads, up to when he started to beat them—tried to remember what details they could. The second car is smaller, about as big as a Corvair or Falcon, but not definitely either one. A dark color, no make on the general shape. Inside, bench seat, narrow, adhesive tape across part of dash and center of steering wheel. Dash lights blue-white. Stick shift. I might add," said Hellenthal, looking up from the papers, "that two of these women had never driven anything but automatic transmissions, and being nervous anyway naturally made a mess of shifting. That seemed to annoy him, and in both cases he made 'em stop the car, and used their stockings and his belt to tie 'em up, put them in the trunk. Oh, and neither car has power brakes or steering. Both oldies."

"Well," said Clock, "that's a handful of nothing. Either one could be any of thirty makes and models. And women and cars —especially when they were nervous, the gun on them—"

"We have to get what we can how we can, you know that," said Kaiser impatiently. The sergeant from the anteroom looked in and said Clock's office wanted him.

Clock took up the phone.

"Pete?"

"There was a kind of clutch purse lying under her," said Petrovsky. "Billfold and slots for I.D. She's a Mrs. Lucille Kane, address in West Hollywood. Driver's license says fifty-two, five-five, a hundred and forty, blond and blue. Fits her. Nobody anwers the phone. How does she sound?"

"Just like the other thirteen I've been hearing about, except that she's dead. Beaten up?"

"Looked that way."

"Damnation. You'd better go and talk to the neighbors. . . . It looks as if she fits your pattern, all right," and he passed that on, putting down the phone.

"Where was the body?" asked Kaiser.

"Corner of Seventeenth and Figueroa."

"Well, well, and again well," said Hellenthal. He turned a slow smile on Kaiser. "And *shalom* to you." He closed the manila folder and shoved it over to Clock. "Homicide has just inherited the Masked Monster, and we do wish you fun and games with him."

"That says something definite?"

"Seventeenth and Figueroa. Oh, yes, Andrew. Within a block of the Stack. Every single one of those women was shoved out of the car within a block or two of the Stack."

"Which just puts it a little higher up in the air," said Kaiser.

Clock said several impolite things. "Yes, we said so too," said Hellenthal.

The Stack, which had created neuroses even in some seasoned residents of L.A., was the place down there where all the freeways began, in a glorious muddle of over- and underpasses, and led off in various directions for all parts of the county and beyond. From the Stack you could start off for anywhere in any direction, intending to go five miles or fifty, toward beach or mountains.

But all that added up to the inescapable fact that the Masked Monster was now Homicide's baby.

Clock got back to his own office at ten minutes to ten, and started looking through all the reports and statements collected over two and a half months on the Monster, conscientiously putting Margaret Williams and everything else out of his mind.

72

He was still reading (the paper work the curse of this deadly century) when Petrovsky came back at eleven thirty.

"Just by the little I know about this joker, it appears you've won the bet."

"Yes, that's for sure now. What did the neighbors tell you?"

"Mrs. Kane," said Petrovsky, "has a perfectly good live husband. Only he isn't home. It's a nice big house, an older place on a nice street, not fashionable but—substantial. Seems she's lived there for twenty years or more, lost her first husband—she was a Mrs. Banning—about four years ago, married Kane a little over a year back. He's around her age, seems to be—I quote the neighbors—a nice quiet fellow. He's got a cabin somewhere up around Big Bear, likes the winter sports, and he went up there last Monday. For a few days. Leaving Mrs. Kane alone."

"Yes," said Clock. "The pattern. Damn it, so it's our baby now." He shoved the bundle of papers over. "You'd better go through all this—and Johnny too. In case— Well, Adam said R. and I. was a broken reed on this one and I can see why. All we know about him really is his general size. The ski mask. Interview all those women again, we'd get nothing more at all—" The outside phone rang on his desk and he picked it up. "Central Homicide, Clock."

"Andrew," said Jesse urgently, "the hospital just called. Mrs. Williams is conscious. Seems to be rational. Doctor says we can talk to her a few minutes."

"I'll meet you there. . . . Pete, the husband ought to be notified. Neighbors have any address for him up there?" That far-flung area of mountain resort took in a lot of territory. "Well, contact the forest rangers—if he owns property there they can locate him. And when they do find him, it'll take him some time to drive back. I'll be in when I can."

"You never know how these things will go," the doctor said in the hall. "She's partially paralyzed, of course—much worse than she was from previous strokes—and it's a little difficult for her to talk. But she seems quite rational. I just thought—I understand it is a case of homicide—if she has any information for you, you'd better try for it now. I don't like the state of her heart. Just be quiet and patient, eh?"

"Yes, doctor."

It was a four-bed ward; the nurse had put discreet screens around the bed where Mrs. Williams lay. She was conscious, and at least she knew Jesse, even in the half light. He bent over her. "Mrs. Williams, we'd like you to try to answer a few questions, if you can. We'll try not to tire you. Will you try to help us?"

"Yes—sir," she whispered. A nurse slipped in and quietly raised the head of the bed a little. "That's—better," the old woman mouthed. One side of her face was drawn down, distorting her mouth. "Please. Please. Is—"

"What is it, Mrs. Williams?"

"Is Sally—all right, somebody—taking—"

"Sally's fine," he said gently. "Don't you worry. We're taking care of her."

"Mrs. Williams—" Clock tried to mute his normally strong voice. What questions to ask her? She'd said Margaret hadn't told her anything on Monday morning—

"Mrs. Williams, you remember that Margaret went out last Sunday night?" said Jesse. "To a party?"

She nodded once. "Yes. Sunday. I had—sit up late—watched TV. For her—help me—bed."

"Yes. When she came in from the party—and helped you into bed—did she tell you anything? About something that happened—" Where? When? Martha Weglund there, and she hadn't—

Surprisingly, slowly, Mrs. Williams tried to smile. "Looked pretty," she croaked, "all flushed up—like that. The party. Nice —party. But she—had to go—work, in morning. Shouldn've—sat up. That—night."

74

"Sunday night? She didn't go to bed right away, after she'd—"

She nodded, breathing heavily. "Couldn'—get sleep. Coffee at supper. Saw—light from—under her door—in hall. Sat up. Papers—papers—heard— She shouldn've—had to go work early—"

"Now just take it easy. Papers? You *heard*—oh, like papers rustling? Newspapers, or—"

She made an effort, but all she got out was, "Papers. Light still on—when—went to sleep."

The nurse had a hand on her wrist; she flicked a glance at them. "Please, I think—"

In the hall, they looked at each other. "Now what the hell does that mean?" asked Jesse. "Papers. Damn it, it suddenly occurs to me that *papers* are pursuing us, Andrew. Paper in magazines. All those letters and carbons. The TV scripts and contracts. Me with no secretary to do the paper work. And now our Margaret, sitting up late after she came home from the party, rustling papers. What was she doing?"

"She'd had a sudden inspiration for a mystery story," said Clock. "Somebody at the party had asked her for a list of good detective novels. She had a premonition she was going to die and was making a will— What bit you?"

"My good God," said Jesse, "I wonder if she did. I didn't draw one for her but—formalities to be observed, as I should have remembered, Andrew. If she had a safety vault at some bank, or— Can I get into the apartment? I'd better have a look. Are you finished there?"

"Oh, I hadn't thought of that either. I suppose you'd better. Come back to the office, I'll give you the keys—we're finished there. And on top of everything else, damn it, my premonition has come true and the Masked Monster is now Homicide's job. He killed a woman last night. The psycho. As I knew he would. And not one single solitary lead that I can see— Well, Kaiser and Adam have been cops awhile, they looked as they could, and there's not a single—"

"*All iniquity is as a two-edged sword, the wounds thereof cannot be healed,*" said Jesse. "My sympathy." But his tone was absent.

At the office, they found Petrovsky and Lopez poring over the collected statements, and Petrovsky looked up to say, "Johnny went out on a call. Somebody throwing rocks onto the Pasadena Freeway."

Clock looked too mad to swear. He handed the keys over to Jesse.

In the Williams apartment, already a little dusty and looking deserted, Jesse prowled through drawers, feeling obscurely guilty. He found a metal box full of canceled checks in the little desk, and in that a receipt for a year's rent of a safety vault in a Security-Pacific bank on Vermont. He called the bank. The lock box had been in Miss Williams' name; they'd seal it and arrange a date for the contents to be formally tabulated; they took his name and address. He supposed he had better act for Mrs. Williams. He wondered if Margaret had made a will.

In the corner of the kitchen he found a little box belonging to Sally: a chewed rubber ball, a fake bone, a wind-up cat that squeaked.

The file case had been taken away bodily. Clock would be checking out everything in it eventually.

Jesse looked around the apartment, the clutter of possessions acquired over the years, the residue of mere materiality left, suddenly so very unimportant. He felt depressed. He doubted that the old woman would ever come back here. He took the box of Sally's toys, locked the door, and went downstairs to talk to the manager.

"The rent's paid up through March first," said Shackleton. He looked distressed. "Old Mrs. Williams not too good, you say? Probably have to be in a rest home, like, even if—"

"I'd think so. The furniture theirs?"

"Everything but the stove. But what'd I better do then?"

Jesse looked out the front door to the place where Margaret Williams had—died? Or her body been left? They didn't even know that. And come to think, he'd owed her two weeks' salary. But aphorisms about that too: the root of all evil. He said soberly, "I'll arrange for everything to be put in storage, Mr. Shackleton—the place cleaned out. Until we know something definite."

"And I'd owe a rebate, first two months paid when they moved in—my God, a matter of twenty years back, time gets away from you. I'd owe a month's rebate. Who'd I give it to?"

"Good question," said Jesse. "I could see it goes to help pay for the funeral." And it would be up to him to arrange for that too. Ask Andrew when the body could be released.

"Just a terrible, terrible thing," said Shackleton, troubled. "All at once. A *murder.* Here. Doesn't seem possible. Yes, sir, you do that, would you?"

"Glad to, Mr. Shackleton."

In the midst of life, he thought . . . He hadn't had any lunch, he had four appointments this afternoon, and still no secretary. He snatched a sandwich, and stopped in person at an employment agency on Hollywood Boulevard. They told him brightly he was lucky, and offered him, in person, Gladys Buck, said to have two years' experience in a legal office. He didn't care for her looks especially but asked if she could come on the job at once, gave her the address, and paid the agency's fee.

At four-thirty, with the last client of the day momentarily expected, he told her to get out. The pungent aura of My Sin she carried about did not cover up the more pungent aura of unwashed Gladys, her skirt was five inches above her knees, and she chewed gum continuously; in her one venture into Miss Williams' spick-and-span files she had replaced the O'Hanlon records under the R's.

She flounced out past the client coming in.

Clock was still talking to himself about the Masked Monster. The rangers in Angeles National Forest had called back at one-thirty: Stewart Kane had been located, at a resort cabin in the Crystal Lake area, and informed of his wife's death. He would drive back to L.A. at once. And just what use that was—of course he'd know nothing.

They now had a new body, and all the paper work to do on that, if no mystery to solve. A knifing in a bar on Main, the knifer picked up by the uniformed men. It would add up to involuntary manslaughter. The paper work went on forever.

Just after the rangers called, a uniformed messenger brought in a new report: the formal autopsy on Margaret Williams. Clock opened the envelope.

The subject (Dr. Van Vogt was thorough) was a healthy female Caucasian—and so on and so forth; Clock skimmed—no history TB, VD, alcoholism, addiction; appendix out, tonsils out; *virgo intacta.* All her own teeth except for two artificial ones on a bridge. Estimated time of death, between seven and midnight last Monday night. Immediate cause of death depressed skull fracture, blow or blows with blunt instrument: probably more than one blow, as area of fracture extensive—precise area— Clock skipped over the Latin. Deceased wearing hat when blows struck— No extraneous matter in wound; hat sent to lab. (Ask the lab if they got anything there.) By secondary indications, deceased may have been forcibly restrained some period prior to death: minor bruising both wrists, none on ankles but stockings could have prevented such from—

"Well!" said Clock, surprised.

Deceased had ingested codeine sometime within twelve to twenty-four hours prior to death. Amount unestimated. Codeine probably in tablet form, ingested orally.

"Now I will be damned," said Clock. He picked up the phone. "Get me Van Vogt. . . . Doctor. This autopsy report on Williams. What the hell about the codeine?"

78

"And so what about it?"

"Well, you give it a leeway, when she took it. Can't you pin it down?"

"My good Sergeant, these reactions so widely vary with the individual person, how soon it goes from bloodstream, how much makes what effect— No, I do not know how much, how many tablets— If it was taken, say, twenty-four hours before, most of it would be dissipated. Tablets, yes, it was definitely. By the mouth. The kind of tablets for pain, the toothache, sinus headache, whatever. For sleeping maybe, a person has such tablets left from a toothache, not? I don't say what I can't be certain."

Well, damn it, thought Clock, it tied together. "She could have taken a couple of tablets as early as, say, Sunday at midnight?"

"That could be, yes. Or Monday at noon. I do not say. The individual reaction—"

That tied together in a way. On Sunday night she'd gone to a party. A fairly big party, by what they heard: gala occasion. He could guess that she hadn't gone to many parties. And by what her mother said—all excited over the party, and sitting up late. It could be she couldn't get to sleep, and so she took a couple of codeine tablets—left over from some toothache (that bridge?) or something—to help her sleep.

So the codeine didn't have a damned thing to do with how she died. That at least explained her sitting up late that night, but—

Fran called at eight o'clock and Nell answered the phone. "I just wondered if he's found a new one yet."

"A— No. They're all impossible. He says he called it down on himself by criticizing Miss Williams. But, Fran, what on earth did Andrew tell him to send him off? He came home muttering about codeine and teeth and papers, and ever since dinner he's had *The Art of the Fugue* stacked on the stereo—you know how he thinks better to Bach—"

"Teeth?" said Fran blankly.

"And something will really have to be done," said Nell exasperatedly, "about that. That creature. A terror. Because Athelstane is getting a definite neurosis."

6

WHEN CLOCK got to the office on Saturday morning he found a note from Sergeant Raven: *Mr. Kane called in 8:10 P.M. was advised show up this morning.* The bereaved husband: and about all the help he was going to offer them was the formal identification of the body.

Kane showed up at nine o'clock, and of course he was shocked and bewildered. He was a good-looking fellow in his fifties, with a spare figure, plentiful graying hair, glasses, conservative dark suit and white shirt. The rangers, of course, hadn't known any details to tell him, and he seemed to have the idea that his wife had had an automobile accident. "But she's a good driver—did you say Sergeant? Of course with all the drunks—but I can't—"

Clock explained. Mr. Kane would have read about those cases, the last couple of months—this fellow abducting and beating those women. "This has all the marks of that one, Mr. Kane, only this time he used a little too much violence."

"Oh," said Kane. "Oh, yes, I saw something—about that. You mean Lucille was—was *killed?* Murdered? But that doesn't—not to—" people like us, he didn't say. And Clock had seen that reaction before too. The violence happened to anybody these days. "You think—the same man who hurt those other women k-killed Lucille?"

"That's what it looks like, sir. Now we'll have to ask you to identify your wife's body formally, but I'd like to ask you just a few questions—"

"Certainly," said Kane with automatic courtesy. He looked a little dazed. "But if I'd been at home! If I hadn't— You see, she didn't care for the—the snow, the mountains in winter. It's very beautiful up there—with the snow. Very quiet and—and so far from any distractions. I have a little cabin up there, I've had it for years. And it wasn't as if Lucille minded—"

"Yes, sir," said Clock patiently. "Don't blame yourself, Mr. Kane. This fellow seems to make sure the women are alone before he—moves in. You'd been away how long?"

"Since Monday," said Kane. "Monday I— I'd meant to go up last week but Lucille wasn't feeling well, coming down with a cold. But she was feeling better, and I left on Monday—about noon. It's only about a five-hour drive up there—"

"Would your wife have been careful about keeping the doors locked, there alone? Or—"

"Oh, of course. We were always careful—the rise in crime— No, Lucille isn't—wasn't a timid woman, but she was sensible. What? Yes, of course she drove—had her own car. You know, we'd only been married a little over a year—she was a widow, and I lost my first wife some years ago. Lucille had the house and, well, investments from her first husband, and as I didn't own a home—"

"You're retired, sir?" Let him ramble a little, settle him down, thought Clock.

"I suppose you could say so, in a way. I've been lucky, I made some lucky investments. I've always been something of a rolling stone, with no family—traveling. Wholesale importing, from the Orient mostly. And it just seemed the easiest thing, with Lucille having the house— But I shouldn't have left her alone—"

"Mr. Kane, would there have been much cash in the house?"

Dumbly he shook his head. "No, certainly not. It's foolish to keep cash at home—neither of us did. Lucille had a little jewelry, not a great deal—mostly costume stuff."

And of course the Masked Monster had not gone rummaging for the articles of value. The cash he had taken, period. "Any idea how much money your wife might have had in her purse?"

He shook his head. "No more than ten or twenty dollars, I wouldn't think."

"Well, have you looked around to see if there are any signs of disturbance at the house?" Kane hadn't, not knowing how she had died; and this following the same pattern, it was very unlikely there'd be anything useful to them in the house, but they had to look.

Clock took him down to the morgue. They had cleaned up the body some, and he saw that Lucille Kane had been a nice-looking woman, regular features and a creamy soft complexion, the silver-blond hair professionally cared for.

Kane identified the body in a subdued tone, and asked painfully if she'd been raped. "We don't think so, sir."

"Well, thank God for that at least. It doesn't seem—" He shook his head.

"Are there any relatives?"

He shook his head. "There weren't any children, and she was an only child. I think there are cousins somewhere but they hadn't kept up. A lot of friends, of course."

"I see. Well, we'd like to look over the house—"

"Surely," said Kane in a dull tone.

Clock and Petrovsky trailed him back to the house in West Hollywood. It was, as Petrovsky had said, an older place, two-storied Spanish stucco, on a quiet dead end street. Old-fashioned, solid furniture. And just a few little things showing to follow out the pattern.

"I hadn't noticed that at all," said Kane, surprised and annoyed. "We always came in the back way— Locked? Of course we kept the screen door locked." The screen door, a fancy aluminum one with decorative grillwork, beyond the solid front door, had had its screen slashed—one long vicious slice down from the latch, the screen bent back so X could reach in quick to unlatch the door.

In the front hall, a small throw rug was bunched up and kicked aside—as she stepped back from the gun, surprised and frightened?

"Where would her handbag have been? In her bedroom upstairs?"

"She carried—different ones," said Kane. "The way any woman— She had a—a purse organizer, I think she called it, she always carried, transferred it from one to another, you know. It has everything all together—place for cash, credit cards, I.D., driver's license— That'd have been in the top drawer of the credenza right here, she kept it handy— She was so kind-hearted, you know, she always bought from the children coming round—the Girl Scout cookies, the tickets to Little League games—"

The drawer was pulled halfway open. She'd never have left it like that, he said. There were two lamps on in the living room; it had been after dark, of course. Kane said he hadn't noticed that either. "It was rather a nerve-racking drive down, in the rain and fog— I came in the back way, had a little meal in the kitchen—after I'd called your office—and went straight to bed."

Clock was annoyed. Fourteen victims, and they didn't really know anything about him at all. And not one single lead to be had. The very anonymous one.

He'd just got back to the office when Jesse called. "Suppose the body can be released anytime?"

"Anytime," said Clock.

"Yes. Better get to the funeral arrangements. Monday, I suppose. But that autopsy report—"

"It could tie together," said Clock, and passed on his idea

about the party, and Margaret wakeful enough to take something to get to sleep.

"Well," said Jesse doubtfully. "See you."

But damn it, that business he'd do some work on at least, thought Clock. Legally the D.A. didn't have to show motive in a murder-first charge, but it was always helpful to be able to: and money was always such a nice motive. That incredible TV thing—those people. Saturday—did they work normal hours like other people? Other people, cops always excepted? He didn't know. He got the Beverly Hilton; he got Schwab.

"You'd like to talk to some of them?" said Schwab. "Well, I can probably locate some of them for you, Sergeant. But if you're thinking of your murder—now that is something—well, these are funny people to deal with. I never know where I am with 'em, and I've been dealing with 'em since—well, since TV, you can say." He sighed. "Sometimes, Sergeant, I regret the TV. Simpler when we just had to concoct the still-life ads for magazines and billboards. Oh, my, yes. Well, I'll call you back."

He called back in half an hour. "I've located the producer, director, three writers, and a Grand Panjandrum of Ace-Ames Productions. At the studio. If we hurry we might catch them still there—or for all I know they might be there till tomorrow morning. Sunset Boulevard." He gave an address.

And Clock didn't understand people like those at all; he didn't know what to make of them. Only a relatively small part of the population of Los Angeles is concerned with The Business: a small nucleus of a world to itself, The Business, and most of the people involved in it apparently blind and deaf to anything outside it.

It was a walled place about half a block square, far out on Sunset: there was a gate, a guard who knew Schwab and let them in. Inside, clutter: small buildings here and there, in no seeming order. Blacktop, cars left parked at different angles, work going on somewhere, pounding.

"What about the program?" asked Clock.

"O-u-t out. These people you can't reason with," said Schwab. "And I sometimes wonder, Sergeant, if we're not just fooling ourselves . . . that building straight ahead . . . and that is heresy, I suppose. But I wonder. Is it really necessary to keep pounding people over the head with TV commercials and billboards and full-page ads in national magazines, to persuade 'em to drink beer—or buy lipstick or cigarettes or T-bone steaks or automobiles? Aren't we just giving natural human impulse a little shove?"

Clock laughed. "Could be."

Alec Toomey was there, in a crowded little office—Clock supposed it was an office, desks and shelves—Toomey talkative and loud. The rest of them somehow stamped with the same brand. The producer, Jay Wilmot, was tall and thin, one of the other writers was a fat slob, the director, Robert Ten Eyck, a nondescript little fellow with a bald head, and the Grand Panjandrum, whose name Clock never caught at all, was a dark-bearded hook-nosed fellow who was busily cutting paper patterns out of folded crepe paper. But they all wore the expensive, rather odd sports clothes, two of them with ascot scarves in place of ties; they all swore a good deal, with the casual obscenities; and none of them seemed to be much interested in what Clock was doing there, or why.

He gathered that they were discussing a new series on the agenda. "You got to have a gimmick," the producer was saying. "A gimmick to catch 'em. Make 'em identify right off. Take if this guy's suddenly inherited a ranch, see—maybe he's from New York or—"

"You can't use Ray Dawson in a Western, for God's sake. He won't hold still for it—"

"Why not? I just thought of this thing, we bought the screen rights years back, but we could *use* it, just the central gimmick, adapt it. This guy from the city, where the hell it doesn't matter, he—"

They looked at the interruption of Schwab and Clock with

dislike and bewilderment. The only one who showed any reaction to Margaret Williams' name was Toomey; and Clock wondered if he knew she was dead. He felt confused: and these men weren't actors, but they were in The Business and it could be everybody involved in that was, consciously or not, an actor. He'd thought, and on the surface fact it was so, that Margaret Williams—in concert with some other, more important people —had done these men some deadly harm. Any of them might have felt vindictive. But they stared at him, annoyed at interruption. Jay Wilmot asked, "Who the hell is Margaret Williams?" The fat writer, staring at Schwab, was momentarily reminded of old grievance and muttered, "Saints we got to make the cops yet." The director peered at Clock without interest and asked Schwab what the hell he wanted *now.*

Clock had his badge out.

"A cop now he brings in. A real-life cop. Enough trouble he handed us with the fake cops. For Christ's sake," said Wilmot, "we're *busy.* Now, the gimmick for this thing— Look, Jesus, do I know Dawson, but we can fake it, shoot him at an angle and use that left profile, he'll get by—we've got all those process shots from that desert thing, and—"

"Not another Western, Jay, for God's sake not another—"

The Grand Panjandrum said, *"Voilà!"* and flicked a wrist to unfold a long banner of crepe paper with a cut-out design of running fleurs-de-lis. Everybody looked at him as if he were mad.

"You don't," said Schwab downstairs, "really think any of them tie up to a murder, Sergeant?"

"I must say," said Clock, "they all seem to have forgotten all about 'Crimefighters,' don't they? All of a sudden?"

"And it's queer to think," said Schwab, "that just now and then people like that do put together a very fine film. Whether it's luck or genius I don't know. Do you think you could get any alibis out of them—for when? Last Monday night. Do any of them remember where they were, five days later?"

"I'm not," said Clock, "right now, thinking it'd be worth the effort to ask, Mr. Schwab."

"No," said Schwab sadly. "Like talking to children, in a way. I'm flying home tomorrow. To tell you the truth, Sergeant, these TV people make me uneasy."

Clock knew how he felt.

He went back to the office and reread some of the statements on their Masked Monster, feeling frustrated. Any use to interview all those women again?

The addresses where the women had been picked up were widely separated: they couldn't fall into, say, a single laundry route, a bakery truck route, a Fuller Brush— And none of the women had indicated in any way that they thought the man was at all familiar, that they'd seen him before, however casually. Well, even if they had, the ski mask would effectively distort both features and voice. That was wild. How was he picking them? All too probably, just at random, driving around looking for a house with few lights on, chinks at shades where he could look in.

On the homicide, however, the lab might turn up something. Occasionally the lab performed seeming miracles, with all their bright-boy chemists and new machines and tests.

"Where is everybody?" he asked Sergeant Pitman.

"Out to lunch mostly," said Pitman. Clock looked at his watch, a little surprised to find it was twelve-thirty. "Pete went out to talk to the Kanes' neighbors again. He said that being a dead end street maybe somebody had noticed the car."

"A long shot," said Clock, and Mantella came in looking amused.

"You'll never believe this, Sergeant," he said. "But never. Sometimes the deck gets stacked in our favor. We've got Henry Nadinger."

"You don't say. Where and how?"

"He got into a fight with a fellow at a bar over on Fourth,

there was some furniture broken, and the bartender called the cops. One of the uniformed men spotted Nadinger from the A.P.B."

"The little pros," said Clock, "doing what comes naturally, I do get a little tired of 'em, Johnny. But I suppose we've got to lean on him, try to pry a statement out of him on Cameron if possible. After lunch—I suddenly realize I'm starving. I suppose he's tucked away all comfy?"

"At the Alameda jail. Don't forget to tell him all about his rights."

"As if I needed to be reminded."

Jesse went up to Forest Lawn in Glendale and talked to a funeral director. He had Miss Williams' bankbooks from Clock; she'd had slightly over a thousand dollars in a checking account, nearly two thousand in a savings account. Eventually he'd get paid back. He wondered again if she had made a will.

He felt a little annoyed at the would-be sophisticates who poked fun at Forest Lawn. A beautiful, green, quiet place it was, like a big park. And the little unimportant material residue had to be tidied away: might as well do it gracefully.

He drove down to Berendo Street and told Shackleton about the funeral. One o'clock Monday, the Church of the Recessional. "I'll see people get told, thanks, Mr. Falkenstein. A lot of us'll want to pay our last respects, sure. I don't suppose her mother'll be able to be there? That's terrible. My wife, she always used to say funerals are depressing, but what I say is, a nice tasteful funeral just shows proper respect, and if dead people know about it—which I think they got to, Mr. Falkenstein—it must kind of reassure them, know what I mean? I'll let everybody know, Mr. Falkenstein, thanks."

The warehouse truck would be coming on Monday, to clear out the Williams apartment, stow all the odds and ends away neatly, to wait until called for. Which they probably never would be. Jesse went upstairs and unlocked the door. That autopsy report. Codeine? Oh, yes?

In the one bathroom, an ordinary medicine cabinet. He opened it. Empirin compound: comparable to aspirin. Milk of magnesia. White's A and D Cream. An eye-bath solution. A prescription bottle labeled *Miss M. Williams, 2 tablets every 6 hrs. Dr. J. S. Hope.* It was empty. (So a refillable prescription, which one for codeine probably wouldn't be?) Jesse copied down the doctor's name. A roll of cotton. Iodine. Four prescription bottles on the bottom shelf, containing various-colored capsules: *Mrs. H. Williams . . . Dr. J. S. Hope.* Codeine, thought Jesse, was yellow; and the police surgeon said tablets.

The last tablets in the bottle? He looked in the little wastebasket there: used Kleenex, a worn-down nub of pale coral lipstick, a broken emery board. Just to be thorough he looked at all the other wastebaskets: one each in the bedrooms, one in the kitchen. No medicine bottles.

And there was also, of course, Dan Purcell.

He locked the apartment and went down the hall to the Lightner apartment. Brenda was there alone; he had surprised her washing her hair. A very pretty girl, fresh complexion without makeup, hair wrapped in a blue towel. "Oh—Mr.—Mr. Falkenstein, you were Miss—"

"Like to ask you a few questions if you don't mind."

She looked surprised. "Well, come in. Daddy's gone to the library, like always on Saturdays. Have the police found out any more about who—"

"Not much," said Jesse. "There were—um—people who didn't like her. But it's rather up in the air. Tell me, Miss Lightner. This Dan Purcell—"

"There were?" she said. "Who didn't like Miss Williams? That's—funny. I wouldn't think— Well, Dan. That really rocked me. In jail for robbery! I—"

"Was he mad?" asked Jesse. "When you turned him down? Told him you wouldn't date him any more?"

"What do you—" She looked at him a little warily.

"Argue with you?"

She was blushing slowly. "Well—"

"Try to persuade you, change your mind?" She was blushing deeper; she shook her head. "Well, how did he react? You implied, you told him you'd found out he had a record so you didn't want any more to do with him. So what did he say?"

She bit her lip in silence, and then the blush faded and she looked up at him with the sudden vulnerability of youth. "I— I was only out with him twice. And"—a gulp—"well, a lot of boys'll, you know, make a pass, you let them know you're not that kind, so they *do* know, and after that they act all right, you still go out with them. I thought—that way, with Dan, when he —the latest time we'd been out. But—well, when I—told him that, then, how I knew he'd been in jail, and in trouble with the police before that, he— No, Mr. Falkenstein, he didn't argue at me. I—I felt sort of dirty about it, that I'd ever—liked him. He just l-looked at me, and sort of sneered, and said so I was the real goody-goody square, he'd already figured, so skip it. I felt— But why did you—"

Indeed, thought Jesse sadly. Which did not sound as if ex-con Dan Purcell was at all interested in how Brenda had found out about his pedigree.

"Well, thanks very much," he said.

And there were no employment agencies open on Saturday afternoons. He now had another will to be typed. The papers talking about unemployment—but the unemployed seemed fairly choosy as to what jobs they would take, and there seemed to be a complete dearth of trained legal secretaries. To think how lightly he had complained about the one he'd had—

He went home. Athelstane, unusually, didn't come galumphing up to wash his face; he was sitting under the birch tree at the end of the yard, with a brooding look on his jowly face.

"Hey, boy," said Jesse, "you don't really mind that little scrap of a girl, do you?"

Athelstane gave him a dark look and thumped his tail list-lessly once.

A little worried about that, Jesse went in the back door and heard Nell's voice from the living room; went down the hall.

"*No!*" said Nell. "You are entirely too hairy for the furniture — Off! You hear me?" She picked Sally off the couch and depos-ited her on the floor, dropped the well-chewed rubber ball beside her. "Understand?"

Sally waved her hairy banner of a tail once. Neatly she picked up the ball, gathered her hindquarters together, and with a rush and scramble just made it back to the couch, where she lay down to chew the ball. She waved her tail politely at Nell, but turned her back deliberately. There was no air of mischief about her at all; merely, Sally did not recognize humans as being necessary arbiters of her behavior at any time. Sally liked humans quite well, and she would defend the humans she lived with against all villainy, but at the moment she had decided to chew her ball on the couch, and she could not have cared less what the humans thought about it.

"Honestly!" said Nell, turning to notice him. "This creature!"

"Never knew a Peke intimately before. Edgar says they call 'em lion dogs. Stubborn as all hell, he said, but brainy."

"And you had to bring one home. Athelstane's scared of her, Jesse. She bounces at him. The poor darling just sits and broods. And watches her from behind things. We've got to find a home for her. We can't—"

"Well, think about it, sure," said Jesse, feeling guilty.

"Come on, come on, Henry, you might as well tell us about it," said Clock. He and Petrovsky and Mantella had been lean-ing on Nadinger for a while, without much result; Nadinger had been questioned in depth by cops before. They had read him the piece about his rights, and they had given him cigarettes and a cup of coffee—he had complained about there being only powdered milk—and they were feeling tired of Nadinger, the pro hood who would be up for murder-second.

"I don't know why we bother," said Petrovsky. "He's tied in very tight by the gun. You know that, don't you, Henry?" he added casually. "Why you shot Cameron in that liquor store heist we don't know—like always the owner'd told all the help, hand over the money, don't risk getting killed. But you did shoot him, that we know, because when you took a shot at the other clerk we got the slug, and it matched the ones in Cameron."

Nadinger looked at them in sullen silence. Since the last time he'd been inside, he had gained about twenty pounds and grown a beard, probably with the idea of changing his appearance from his official mug shot. It wasn't much of a beard. His hair was thin, he was more fair than dark anyway, and after the years of shaving, the sparse weedy growth of sandy hair on his face had sprouted in several directions at once. He wasn't a handsome man to start with, a bulbous nose and little pig eyes and ears sticking out; and the attempted beard made him look a little like a moth-eaten muskrat, patches of bare skin showing through, tufts pointing up, down, and sideways.

"And we now have the gun, don't we?" said Mantella. The gun had been on him: an old Colt .38 revolver, which had been one of several guns Ballistics said it might be.

"It doesn't matter whether he talks, we've got him nailed for it," said Clock. "Leave it lay. Waste of time. He shot Cameron just because he's a mean bastard." He turned away.

"That ain't so," said Nadinger in a growl. "I never. I never aimed shoot nobody—I was just after the loot. No, he didden try go for a gun or nothin'. That other guy did, but that one didden. He handed over the loot right off."

"So why'd you shoot him, Henry?" asked Petrovsky mildly. "After he'd handed over the loot?"

"He hadden no *call*," said Nadinger resentfully. "No *call* to get personal. With me holdin' a gun on him, damn it, he hadden no call *laugh* at me." He blinked up at them. "Laugh at me— handin' over the loot. Laughin' *at my beard!* He says, what-samatter, big man, moths been at your whiskers, he says. He says, my dad's old billy goat grow a better set o' whiskers than that! He laughed at me—that damn—"

They looked at each other.

Sooner or later, cops saw and heard everything.

At least part of Jesse's reason for calling Martha Weglund on Sunday morning was, of course, Sally.

"Oh," she said. "Well, anything I can tell you, Mr. Falkenstein —but I really don't know what—"

He told her about the funeral and she thanked him. "Of course there are a lot of people who'll want to be there. I'll call Mrs. Rathbone at once, she'll— Well, I suppose you can come around if you like, now is as good as any time, but what I could—"

And in her ordinary neat Hollywood apartment, she looked at him in surprise and said she couldn't imagine why he wanted to hear about that. "It was the next night she was— And what could that, anything in her personal life— But that police detective said— *Was* it? Something—personal? *Margaret?* That doesn't seem—"

"Just take it we're collecting—data," said Jesse vaguely. And he felt amusedly put in his place when Martha Weglund looked, for the first time, at lank and lean and unhandsome Falkenstein and said in a bewildered tone that Margaret had thought a good deal of him. He felt flattered that she had. (People underestimated Margaret.)

"Sunday night?" she said. "The reception? Well, it's an annual affair, of course. There are regular monthly luncheon meetings, not everybody gets to all of those. It's mostly a social club, there's a bimonthly newsletter and the Silver Tea in April and

— Professional Women," and she laughed briefly. "It sounds—but actually it's mostly a social thing. Some of the women aren't working at all now, if they did once—secretaries, office managers, any sort of job. Sunday night—a week ago today—it was the usual jam. Four or five hundred people, at a guess. Husbands and guests, and the speaker was Dr. Alice Wolinsky, the psychiatrist—" She grimaced. "Rather boring, I thought. What? Why, we borrow the clubhouse owned by the University Women's Association, it's on Fairfax. No, not a dinner—eight to eleven, and—"

"Well." The old man said find out more about the party. What? "A reception for whom?"

"The incoming president. Mrs. Helen Rathbone. Well, of course neither Margaret nor I knew everybody there—it's a large membership. Women in all sorts of jobs. Women who've ever worked at a professional job. I don't know why I'd kept up my membership really. No, there were a lot of people there I didn't know, it'd be the same for Margaret. And she'd know some women I didn't. Well, of course a few women who'd been at college with us, in our class or just at the same time. Time— It doesn't seem possible, twenty years ago," she said suddenly. "Margaret's father was alive then, he was a pharmacist, you know—"

"People there Sunday night," asked Jesse, "she knew—you know she knew, even if you didn't know them? You were both there at the reception, but not together all the time?"

"Well, no. She got there before I did, there was a lot of milling around, you know how it is, and then when the program got under way Margaret was sitting with the Enrights across the aisle from me. Well, people we both knew. The Enrights. Dick Enright married again after Sally died last year, I don't know the wife, her name's Ruth, I think. Mrs. Rathbone, both Margaret and I knew her. May Foster, of course, and Estelle Sparr, and Joan Pitt, and Stella Robbins—we knew all of them— But what on earth you should want to know that for—"

"Well, thanks very much," said Jesse. "Er—Miss Weglund— you know Mrs. Williams isn't going to be able to take care of the dog. Margaret's dog. I wonder if you'd be int—"

"That Peke?" she said. "That lapdog? Thank you, no, Mr. Falkenstein! I couldn't keep a dog anyway, gone all day at work. But if I could, the last dog I'd want would be—"

"Look, family feeling," said Jesse plaintively. "I've got another will left over from Friday, and letters, and seven appointments today with God knows what kind of paper work turning up, and nobody to do it."

"And I'd just been finding out what heaven it is to have no regular job," said Fran. "There must be scads of legal secretaries around—"

"Hiding where I can't find them. Come in, Fran. You understand the electric typewriter."

"Oh, damn!" exploded Fran. "Of all times for you to lose a secretary—"

"Desperate situations—" said Jesse meekly. Maybe, Nell had said this morning, they could give Sally to Fran and Andrew, extra wedding present. As if Fran, much less Andrew, would give houseroom to—

Of course neither of them had really met Sally. As Jesse and Nell were coming to know her.

"I'm calling all the agencies in the yellow pages," he said hastily. Somewhere in the environs of L.A. county, in upwards of eight million population, there must be one available, reasonably efficient legal secretary?

"Oh, damnation," said Fran. "All *right.* I'll be in. As soon as I've done the breakfast dishes."

Jesse put the phone down. Monday morning . . . Just a week ago today, about now, Miss Williams phoning—underestimated Margaret. Saying an extremely urgent matter, must tell, it

96

wouldn't take more than an hour. Saying had to look up the address, West—

Saying, he remembered suddenly, "I must tell her." Who? And what? Something to do with the party the night before? Sitting up late, said her mother. Over papers.

7

"CERTAINLY I WAS terrified," said Patricia Morgan. "I couldn't scream, my throat sort of closed up. Even just thinking of it, I get mad all over again that I couldn't scream! But I tried to keep my head. The doorbell rang just as I was looking at 'Dragnet,' it was a quarter past seven, the commercial had just come on. After dark, and I didn't just open the door, of course. There's one of those peepholes in the door. I opened it and asked who it was. Well, you can see I'm not very tall"—Mrs. Morgan, fifty-one and not looking it, with a trim figure and blond curls, was a diminutive five feet, one hundred pounds even—"and I couldn't really see much but the top of his head, a wool cap I thought, but it was a cold night. And when he said, Western Union, of course I thought of Anne—my sister in Boston, she hadn't been well—and I was frightened, I opened the door and —there he was."

"In his ski mask," said Clock.

"Oh, my goodness. And the gun! He came in like—like lightning, and he said, 'Don't scream, lady, go get your handbag. Move!' Well, I moved. I was alone in the house, Ken was out of town for the company and Cissy was in the hospital overnight for a shot and grooming—"

"Cissy."

"Our poodle. And in a way I was glad she was, he might have shot her if she'd tried to— Well, of course I thought he was just after the money, but after he'd taken it from my purse he grabbed me by one wrist and said, 'Come on, we're going for a little ride.' And—"

"Just a minute, Mrs. Morgan. Now at the time, you gave Lieutenant Hellenthal a description of the man, as well as you could. Memory's a funny thing. Sometimes after you've thought a thing over, you'll remember something more— I'd just like you to describe him again to me. What you could see of him."

"Well—" She made a grimace. "I tried to keep my head. I've never been one to fall into hysterics, and of course I'd read about this man in the papers—he'd already kidnapped four other women. And when I realized it was probably the same one, when he said that, I just said to myself, You're going to keep your eyes open and remember every little thing you can, to tell the police. Always assuming I got out of it to talk to police afterward! But you couldn't tell much about him, Sergeant—as I told the other man then. Judging by Ken, who's six feet even, this man was only about five-seven or eight, I'd say. He was only in the light, in the entrance hall, maybe a minute—my handbag was right there on the hall table. He had this black ski mask on, you could only see his eyes moving—it was rather horrible— and a dark suit, charcoal or black, with a dark turtleneck sweater instead of a shirt. He's not fat or thin, just medium— but I'd guess, by the way he moves, he's fairly young. Well, when he said that, he pulled me out and banged the front door and said, 'You're going to drive us, lady,' and handed me some keys. Then I was sure who he was—from what the papers said."

"So, the car," said Clock.

"Well, I tried to get a good look at it, but that was impossible too," she said apologetically. "It was right at the curb, side on to me, but there's not a street light very near and the car was a dark color. And he shoved me into it so fast, and dived in after me— It was a strange car to me. A small car. Vaguely the size of a Falcon or Corvair . . . Oh, I drive a Dodge two-door. And there were strips of adhesive on the dash and in the middle of the wheel. I was nervous, and I hadn't driven a stick shift in years, but I finally got it started and found the lights—the dash lit up bluey-white, and— Oh, one thing, the speedometer wasn't working."

"Oh?"

"It was dead—didn't show at all. He said to be careful, take it easy, we didn't want to get stopped for speeding, did we?"

"Could you tell anything about his voice? Accent?"

She shook her blond head. "The mask— He spoke very low, but it was just a medium voice, not deep or high. He told me to get up on Mulholland. Well, I could guess what was coming, and I was frightened, I'll never say I wasn't but I thought if I could do something—attract a police car or— But when I got onto Sunset and speeded up he—he dug the gun in my ribs and said, 'Take it slow, lady, slow and easy.' And I hadn't any choice, I turned up Laurel Canyon Boulevard and that runs right into Mulholland—and we might have been a thousand miles from anywhere, you know how it is up there at night! When he said to stop, I did, and I thought I could try to run, but he had hold of my wrist, he shoved me out of the car onto the shoulder of the road and began hitting me—"

"Did he begin hitting you in the face first, or—"

Patricia Morgan's hand strayed to her temple. "He certainly did, Sergeant. He hit me here with his fist, and he still had hold of my wrist with his other hand, and I got mad— I'm afraid I've got a temper, and I know I'm not very big, but suddenly it seemed so silly just to stand there and *let* him—bully and coward like that, lunatic or not—and I hit him back as hard as I could, I slapped him hard, and I *swore* at him, and he began hitting me with both hands, and then I slipped and fell but I pulled him down with me—it was like a sea of mud up there, we had so much rain in December—and I tried to bite him, only I just got his sleeve," she said regretfully. "I only had one idea, if I could *mark* him some way—and I know I scratched his face. But then he hit me on the head with something, the doctor afterward said probably a rock, and I went out."

"Yes," said Clock. Mrs. Morgan was, in fact, lucky to be alive. She had sustained a skull fracture if a minor one, a number of bruises, a broken nose, one front tooth knocked out, and a pulled tendon in one shoulder. "You couldn't estimate how long?"

"No idea. When I came to, I was vaguely aware I was in a car, moving—after a while I remembered what had happened, I guess I groaned or something—but I don't remember seeing him again. I was sort of propped up, half lying across the seat, the front seat—and the car stopped and he—all I remember is a *shape*—leaned in front of me and I suppose opened the door, and—pushed me. I couldn't save myself, I fell right out headfirst, and he pushed me again and then I heard the car door slam and the car drove off. A car. It was dark and cold and I felt so weak—but you have to keep trying, the best you can, don't you? I felt around, there was a curb, so I was in a street somewhere—the gutter all wet and slimy. I managed to crawl up onto the sidewalk, and there was a light—it looked so far away but I kept trying to crawl, and all of a sudden this dear dog came up and found me and barked and barked, and it was Mr. Galluzzi's dog, he had him out for a walk, and he called the police and an ambulance. It was the corner of Oak and Fourteenth, right downtown—" Just a block from the Stack, of course.

Clock regarded Mrs. Morgan with respect and frustration. He had picked six of the Masked Monster's victims, by their original statements, as being possessed of more than average common sense and courage; he and Petrovsky and Mantella were reinterviewing them. And here was Patricia Morgan, certainly common-sensible and brave, keeping her head and remembering details, and she gave them nothing at all. Just as she hadn't at the time.

"Had you had any peddlers around that day, Mrs. Morgan, do you remember?"

She shook her head. "We don't get many up here." This was Londonderry Avenue above the boulevard.

"Any telephone calls—besides personal ones?"

She thought, and smiled. "Only the man who wanted to sell us a family plot in Forest Lawn."

"Well, thanks very much for going over it again. I'm sorry if I reminded you of—" Clock got up.

"I didn't help, did I?" She looked sorry and angry. "And now he's murdered this poor woman. I wish I could help you more, but"—she made a helpless gesture—"with that ski mask over his whole head—"

"Yes, I see, thanks," said Clock dispiritedly.

He drove across Hollywood to an apartment on Los Feliz Boulevard, where he heard substantially the same story from Helena Baynes. Mrs. Baynes was a widow of fifty-seven, and twice the size of Patricia Morgan, and she hadn't had any qualms about opening her front door because it was in an apartment, people all around. But the masked man had grabbed her, got his hand over her mouth right off, and said if she screamed he'd shoot. "I don't deny I was scared," she said. "I didn't have the breath to scream then." And when he'd dragged her out to his car—the apartment was on the ground floor—and told her to drive, she told him she didn't know how to drive; she'd never driven a car. He'd pushed her into the back seat then and tied her wrists and ankles with something that might have been neckties, she thought, and thrust a handerchief into her mouth as a gag. (About that handkerchief Clock knew: it had been still in her mouth when she was found, and the lab had spent quite a while over that handkerchief—which had turned out to be the kind of men's plain white cotton handkerchief on sale at any dime store for ten cents.) Mrs. Baynes had tried to keep her head too, but all she could say about the spot where he pulled her out of the car and started to beat her was that there were a lot of trees and bushes, it was dark, she could hear traffic quite near but saw no lights. Barnsdall Park, right in the middle of Hollywood?

"Wait a minute," said Clock suddenly. He had her original statement with him; now he thought there were a couple of questions she should have been asked. "You said the back seat of a car. The car parked right on Los Feliz?" That was a busy street and well lighted, somebody should have—

"No, round on the side street, Catalina. He just marched me around—"

"The back seat. Was there a rear door, or did he have to push the front seat forward, to shove you into the back?"

"I don't know much about cars," she said doubtfully. "I can't recall— It was a kind of a tight fit, I know he bruised me a good bit shoving me in, but there, I'm not all that slim any more."

And did that say, for seventy-five-percent sure, a two-door? Maybe.

And the only difference to the rest of the story was that Mrs. Baynes hadn't remembered being shoved out of the car, had regained consciousness in the ambulance. She'd been found by a dime-store clerk coming home from work, near the corner of Bonsallo and Cherry—a block from the Stack. Of course. And she had tried to remember details for the police, but the same things came out: medium-sized, black ski mask, dark suit, dark sweater. She thought crepe-soled shoes, he was so quiet. Low voice.

Clock sighed. He suddenly thought of something, and asked her, "Gloves?" She said no. "Well, do you recall seeing a ring?" Mrs. Baynes couldn't say; it was dark.

It was getting on for noon. Clock drove back downtown and met Petrovsky and Mantella just turning into the parking lot. They all got in the Pontiac and went up to Gino's for lunch.

"So," said Petrovsky, "a big fat nothing, Andrew. These were the women who didn't panic—he didn't rape any of these— they tried to use their heads and remember things. They give us the most details—and the same details second time round—and it adds to nothing." He lit a cigarette and produced his notebook. "Ski mask, dark suit, dark sweater, rubber-soled shoes, medium-sized, low voice. The car. A light color, back seat but no definite idea two- or four-door, no guess at the make. Not a new car. Dash lights green. Adhesive tape. Is this a psycho at all? He's very damn cute."

"Sometimes the psychos are. Johnny?"

Mantella shook his head. "I needn't waste time repeating it. One of my girls had a ride in the light-colored car, the other one in the little dark-colored one. The only new thing I heard was about that. Mrs. Ida Jenkins, who drove that one up to Mulholland Drive, says it needed a tune-up and a brake job. The brakes were loose, she says, and the engine was running loud and rough."

"Timing off," said Clock. "And that gives us nothing too." Well, these anonymous ones were always tough to work.

"So where do we go," asked Petrovsky, "from here?"

"This time we've got a corpse," said Clock heavily. "See what the lab turns up on the clothes and so on. What the autopsy shows."

Petrovsky made a derisive sound.

Jesse was in court until noon. He bolted a sandwich at a drugstore and drove up to Forest Lawn to attend Margaret Williams' funeral. He couldn't altogether agree with Mr. Shackleton about funerals: the residue had to be tidied away, but no need to make such a production of it. Mrs. Hulby had said when the Williamses went to church, which was seldom, they'd gone to the Episcopal church on Sunset, so he'd asked for that minister. He was a tall man, impressive in dark robes, and he read Scripture in a beautifully modulated voice.

The church was well filled. Several of the people from the apartment; Martha Weglund, and a large contingent of, probably, the Professional Women, some with husbands; people he didn't know, who might be other neighbors, people from the church. Surprisingly, Roland Henry was there, in a conventional dark suit.

And Jesse had told Nell that if he happened to shuffle off before she did, if she let the damn undertaker leave the coffin open for people to file by and stare at him, he'd haunt her; it was a barbaric ritual he deplored. But on this occasion, he was curiously grateful for a chance to look at Margaret Williams again. . . . Underestimated Margaret, the very unsuspected quality, fluttering around him for nine years, and Falkenstein blind and deaf to the woman beneath the surface. Of course she hadn't advertised herself. . . .

The undertaker had used more cosmetics than Margaret ever would have. In death she had dignity, at least: the dark curls stiffly arranged, lids down on the pale-blue eyes. For the first time Jesse noticed that she'd had a stubborn jaw. But the essential self, of course, was gone; the corpse had nothing to say to him.

He filed out with the others, and most of them drove up the hill for the graveside ceremony. It ended, the minister turned away, and the mourners straggled after him down the slope toward the cars parked in the narrow curving road.

"Mr. Falkenstein?" said a subdued voice. Jesse turned, stumbling over one of the inset bronze plaques that were the only markers permitted in this cemetery.

"Mr. Shackleton." The tall bald old man looked different in formal dark clothes, a white shirt, discreet tie. "You satisfied with the funeral?"

"It was a very nice funeral, I'm sure Margaret would be pleased," said Shackleton. But he looked uneasy. "Mr. Falkenstein, I've been talking with Mrs. Hulby and Brenda Lightner, and something they said—and something you said the other day — Is it a fact, the police are thinking it could have been a—a personal thing? I thought it was just what they call a mugger, attacking lone women—but if it was something like that—somebody who knew her— Do they think that?"

"Afraid it looks that way, Mr. Shackleton. More likely. Needn't go into all the reasons, but that's so."

"Now that's awful," said Shackleton. "And seems— Margaret Williams, last woman you'd think— But if that's so, Mr. Falkenstein, I guess there's something I'd better tell you. Don't sound like much of anything, but I guess you never know. Maybe the police'd want to know."

"About what?"

"Well"—Shackleton looked uneasier—"it sounds silly, but she'd had quite a lot of trouble with that new tenant in six B downstairs. Mr. Gallagher."

"She had? Just recently? Haven't heard of Gallagher before."

"He just moved in last month. I got to say I didn't cotton to him much, but he's been a quiet tenant so far, until acourse he had this ruction with Miss Williams. Since a couple of weeks before she—got killed."

"Him with her, or vice versa? What about?"

"Those damn dogs," said Shackleton, exasperated. "I'm fond of animals myself, Mr. Falkenstein, and I never thought 'twas fair—say No Pets just because it's an apartment. But some people take good care of pets, and show some consideration for other people, and some don't. Miss Williams lived in my place for twenty years, I guess she had some priority over a new tenant. But Mr. Gallagher came complaining to me, she wouldn't listen to him, there wasn't any reason they couldn't make an agreement about different times to use the yard—see, the back yard's fenced."

"Use the yard. To let the dog run in."

"Yes, sir. Miss Williams liked her little dog to get some exercise outdoors, acourse. She'd put her out in the yard when she came home from work, in summer when it was still light, and weekends she'd take her on walks. Well, Mr. Gallagher says to me that dog o' hers is vicious and frightens his, and he's afraid

106

Miss Williams' dog'll hurt his—and a poor excuse for a dog that one looks to be, all right. It sounds silly, but Mr. Gallagher blew it up into a real ruction, he said some nasty things about Miss Williams."

"I see," said Jesse. "Well, it probably doesn't mean anything, but thanks, Mr. Shackleton—I'll see the sergeant hears about it." He wandered on down the hill to where he'd left the Ford. That Sally, he thought. Dogs and people got to be alike, all right: Sally, like her late mistress, getting underestimated. Looking so harmless and little.

There was somebody waiting for him in the passenger seat of the Ford. "Well, I didn't spot you," said Jesse, sliding under the wheel.

"Got there late—sat in the back," said old Mr. Walters. He was puffing on a cigar. "Had the fancy to see what kind of people she knew. Who might turn up. Who was that talkin' to you just now?"

Jesse told him about the dogs. "Hum. Does sound silly, but murders've been committed over sillier things. No harm to take a look at Gallagher. You found a new girl yet?"

"I have not," said Jesse. "They seem to be scarce as hens' teeth. Decent efficient ones, at least. I've got applications in at every employment agency in town. Meanwhile Fran's sitting on the office feeling cross at big brother."

Mr. Walters laughed. "Fran anxious to start bein' a plain housewife," he said approvingly. "You got any immediate appointments? I'll buy you a drink."

"I could use one. And you haven't heard about the autopsy report. . . ." Over the drink, in a booth at a very olde English bar on Sunset Boulevard, he relayed that and their old maestro mulled it over. "I want to talk to the doctor—evidently a family doctor, they both went to him."

The old man replenished his glass from his private bottle absently. "Codeine. Apparently not a very big amount. I don't know that I'd take a bet, Jesse, that you'd find this doctor ever

107

gave her a codeine prescription. . . . I didn't spot anybody at that funeral who looked like a mystery story writer. That writers' club—"

"Just one, and a very nice fellow. Roland Henry. It was good of him to come," said Jesse. "Pure formality. He's a very nice guy."

"Um," said the old man. "Wonder if Andrew's turned up anything more interesting in her letter files. Damn it, Jesse, she looked like such a nonentity of a female—"

"Same like her dog," said Jesse. "Edgar, would you like a nice little Peke? Do you good to exercise her every day—"

"A Peke? Listen, boy, for my sins I live with some of that family o' mine. Hardly let *me* off a leash, like to call the police if I'm not home by dark. And Betty with that damn feisty little shy-wah-wah, that Peke'd make one mouthful of it. Don't I know! Doesn't Nell like her?"

"It isn't Nell, it's Sally. Athelstane's afraid of her. He broods."

Mr. Walters laughed long. "It figures, though. . . . There was something somebody said that struck me, y' know. Just as a kind of profound remark, though I'm damned if I can see how it might apply. You reportin' all this at second hand—that Brenda girl, who said— And be damned if it wasn't Miss Williams said it, if you got it straight."

"Said what?"

"Well, she said to Brenda—if Brenda got it straight—that you had to be careful, in a city. Said in a city anybody might be anything." The old man drank reflectively. "Which is absolutely right. Never know who you're rubbing elbows with."

"But what could that say—"

"Don't know. Just something to keep in mind. What sticks in my mind, Jesse, is that damn queer thing—the magazine cover. In her *mouth*. Why? Pretty poor excuse for a gag. What's it mean?"

"God knows," said Jesse, and finished his drink.

108

"You can see the edges join up," said Winter. "It's the piece from this magazine cover, all right. What the hell does it mean?"

Clock said he couldn't even guess. He looked at the lab exhibit with gloomy interest. With their usual finicky attention to detail, the lab had pressed and dried the now somewhat dilapidated piece of stiff shiny paper which had been wadded up in the corpse's mouth, and it was laid out under glass along with the rest of the cover from the magazine in the back of the loaner car. The remainder of the cover, still attached to the body of the magazine, had been carefully removed and lined up with the other. With the naked eye you could see the alignment, blurred here and there where a minute piece was missing.

The whole cover was about eight and a half by eleven inches. Across the top of it was a line of print: *Virginia's Puzzle of Teen-age Rape-Slayer.* Then the words in larger, bolder print, MASTER DETECTIVE, and the current month and price of the magazine. The tear began just under the small 60¢, and ran down diagonally right across the next line of print. Remaining attached to the magazine had been *Beauties,* and lower down, *Den,* and lower yet, *Sex.* The larger piece, on which creases and stains still showed, had been flattened out and joined up. Aligned, the whole cover was reconstituted sensibly: *Beauties Abducted from Denver Restaurant—Sexual Maniac Loose in Georgia!* "Oh, yes," said Clock. "So it matches. It tells us nothing, why it was in her mouth."

"Well, it tells you the piece in her mouth was from the magazine in her car. It's interesting. A very unusual little clue, Sergeant."

"What else have you got, if anything?"

Winter moved over to a desk away from the long lab table. "Give you this and that. We've been going over her clothes." He picked up a couple of the little plastic bags used for evidence. The plain beige dress, tan stockings, black coat and hat, and presumably the respectable female underwear Miss Williams had died in. "Couple of things showed up, I don't know how much they'll say to you. First, on the hem of the dress, a few granules of moth crystals."

"Moth crystals? You mean the stuff to kill moths?"

"That's right. I don't know what they call the things, but they're like a big cake—about the size of a bar of soap— I think the principle is that they keep releasing fumes of some sort. For moths and silverfish. Anyway, we isolated the brand for you."

"The hem of her dress— Hell," said Clock, "it could have come from her own closet. Dress dropped on the floor there once."

"Could be. From the coat, caught under the collar in back—" Winter offered a little bag, dropping it on Clock's palm. "Sequins. Four multicolored sequins, such as are found on—well, what? Ask our wives—I understand you've just acquired one of those, Sergeant, congratulations— Evening jackets, fancy sweaters, fancy handbags—whatever."

"And damn it, that could also have been from something in her own closet, the coat hanging next to it."

"Well, we don't always produce miracles. There are various stains and dust we're still analyzing."

Clock, suddenly remembering the warehouse truck, fled back to his office and called Jesse.

"I just got back from the funeral. What? Sequins? Moths? Yes, I've got that. Somehow I don't connect sequins with Miss Williams, but I suppose—it's nothing like evidence, Andrew, sequins there or not. She may once have had something with sequins, I don't suppose it was a new coat. Well, there's something else I want to look at there anyway. No, I haven't found a new one yet."

"Well, you'd better," said Clock. "I only agreed to marry the girl on condition she swore off being a career woman."

"Whoso findeth a wife findest a good thing," said Jesse. "I'm trying, Andrew. Will continue to try with fingers crossed."

Fran was busy at the typewriter in the outer office. "I'm going on an errand for your husband, so don't accuse me of goofing off."

"I just hope the potential new one shows up while you're out," said Fran crossly. "You haven't got any appointments the rest of the day, of course."

"Yes, you could make quite a good one, put your mind to it." Jesse ducked out the door before her baleful look.

He was just in time, down on Berendo Street, to forestall the warehousemen in Miss Williams' bedroom. He thought in sudden distaste, all this stuff should be given away, disposed of—silly to put it in storage. Rummaging through her closet, unwillingly prying into her privacies, he felt guilty. And there were no sequins to be seen anywhere. Practical dresses, plain shirtmakers, skirts and blouses, practical low-heeled shoes, and the plain nylon underwear minus lace or frills. Nylon stockings in drawers with the underwear, a little pile of handkerchiefs: in the bottom drawer, under some odds and ends, a knitted white stole, a pair of white lace gloves, an evening bag, plain gold metallic vinyl. He sniffed in the closet. No mothproofing that he could discover.

He came out and told the warehousemen to carry on. In the hall downstairs, Shackleton intercepted him.

"I saw you go up. Mr. Falkenstein, that Gallagher just came in. If you want to see him."

"I do. Do you know where he works, by the way?"

"Asked him when he moved in, sure. At one of those art galleries out on Santa Monica. Shouldn't think there'd be much money in selling pictures. Specially the kind of pictures people seem to paint nowadays."

Silently agreeing with that, Jesse went down the hall to apartment 6 B and pushed the bell. After a moment the door opened. "Yes?" said an impatient voice.

"Mr. Gallagher." Jesse presented him with a card. "Like to ask you a few questions if I may. About Miss Williams."

"What about her? Thank God they've gone," said Gallagher. "With that vicious bully of a dog. Really, if it had gone on I'd have had to move. Again. It was quite impossible. Tina's a very delicate animal and—"

"Understand you had a little trouble about the dogs," said Jesse. "This your dog?" He looked at the animal pressed against Gallagher's legs. He suppressed a grin, with a mental picture of Sally bouncing at it. And he wondered about dogs and people: did people pick dogs who were like them (physically or more subtly), or did the dogs just get to be like the people?

"Tina," said Gallagher, "is an Italian greyhound—they're very sensitive, delicate dogs, and that brutal little bully of the Williams woman's— Of course she was quite insensitive to *my* feelings, *or* Tina's—there was no reason we couldn't have agreed, alternate days or something. But she was a terrible woman—calling Tina a miserable brainless—" Gallagher went crimson in remembered fury.

"That so?" said Jesse. Gallagher was perhaps twenty-eight, thirty. He was a tall willowy young man, not quite handsome, with a receding chin and a too small mouth and nice wavy golden hair; he was impeccably dressed in pale fawn sports clothes, matching slacks and shirt. And the dog shivering against his legs was pale fawn like his clothes, a thin bony short-haired dog with a narrow foxy face and big ears half-dropped and a thin whippy tail and a narrow head (not much room for brains) and timid dark eyes. It shivered and whined, and Jesse thought of Sally and was surprised Tina hadn't already suffered a nervous breakdown after a month of being bounced at. Sally, like her late mistress, would have given Tina short shrift.

"I can only thank God it's resolved itself," said Gallagher. "Fate. That woman getting mugged. Someone has taken that horrid vicious dog away, thank goodness, and Tina can have the yard to herself. Can't you, my pretty? That's Terry's good sweet girl." He picked up the dog, caressing her, and she whimpered in falsetto, whipping her tail.

112

And Jesse didn't like Mr. Gallagher. Not worth a damn. His pretty sports clothes or his accent (which was fake Eastern Seaboard) or his poor little idiot of a dog. Mr. Gallagher was so evidently self-centered: the egotist—and what else? Possibly . . . and if so (of course the fags didn't always look like fags), maybe the egotist who couldn't stand being crossed?

"But what do you *want?*" asked Gallagher.

"Nothing right now," said Jesse meditatively. Tell Andrew about Gallagher. Because just possibly—

Gallagher shut the door on him with a little bang.

"Jesse—"

He looked up, phone in hand. "I've got that doctor."

"I've run out of cigarettes," said Fran. "I'm just going down to the drugstore. Back in ten minutes. I want to finish getting out that will if I can."

Jesse waved her out. Dr. Hope came on the line, and was outraged at hearing about the Williamses. Both the Williamses. He sounded elderly and very competent. He had been the Williams family doctor for thirty years, and why nobody had thought to contact him— *Homicide?* And certainly he knew who Mr. Falkenstein was, and why Mr. Falkenstein should have deliberately kept him ignorant of all this— Mrs. Williams had missed her regular appointment with him last Thursday and his office nurse had been calling the apartment— Central Receiving? He would most certainly —

There was a good deal more to that effect, with Jesse trying to get a word in here and there. Finally the doctor snorted, "Codeine? Codeine? Margaret Williams? Healthy as a horse, that girl—I never gave her any codeine prescription! *Or* her mother—with her heart in that state? And why nobody informed me—" He banged the phone in Jesse's ear. Jesse sat back and lit a cigarette. So no codeine. Where had she got the codeine, when and why?

The outer door opened. Fran had been quick.

It wasn't Fran. Into his office breezed a female, buxom, confident, and hearty. "Mr. Falkenstein? You asked Bryant and Levy for a secretary. Well, I'm your gal! Willing and able, me—your new gal Friday! Small-time setup you got here—just you? Well, that's O.K. by me, I'll be just as happy, no stupid little file clerks. One-girl office just my meat, Mr. Falkenstein, I'm a glutton for work, I admit it!" She uttered a laugh that rattled the windows. "Dictation any speed you please, expert typist, any machine, I'm even a damn good amateur repair artist on typewriters, and I don't care what overtime I do. Except Mondays, Wednesdays, and Fridays—night school, see?"

Jesse regarded her dumbly. She was short and plump and dark and jolly. She had a florid complexion and bright shoe-button black eyes and a loud raucous voice. Somewhere in the twenties but she'd probably go on looking the same for years. She was wearing a bright red pantsuit with brass buttons down the front, and a shoulder bag, violently fringed, of dark maroon suede, and yellow flat-heeled shoes, and her lipstick was bright orange.

"Maybe you'd like to talk partnership come next year," she said breezily. "Me, I'm up for the bar examination next February—*and* I aim to pass cum laude. Of course we'd have to get bigger offices—" She glanced around disparagingly. "And a couple more girls. But that's all for later on, little Jessie's never one for stepping on any toes— Should've said, excuse me, I'm Jessie O'Ryan, Mr. Falkenstein, very happy to—"

Jesse stood up. Suddenly he knew exactly how Tina felt, being bounced at. "Er—as a matter of fact, Miss O'Ryan, the position—"

"Place could stand a coat of paint," said Miss O'Ryan with a sniff. "Wouldn't mind doing it myself over a weekend. Turn my hand to most anything, I—"

"I'm afraid the position is filled," said Fran sweetly from the door. "You're just too late, what a shame, Miss O'Ryan. But I'm sure anyone so capable won't have any difficulty— Thank you so much for coming. Good luck in finding something else. . . . *Honestly*, Jesse! If I hadn't come in just then, that harpy inflicting herself—"

"Now, Fran. Not a fool or a coward, I'd have got rid of her. What a female. But thanks so much for the rescue. And that reminds me—Fran, would you take Sally? You and Andrew? Extra wedding present, call it?"

"Sally? You mean that brainless lapdog? For heaven's sake, Jesse, if I wanted a dog that'd be the last—"

Jesse muttered, "If you knew Sally like I know Sally— Just a thought, Fran."

8

AND WHEN Clock told himself there was nothing to do on the Masked Monster (God, what names the media could dream up!) he meant, of course, nothing specific. In general, there was all too much to do. Routine, it was called.

A lot of the time, the only handle they had to something could be summed up in two words—*modus operandi*. And the computers were a big time-saver these days. They asked R. and I. what names were in their files to match the M.O. (or a general description, or some other vague lead) and started finding those people and questioning them.

Hellenthal, of course, had been before Homicide on that. Since November he had been at it with some of his own minions. What they had on this X was his M.O.—robbery and abduction at gunpoint—the few rapes, the fact that he picked middle-aged women as his victims. Hellenthal had fed that into the computer, and of course been handed back a small mountain of names from records. There were a lot of sex deviates here, a lot of heist men, a lot of men harboring an impulse to violence in general. And some of the names turned up had since been cleared away by Hellenthal's routine, men found to have alibis for one of the crimes, men in jail or hospital. More were left on that list of possibles, with no clear-cut evidence to say yes or no.

Clock, inheriting the case last Friday, had decided after rumination that the key points in this M.O. were the violence and the middle-aged women. Obliging clerks down in R. and I. reset the computer and handed him a new list. The lists overlapped to some extent, but when duplicate names were weeded out they still had some hundred and forty men who *(a)* might conform to the very vague physical description they had and *(b)* had records of using violence against *(c)* middle-aged women. Obviously, some of them would have picked the middle-aged victims merely by chance.

Since Saturday, with a few intervals out, Petrovsky, Mantella, Keene, and Dale had been chasing around looking for those men, bringing them in when they found them, and questioning them. Nothing definite had showed except that three of them had alibis for Thursday night. Most of the others remained possibles for the M.M., as Petrovsky had taken to calling him, if only just possible.

And the devil of that was that there was no guarantee he was in their records. This might be the first time in his life that he'd gone outside the law. Or he might be in somebody else's records, New York or St. Louis or wherever.

They had to work the job as they could, and routine broke a lot of cases.

But there was also Margaret Williams, and that was shaping up to look like something offbeat. That lab exhibit, the magazine cover, stuck in Clock's mind.

So when he had heard about Terry Gallagher from Jesse the night before, he thought about that interestedly.

"Don't say it could mean anything," Jesse had said. "I don't know. But motives are funny, Andrew. Heard you say often enough. Gallagher's self-centered, spoiled boy, I shouldn't wonder. Don't know if he's a fag, but he's got a temper—no empathy for people. Just saw it, you know—if maybe he had Tina out for a run before bed, when Margaret came home—"

"This is forgetting where she'd been, and the magazine cover?"

"Don't know," said Jesse. "Just, I didn't like his smell."

Neither did Clock, at second hand: Jesse got nuances. With Petrovsky and the other boys still out hunting for the possibles, and Lindner left to mind the store and take whatever new calls might go down, Clock visited R. and I. on Tuesday morning and asked if they had anything on a Terence, or Terry, Gallagher. He got handed something ten minutes later.

And it sounded like the same boy Jesse had described. Terence William Gallagher, twenty-seven now, male Caucasian, five-eleven, one sixty, blond and blue, no marks. The pedigree shot his brows up. A j.d. record, petty theft, shoplifting, vandalism. That was all listed from the Van Nuys station: address then given as Canoga Park. After he turned adult legally, there was a D. and D., petty theft (notation on that, resisting arrest and assault of arresting officer), and then something more serious, forgery. Clock read between lines. The forgery complaint had been signed by Mrs. Mary de la Croix; and on the j.d. record, Gallagher's guardian was listed as an aunt, Mary de la Croix. He'd got a one-to-three and served fourteen months at a minimum-security facility. That was five years back.

A temper, Jesse said. Clock sometimes got nuances too, and like Jesse he could see a little picture here. Underestimated Margaret—on the surface dithering (only at times) but actually a practical female, even a common-sensible female. And damn where she'd been on Monday, there she'd been coming home maybe as late as midnight; she'd probably been tired, and if Gallagher, coincidentally taking his dog for a run as she turned in, had tried to renew the argument, she might have been pretty short with him.

Clock rather thought he'd like a look at Gallagher. He called Shackleton and asked if he knew what art gallery Gallagher worked for. Shackleton did. The Diadem Galleries.

Out of Santa Monica toward the city line there was a scattering of those galleries, and Clock wondered how they managed to stay in business. But a lot of them had been there for years, most having sideline businesses of antiques, Oriental rugs, the art objects. Diadem Galleries was housed in an old two-story building, one of a row a block long, needing paint and cleaning up. Clock parked on the street and walked back. Inside, it was unexpectedly bright and airy, high-ceilinged and empty except for a pair of couches with a coffee table between them in the center of the room and all the pictures hung round the walls, mostly violently surrealistic ones.

There were three men standing at the far end of the room, talking; at Clock's entrance one broke away and came to meet him. "May I help you, sir?"

This looked like Gallagher: tall and willowy and such a pretty, pretty boy. "Would you be Terence Gallagher?"

"Why, yes—" Gallagher looked at the badge, surprised; sudden fear showed in his eyes. "What do you want? I haven't done anything!" His voice shot up half an octave.

"I understand," said Clock, "you're feeling thankful about the Williamses' being gone from the apartment. Thankful that one woman's dead and another in the hospital, Gallagher?"

"What do you—"

"Maybe they were annoying you enough that when Miss Williams came home a week ago last night, you started the argument all over and ended up killing her?"

"What? That's not so—you can't say a thing like—that's c-crazy!" Gallagher backed away. "You can't—"

"Well, I'd like to ask you a few questions. Were you at your apartment that Monday night?"

"Yes—no. I don't remember. You're just picking me to be a fall guy because—" Gallagher went on backing away. Now he looked terrified. "J-just on account of the d-dogs—that'd be—I —" And suddenly he broke and ran for the end of the room. Clock walked after him. "Bernie, it's a c-cop, he's trying to pin

119

that killing on me, you know I told you how that woman got—Bernie, you got to show him— It wasn't me, I wouldn't—"

"Hey now, you take it easy. You didn't do no such thing, so they got no evidence, calm down." The man Gallagher had run to looked at Clock measuringly. A tall dark man in his forties, Clock sized him up, and his shoulders probably the result of tailoring rather than exercise. He was sharply dressed; he had a lined cynical tanned face with a pair of very cold dark eyes. "What d'you want to go upsetting Terry for, Captain? He wouldn't no more do a murder than fly."

"Would you know?" asked Clock.

"Sure, sure. He's worked for me a couple years, I know Terry. He gets upset at a cross word."

"And that says he couldn't kill somebody. What's your name, sir?"

"Deacon—Bernie Deacon, I manage this place. You're sure reaching, try to pin a homicide on Terry." All this while Gallagher had been clutching Deacon's arm, breathing heavily; now Deacon brushed his hand off. "Here, kid, you go in the back, have a little drink to calm you down. The cop don't mean anything, he's just sounding you out."

"And you'd know about that?" said Clock. Gallagher went off obediently, head down.

"Oh, for God's sake! This is when, the homicide? Yeah, yeah, week ago last night. So I can tell you where Terry was, he was with me, see. There was a lot of people at my place at a party, Terry was there too. Till about two A.M. So you got an alibi for him, Captain. Satisfied?"

"For the moment," said Clock, which was a lie. He drove back downtown wondering about the art gallery (in quotes?) and Deacon, and Gallagher. The third man there rather Gallagher's type, young, nattily dressed. Fags? Some queer things went on in the big city these days—it wasn't so long ago that Wilcox Street had uncovered that ring of male prostitutes. Or the place could be a drop for something. But Jesse's estimates

120

were quite right, there was a wrong smell to Gallagher. *And*, to Clock, to that art gallery. Jesse right another way: Gallagher just the type to lose his temper and lash out suddenly.

Damn where Margaret had been on Monday. Clock had never thought that was all that important; Jesse saying a nine days' wonder, her just taking off. It might have been unusual, but surely not unprecedented. She'd intended to get back to the office, got delayed, and not come back at all; turning into the drive late that night, possibly Terry Gallagher there with the dog—

Back at the office, he was about to look over various reports left on his desk when Sergeant Pitman rang him. "Stewart Kane on the line," he said tersely. "You've got the autopsy report."

"Yes." Clock had just found it. "Mr. Kane?"

"I just wanted to ask when—you know—the body can be— The funeral director told me there'd be some formality— I didn't know that."

"Yes, Mr. Kane. The body can be released to the undertaker anytime now. All you have to do is tell him, he'll take care of the details."

"I see," said Kane thinly. "Thank you. I—it's just, everything's so sudden, if you understand me, Sergeant. Everything— changed overnight. I know it sounds—naïve—to keep saying it doesn't seem possible. Five days ago, I was just getting out my skis when that ranger—and here I am talking about a funeral. Lucille. Why, if we ever thought about it, years ahead of us— she was only fifty-two." He was silent, and then he said painfully, "When Betty—my first wife—died, it was cancer, you see, it was months she was ill. This— Well, it isn't any of your trouble, I'm sorry."

"I'm afraid it is, Mr. Kane. It's my business to try to find the man who killed her."

"Oh—yes. Have you—any new information?"

"We're working on it, Mr. Kane."

"Yes, I suppose so. Well—thank you."

The autopsy report on Lucille Kane— Clock picked it up in one hand, sorting over other reports, thinking of what Pitman had said as he came in. Other bodies for Homicide to look at now. Another suicide. Another unidentified corpse over on the Row. A body, probably dead of natural causes, in a cheap rooming house on Temple. And the routine to be done—the inevitable paper work mounting up.

Jesse had expected to spend the morning in court—divorce court; but the judge had been taken ill (unkind rumors said he had a hangover) and that court would not be in session. Jesse apologized to the client and went back to his office. Fran had just come in.

"I know you've got to have somebody here to answer the phone if nothing else, but I can't understand these agencies," she said. "I'd have thought efficient office help falling over itself after the jobs. It's not as if you're not offering a decent salary."

"Don't ask me to explain it. Don't understand it myself. Tell you one thing," said Jesse. "I'm thinking I'd be a lot safer with two girls, Fran. Me so lightly criticizing our Margaret, when she was never off a day with a cold or anything, and those beautiful files— I mean, a lesser secretary might be subject to migraine or something, and there I'd be. I think when I do find a new one, I go looking for an extra steno or file clerk to share the office with her."

"I think you'd better," agreed Fran. "I keep having these awful visions of you calling and saying, Please, Fran, my secretary's got flu and there are all these wills— Look, so I can type—the legal bit I'm not familiar with and all the Latin scares me."

"Hold good thoughts. Having the morning free, I think I'll— well, call Andrew and see if he turned up anything on Gallagher."

He heard with interest what Clock had turned up. "The little hint of tendency to violence," he said. "Suggestive. Is he a fag, Andrew?"

"You can't tell on looks. Couldn't say. But even if so, you know, a lot of them are chancy boys. Unstable to start with—"

"Mmh, yes, filling in blanks for myself. What's that woman's name? In Canoga Park?"

"Why do you—" Clock read name and address to him. Jesse handed the phone to Fran.

"So you can bill and coo with your bridegroom— I'm off."

"Over the *phone?*" said Fran as he picked up his hat. "Darling Andrew, Jesse hasn't got a new one yet and I'm— Jesse! You've got an appointment at one-thirty!"

Jesse flicked his hand at her and went out.

He had some difficulty finding the address in Canoga Park, but located it finally down a rutted half-paved road on the outskirts of town. A neat small white cottage set back from the road it was, surrounded by immense old live oak trees. There was a white picket fence around it with a gate standing open. As he walked up to it he saw that there was someone on the porch. He went through the gate and up to the porch steps. "Mrs. de la Croix?"

"That's right." She was sitting in an old-fashioned wooden rocker shelling peas into an enamel bowl: a little white-haired old woman, dumpy and grandmotherly, glasses on the end of her nose. "And who might you be?"

Jesse told her. "Interested in your nephew Terry. I—"

"He a client of yours? You better keep an eye on him," she said crisply. "He can be tricky."

"No. It's barely possible he killed a woman last week. During an argument. Tricky, is he?"

She dropped a pea pod and said, "Killed somebody! Terry? You mean, meaning to? Well, you're wrong there, mister. That boy's too much of a coward for that. Sometimes I do wonder if

123

those old folk who believed in changelings weren't right. My brother was as fine a man as ever stood up, Mr.—what say?— Falkenstein. A fine man. Hard-working and respectable and decent, not a wrong thought in his head. And his wife was a good woman, from a good family. Maybe it was because they were married nearly twenty years before the boy come, I don't know. Maybe his mother spoiled him. All I know is, by the time he come to me—his mother and dad getting killed in that accident—it was too late to change him. He was fourteen then. I couldn't do anything with him. Do you really think he—" She looked at Jesse curiously.

"Don't know. He could have."

"Now there I think you're wrong. Don't tell me the police think that?" She started shelling peas again. "He's been on the wrong side o' the law, maybe you know—stole some money from me once. I washed my hands of him, he don't bother trying to wheedle any out of me again. But Terry killing somebody?" She looked over her glasses at Jesse. "He's a coward and a sissy-boy, mister. I could overlook this and that in a man— My late husband, he'd get drunk now 'n' then and maybe have an eye or a bit more to a pretty girl, but he was a *man*, know what I mean. One thing I guess most women couldn't forgive in a man is bein' a coward. And Terry's a coward to end all. 'Less it happened by accident someways, he'd be scared silly, think of a thing like murder."

And so where had that got him? Jesse, tooling at moderate speed back toward Hollywood, thought that Terry Gallagher might be very much a side issue. Extraneous. They had turned up some surprises on Margaret, but hadn't the old man said where she had a couple of people mad at her, there might well be others? Only one of them had done something about it. And Jesse had been telling himself that that magazine cover really could be explained without reaching very far: she had possibly, by the autopsy, been tied up somewhere for a while, and somebody could have grabbed that to use as a temporary gag—

124

But facts, the cold facts that lab had turned up, couldn't be reasoned away. The magazine cover had originally been on the magazine in the back of her car. A struggle in the car? X subduing her, casting around for a gag—

He could just see that. Only just. Could vaguely see X using his belt, his tie, to immobilize her. But why? Well, that explained itself in a way. The mugging setup: that couldn't be arranged until after dark.

Suddenly Jesse stepped hard on the brake. A squeal of brakes behind him, and a new T-bird swept around the Ford, its driver throwing Jesse an angry look. Jesse pulled the Ford over on the shoulder and examined the sudden new idea which had presented itself to him.

Wasn't that Q.E.D.? If any of that held water at all, it was part of the truth: it could explain away part of their mystery.

Clock—Jesse was well aware—didn't necessarily see Miss Williams' unprecedented vanishment for a whole day as part of the mystery; he hadn't known her as well as Jesse (only it seemed Jesse had seen only—as the old man said—the one-tenth of her above water, at that). But that had to be part of it, because it *had* been quite unprecedented.

But think back over it. Miss Williams not coming to the office, after leaving at the regular time, saying nothing to her mother about not coming to work. Calling Jesse, saying she had something extremely urgent to do. And it "shouldn't take more than an hour." And then not appearing at all—until she turned up dead, probably after midnight, in her own driveway.

Couldn't that say that she *had* been immobilized somewhere, for some reason, and that was why she didn't show up after she'd accomplished the extremely urgent errand?

And then Jesse remembered the actual wording of the autopsy report, and swore. It could not say any such thing. Because the only thing that even suggested that she'd been tied up—bound and gagged, it sounded impossibly melodramatic,

Miss Williams—was a few faint abrasions on the wrists. No marks on the ankles. And what was that?

Pass the idea on, see what Edgar thought about it.

He came into the office at twelve-thirty. "I'll sit on the phone while you have lunch, if you're hungry."

"I ought to skip it," said Fran. "That five pounds—"

Jesse laughed. Fran still very much the glamour girl, the five pounds not visible. "You've got to keep up your strength. Go. I hate to break the news to you, but the one-thirty client wants to make a new will."

"Oh, damn!" said Fran.

"Well, sort of integral part of a lawyer's—"

"I didn't mean damn about the will, though I could have. Damn about your infernal machine—it bit me." She opened her hand to show him a long scrape on the inside of her slim wrist. "This typewriter—"

"And our devices are but uncertain," said Jesse softly. "I will be damned."

Clock was feeling very tired of the thankless job. He was trying to keep his mind off slim, svelte, cool-voiced Fran, and the orderly comfortable apartment up on Edgemont where he couldn't go for another three hours—if then. But nobody had twisted his arm to make him take the oath, and the job was there to be done. . . .

He had read the autopsy report on Lucille Kane, and felt a little surprised at it, and wondered why. A lot of detail, but the facts simple—as he had expected. She had died of multiple skull fractures: three principal blows, other glancing bruises. There were traces of wood splinters in the wounds. Two-by-four or something, rough wood? Healthy female specimen aside from some slight emphysema on one lung: it wouldn't yet have been causing her discomfort. Stomach contents were practically nil: small traces of beef broth, soda crackers, orange juice. And both wrists and ankles showed evidence that she'd been tied up. Traces in mouth of loose cotton fibers—also gagged.

After a minute Clock had said to himself, "Oh." What had vaguely bothered him was the absence of stomach contents, but now he remembered that Lucille Kane had just been getting over a cold. Feeling better when he left on Monday, said Kane, but possibly she had just said so, knowing he wanted to go to the mountains; or possibly she'd had a relapse. At any rate, she'd obviously been nursing the cold—old saws be damned, all a doctor ever said was plenty of liquids, and rest. The estimated time of death was eight to midnight last Thursday night.

About then Petrovsky came in with one of the possibles from the list, and all of a sudden he was looking very possible indeed, this one, so they started to question him hard.

He was one Edward Atwell, he was thirty-two, five-eight, thin, and he had a pedigree of robbery with violence: two counts of mugging, one heist job. He had served exactly sixteen months in a minimum-security facility; Clock said things about the courts. He was furthermore driving an Opel Kadett, dark green. That one would be about the right size for the second car the women described.

They'd asked for a search warrant as soon as Petrovsky found him and fetched him in.

They stood over him in an interrogation room and questioned him, and it went the way it usually did with the pros used to being questioned.

"Come on, come on, Atwell. You can save us all a lot of time and trouble, just tell us where you were last Thursday night."

"I don't remember." Atwell was sandy and nondescript: a thin little chin, shifty light eyes. Of course he hadn't any record of sex deviation, but that said nothing. "Oh, well, I guess I was just at home. My room."

"Anybody with you?"

"No. But I was. I been clean since I got out, you can't put

nothing on me. I got a job, I'm selling vacuum cleaners and stuff. Straight. You can't—"

After a few rounds of that, Sergeant Pitman looked in and handed Clock an envelope: more background on Atwell from the parole office, and his probation officer back when he was still a j.d. Clock glanced through it and beckoned Petrovsky with a jerk of his head.

"Something?"

"Something," said Clock, "Maybe significant, Pete. I get a little tired of these head doctors trying to explain why the wrong ones went wrong because Mama spanked too hard or Daddy was overprotective, but now and then— He started a pedigree at fifteen. And Mama was had up for child abuse twice, when he was six, and eleven. She did three years for it. Beat him with an electric cord. No daddy visible at any time."

"Interesting," said Petrovsky, his round face placid. "Implying that he's maybe got a subconscious grudge on all mother figures? And the rest of the Freudian bit? I understand even the head doctors don't go along with Freud any more."

"Well, it's something," said Clock.

"Sure."

They went back to questioning Atwell, and it was uphill work. He went on saying he'd been in his room alone, and they hadn't anything on him. Which they hadn't, of course.

The search warrant came through at four o'clock, and with relief they abandoned Atwell, and collected Mantella, and went to look for tangible evidence—the ski mask, the crepe-soled shoes, et al.

Atwell was renting a room in an old house on Darwin Avenue in Boyle Heights. He didn't have a garage for the Opel. The room wasn't very big, and it didn't take long to search. They didn't find the ski mask, the rubber-soled shoes, or any blunt instrument—of course by what they had, when their X had used anything but his fists he had grabbed up something handy at the scene, a rock or a stick. There was a dark gray suit in the little

128

cardboard wardrobe, but the only turtleneck sweater was blue. They searched the Opel standing at the curb outside. It wasn't very clean: it was probably at fourth or fifth hand Atwell had acquired it, and it had a few dents and needed washing; but in their language it was depressingly clean, nothing suggestive in it at all. And the upholstery was beige vinyl, to show stains: bloodstains cops would recognize, and there weren't any.

"So he looks fine for the description, but what the hell's the description?" said Mantella tiredly. "How many men are there in this town middle-sized and thin, which is all the description —I could call it other things—we've got?"

"All right, I know," said Clock. "We do it the hard way."

They let Atwell go.

Clock went home, and Fran was there waiting.

"Have to do something," said Nell, troubled. "Look, Jesse, I'm sorry for her, she's cute and I like her, but Athelstane's *our* dog and he doesn't. She simply demands attention away from him, and he's always been first, and he can't understand it, poor darling. And, Jesse, the baby due so soon, it'll be hectic enough afterward—getting him used to the baby—I'm afraid it'd make hopeless complications if—"

"I know, damn it." Jesse contemplated Sally, hairy and insouciant, chewing her ball on the couch, and the unhappy jowly countenance of Athelstane peering from behind the armchair. "What the hell could I do? She had to be looked after. And finding a good home isn't so—"

"We can advertise, I suppose. But how could we be sure it *was* a good home? I always thought they were silly lapdogs, but she's a darling really—only Athelstane—"

"*Man is born to trouble, as the—*" said Jesse, and the phone rang. He went to answer it, and Athelstane plodded after to sit on his feet and listen, but not as if his heart was in it.

"Jesse? Shackleton just called the office—some row going on down there, squad car called out—"

129

"I'll meet you," said Jesse instantly.

"I could hear him," said Shackleton, "and I was worried, see. Mr. Felton going off the rails, like they say, since the poor lady died. A nice fellow, never a drinker before, and we all felt sorry, even though it's made trouble. But his apartment's right over mine, see, and tonight it was something different, all the noise, him banging doors and cupboards, I couldn't figure what he was up to—and finally Mr. Lightner, he called down about it, and I went up—" He looked distressed. "They didn't go to church," he said irrelevantly. "Not I guess that you got to go to church to be convinced of that. I got it figured, he doesn't believe you don't really die, see. That she's still somewhere, and he'll meet her again. So it took him like this."

Clock and Jesse exchanged a glance. "When I went up and knocked, I knew he was there but he didn't answer, and I went in—the door was open. He had the gun in his hand," said Shackleton. "He had the gun in his hand—all ready—I just took it away from him, and I figured I'd best call you. I don't think he knew what he was doing," but that sounded a little hollow.

The uniformed men were with Felton, watchful of him in the living room of the apartment upstairs. The apartment probably once dusted and tidy and cared for, but now it had accumulated dust and clutter, since he'd been in it alone. Robert Felton was sitting in the one big armchair, leaning back with eyes closed; he looked white and ill.

Shackleton had given Clock the gun: a Smith & Wesson .38 revolver, fully loaded.

They would take him into protective custody, thought Jesse, and it just could be that that would help him over this crisis, that with no liquor available he'd get hold of himself and back on an even keel. And quite possibly Shackleton was right about the reason. Jesse looked at Felton with remote pity.

130

"Mr. Felton," said Clock. "Are you feeling well enough to talk? Mr. Felton—"

"Don't bother the poor devil, Andrew," said Jesse.

Felton opened his eyes slowly. They fell on Jesse first, and after a moment he sat up with an effort. He said, "She worked for you. Lydia—my wife—liked her, you know. I was *sorry*. I was—but it was—the—last straw."

"Margaret Williams, Mr. Felton?" said Jesse very quietly.

"Yes. My wife—Lydia—they were friendly. I had been trying," said Felton painfully, "to sort things out. Lydia's things. Tonight. I should have done it before—but I couldn't bring myself to—all her clothes, her handbags, the costume jewelry, and the album of her family pictures—but there's no one to care, to value them—we never had children, you know. And I —haven't—had—a drink—today. I haven't. But I couldn't stop thinking about it. A friend of Lydia's. *Because* I hadn't had a drink. Since—since it first came to me"—he blinked up at Jesse painfully, squinting—*"it might have been me."*

"Might—"

"I don't *know*. It was the last thing," said Felton slowly. "That. Mortgage—the store. Fines—tickets—bail—I don't know. Then—her car. The money, all that money— I'd never —and it wasn't my fault, she'd left the car nearly across the drive, anybody might have— The last straw. I remembered— arguing with her. But Lydia liked her." Suddenly he leaned forward and put his head in his hands. "Somebody said—I don't remember—killed. Mugged, they call it. Right outside, in front. And I got to thinking—to wondering—"

"What, Mr. Felton?"

"If it was me. Did that. I don't know," said Felton rather wildly. "I don't remember. Lydia liked her—and I'd been hating her— God forgive me, just that money, why was I fussing about the damn money, nobody for the store to go to or— But if I'd done that, a thing like that—" He raised haggard eyes to them. "And I don't know," he said. "I was drunk that night. Here. The last I remember. If I only knew—whether it was me —did that—"

9

"VERDICT?" said Jesse. They stood on the sidewalk outside the apartment; he blew out a stream of frosty smoke thoughtfully. It had stopped raining on Sunday, and turned progressively colder ever since.

"Well, we were talking about Felton at first, weren't we?" Clock massaged his jaw. "It's a possibility, I suppose, but would Felton—drunk enough to pull a blank—have set up the fake mugging?"

"Thought twice about that too. Near as I can figure our old maestro's rules about thinking out mysteries, one of 'em seems to be think simple—the simpler the better. And—"

"And from my experience I'd say so too. The simplest explanation is usually the right one. Not always."

"Well, Andrew—that fake mugging. We looked at her there, handbag open, et cetera, and we said robbed. And then we said the setup faked. How do we know—or know she was robbed? She could have dropped the handbag as she fell, and it came open and the coin purse, a few other things, fell out. Maybe she didn't have any bills on her when she came home that night. From wherever."

Clock stared at him. "Now that—I suppose that's possible too. A new thought anyway. One thing I'll contribute on Felton.

Also from experience, I'd say that you never know just *what* a drunk might do."

"Also a thought," said Jesse.

He went home and told Nell about that. She was not, as usual, sitting in bed reading because Sally would promptly get up with her and growl at Athelstane when he approached. Sally had come bouncing to greet Jesse.

"But, Jesse," said Nell, wrinkling her brow, "it seems fantastic that all these different motives and—and potential enemies should turn up on any one person, let alone Miss Williams."

"Not fantastic at all," said Jesse. He sat down in his armchair with Sally on his lap; Athelstane was leaning on Nell having his stomach rubbed. "Motives—hardly a soul walking around somebody else hasn't some reason to want out of the picture. Vast majority of people never do anything about it, of course. Motive —it depends who has it, whether it triggers murder. Murders done over anything or nothing. Most of us create a little friction as we go through life. The funniest thing about this to me is that —well, no motive really strong enough for murder, but the biggest one showing here seems to be the TV bit, the 'Crime-fighters'—all that money down the drain, a lot of people affected—but apparently that wasn't the trigger for the kill. Andrew said like a bunch of kids, forgetting the whole thing, wrangling about something entirely different. . . . I tell you, if Felton is X we'll never prove it. But I don't think it's just as simple as that. Damn it, Nell, what she was doing and where, that Monday, has to be something to do with it. An extremely urgent— What the hell could it have been?"

Homicide was back at the endless routine on Wednesday morning. A couple of the possibles had been found and brought in, and were being questioned when a new call went down. Petrovsky took that, and called in twenty minutes later to ask for a mobile lab. Wholesale slaughter of an entire family, he said; it looked as if the head of the household had committed murder and suicide—wife, two kids, himself. No background yet, but somebody had better come out to help him question neighbors and locate any relatives.

Clock swore: he wished real life would behave more like the paperback mysteries, where the cops were let alone to solve one crime before they got handed another. But that was how it went. Neither of the possibles looked very possible; he let them go and sent Mantella to join Pete.

But he was now back to thinking about Gallagher, and rather liking him for Williams. For one thing, he was there on the premises: at least he lived there. And Clock didn't swallow that patently fake alibi Deacon had offered so glibly. He could so easily have been right there outside when she came home, airing the dog before bed. Could so easily— A chancy one, Gallagher, excitable and unstable. Clock sat at his desk, rummaged in the tray, and brought out the manila envelope of eight-by-ten shots of that scene.

He was struck by Jesse's afterthought—quite possibly she hadn't been robbed. Keep it simple, yes. She'd been out all day, she might not have had any bills in her purse, only a handful of coins. That needn't have been a set-up scene at all. Gallagher impetuously stopping her there, renewing the argument, her getting out—on the side where he was, in the front yard—to talk to him. Gallagher hitting out, knocking her down. Weapon? thought Clock sadly. There needn't have been any intention at all—and she'd been wearing that damned hat, so no traces in the wounds of any weapon.

He looked at the photographs. Not far from the body, a couple of feet toward the center of the lawn, was a big white synthetic-stone boulder with the street address painted on it. So, thought Clock, Gallagher hitting out, she fell and maybe hit her head on that. Maybe Gallagher didn't realize she was badly hurt—you didn't necessarily die right off of a skull fracture— and she could have started to crawl back toward the car. No traces on the synthetic stone; but the hat. It could be just as simple as that. Ask the lab if they'd found anything on the hat.

If it was, however, the chances were that Gallagher could be broken down into admitting it; and it would only add to murder-second.

The ones like Gallagher unstable: easy to pry apart. And considering all the damn routine on this Masked Monster, the quicker they cleared up Williams the better. Clock decided to work on Gallagher a little, and sent Keene over to that art gallery to pick him up if he was there.

He was. He was looking very nervous when Keene brought him in, and he attempted to bluster at Clock. "You can't do this, you haven't any right to accuse me—about that Williams woman? That's just crazy, I—we told you where I was that night, I was at a party at Bernie's, that's an alibi, you can ask anybody who was there— I couldn't have—I wouldn't *kill* anybody anyw—"

"Maybe not meaning to, Gallagher. Sit down." Clock stood over him, and of course the very look of Andrew Clock, Neanderthal-jawed and heavy-shouldered, made some people nervous; obviously he made Gallagher nervous. "Sure you didn't happen, say, to be there when she came home that night? Got to arguing with her again? Had a little struggle, maybe knocked her down? And—"

"No, no, that's— I didn't, I wasn't! You can't prove that, it's not so! I was at Bernie's! You— Don't you hit me!" Gallagher was shrill, shrinking away. Clock and Mantella looked at him in distaste.

"No intention of hitting you, we don't operate that way," said Clock. "So tell me where you were that Monday night. From when to when."

"I was at Bernie's! There was a party—we told you! I got there ab-about eight, I was there way past midnight, you can't—"

"Sober?"

"What do you *mean*, s— Of course I was! I don't get drunk! I was—anybody could say I was there, you just ask—"

"Everybody there sober?"

"Well, I—well, maybe Eddy was a teeny bit high, but— Bernie can say! He *told* you I was there! I couldn't have— That awful woman, calling Tina— I wouldn't have, anyway! You ask, everybody'll say—"

"So who's everybody, Gallagher? Give us some names."

"Bernie—"

"Somebody else."

"Eddy Wells." Gallagher was sullen now but still frightened: the whites of his eyes showed. "Uh—Ken Goodis. Bert Lingenfelt. Roberto Reyes. Some guys I hadn't met before, friends of theirs—I don't remember—"

"No females," said Clock genially. "Stag party? What'd you do for entertainment? Dirty movies maybe?"

"No, of course not! We—well, sure, we had a few drinks but nobody was— Well, we just— Well, I was *there*! I wasn't out killing anybody and you can't—"

"So suppose we have some addresses to match the names, Gallagher. We'll go and ask these fellows and—"

"*You can't do that!*" Panic flared in his eyes; he jumped up. He was panting and ready to bolt, if there'd been anywhere to run. "*You can't—*"

Clock opened his mouth; and Sergeant Pitman looked in the door of the interrogation room and raised his brows. "O.K. Johnny," said Clock, "you watch him for a minute, I'll be back." He went out to the hall. "What's up, Bob?"

"Lieutenant Kelleher, in your office. He's looking annoyed," said Pitman.

"Oh?" Clock went down to his office. Lieutenant Tim Kelleher belonged over in Narcotics. He was a little older than Clock, a deceptively dapper-looking dark man with a long Irish jaw and heavy eyebrows. "Do for you, Tim?" asked Clock.

"It's more what you're doing to me, Andrew. I never did anything to you," said Kelleher plaintively. "Try to cooperate like we're supposed to. Just why, Andrew, did you go marching on your flat feet into a case of mine? And maybe shot it all to hell? I can't move until we find the pretty bird to sing us a song, but meanwhile, of course, we've been keeping an eye on the principals. And a couple of the principals are long-time experienced pros who can smell cop at a distance, so that hasn't been so easy. And then you come barging right in the front door, badge in hand, and I only hope to God you haven't scared 'em into breaking and running. Why, Andrew?"

"Oh, my God," said Clock. "You don't tell me—not that damn art gallery?"

"That's just what, Andrew. It's a drop for a wholesale supplier. A big boy. We think that hundred-pound parcel of H we heard about from Frisco got landed there last week. We hope it's still there. We—"

"But my God, how the hell could I know, Tim?"

"Well, you couldn't. But what in God's name led you there? On a homicide? Listen, these boys don't operate like those old-time gangsters. All very quiet and discreet, no gunplay. I don't say—"

Clock explained. "And damn it, I've got this pretty boy down the hall in a panic, I've been going at him a little hot and heavy. If I go back and say O.K., trot along, we're finished with you, maybe the big boys smell a rat? What the hell do they use Gallagher for? Another one like him there yesterday morning. The pretty boy. Fags?"

"I couldn't guess—we haven't looked that close yet. Could be —all's grist that comes to their mill, you know, make addicts where they can. And I could have the educated guess they'll pay off partly in the supplies. . . . That's awkward, Andrew. I'm sorry to ask you to waste the time, but I think the best way to play it—you go back and question him some more, but easy and gentle. The innocuous questions. You begin to believe him. You let out inadvertently that this new evidence just in changes your ideas. And presently you let him go. That should calm him down, and relieve Bernie's mind. Bernie? Oh, he's not one of the big boys—just runs this particular drop. We're waiting to pick up a fellow we know had a fight with one of the big boys back in Philly. Six forces back there all hunting. We have it on the grapevine he'll sing loud and clear when we lay hands on him. Then we move in on Bernie and company. And I'm sorry to intrude on your business. The pretty boy really look hot for a homicide?"

"Now you tell me he could be hooked on something," said Clock, rubbing his jaw, "I'm thinking it's just more than possible, Tim. Well, can't be helped. You'll keep me posted on your end."

Jesse sat in divorce court most of Wednesday morning, and thought about Margaret Williams. He was inclined to write off Terry Gallagher, for a couple of reasons. He agreed with Mrs. de la Croix—the complete coward. That kind, and Gallagher's kind in general, apt to be very careful of their own skins. Temper or no. He could see Gallagher, in a fit of temper, hitting out at somebody, but like a woman, the petulant slap, hardly the killing blow.

Felton? That was just barely possible—and if it had been Felton they'd never prove it. But despite all the rules about keeping it simple, Jesse thought there was more to it than that because, damn it, her disappearance that day must have something to do with it. Her extremely urgent errand.

The interlocutory granted, he went back to the office to find Fran chatting with old Mr. Walters. "Still keeping Fran's nose to the grindstone, I see," said the old man.

"The damn paper work's got to be done, maestro, and you know Nell doesn't type."

"And even if she did, I should hope you'd have better sense 'n to bring her down here, with the baby practically round the corner," said Mr. Walters severely. "You just got to try harder."

"Well, I don't mind if it isn't for long," said Fran.

"And I s'pose you can't come to lunch with us? Sit on the

phone and make appointments for Clarence Darrow here? Well, all right. Come on, Jesse, I want to talk this over, hear what else Andrew's got."

"Well, he hasn't got much," said Jesse. . . . Settled in a booth at the Brown Derby, he told Mr. Walters about Gallagher, about Felton. "Say anything to you?"

"Not much." Mr. Walters sampled his bourbon and water. "Don't think it was anything that simple."

"Neither do I. Because it was—wild, her disappearing like that. Andrew doesn't see just how wild. Nine years, Edgar, and she'd never been off a day with a cold. And me criticizing her because she got flustered sometimes! My God, not knowing when I was well off. But she'd never even overstayed her lunch hour—regular as clockwork, on the dot at eight-thirty. And there she was phoning, an extremely urgent— What the hell could it have been?"

The old man looked at his glass. "Say this much. All we know about her now, she had common sense, Jesse. If she got flustered. She told you it was somethin' extremely urgent. Inclined to think it really must have been. Or, if you take me, she wouldn't have taken such an unprecedented step, stay away from work—call you."

"All right, I'll go along with that. But there's no way I can see to find out what it was or where it took her."

"Tell you something else funny." The old man absently brought out his private bottle to replenish his drink. "That TV thing. The 'Crimefighters.' Evidently she didn't realize at all what she'd—um—accomplished there, the magnitude of it, as it were—quarter of a million down the drain, that fellow said to you, my God—nobody bothered to tell her. Once that was set in motion, it was the fellows at the top concerned over it, that TV studio, the Weinstraub chairman, that advertising fellow. Don't think Miss Williams ever knew about the row. I'll bet you, time Andrew looks all through her files, he'd find the follow-up letters on that."

"Could be. Which says?"

"I'm just ruminating," said the old man. "Sort of at random. But all right, say whatever the errand was she had to do, it really was important and urgent. When did it come up? When did she find out about it? Whatever it was?"

"That's why you wanted to hear more about the party. Well, I don't know, it sounded like a pretty ordinary affair. Bunch of women being social—excuse for a party. Boring guest speaker."

"And I'd like to hear more about that party than I have heard, at that. But somethin' else occurs to me now. She does just as usual that morning, helps her mother out of bed, gets her dressed, fixes breakfast, says nothin' about not going straight to work as usual, leaves at the regular time. . . . And then about an hour later she's calling you explaining about the urgent errand." The waiter set their plates in front of them. "Jesse, when's the mail delivered to that place?"

"My God," said Jesse. "My God, it never crossed my— I can call Shackleton." He went to do so before he started on his sandwich, and came back five minutes later. "You do have ideas. As a rule the mail gets delivered about eight A.M."

"Well, is that so? That's interesting. She'd have left about ten past, give herself time to get to the office. So maybe pick up the mail as she left. And go through it at the office or in her car, if she had time. Could have been something in the mail that morning that sent her off on the urgent errand." Having gobbled down his sandwich, the old man splashed bourbon into his glass, sat back, and drank.

"But what, and how we could ever—there wasn't any letter, anything like that, in her bag."

"Doesn't say there hadn't been. And damn it, mail or no mail, I'd like to hear more about that affair the night before," said the old man wistfully.

Well, their old maestro sometimes pulled rabbits from hats. Jesse said obligingly, "I haven't an appointment till three. Drive down to Commerce and introduce you to Martha Weglund."

141

"And I don't know if she could tell me anything relevant, seeing what she told you, but on the other hand—that'd be fine, let's do that." He finished his drink.

Martha Weglund looked at them in bewilderment. She had led them down to the big comfortable lounge with the Coke machine, the cigarette machine. "Well, any way I can help you —" She looked at fat, untidy Mr. Walters in surprise.

"This is a colleague of mine, Miss Weglund. Sometimes knows the right questions to ask better than I do. We'd be obliged if you'd—"

"Well, whatever I can— About Margaret? But I told you—"

Mr. Walters had found an upholstered chair. " 'Bout that party on the Sunday night, Miss Weglund," he said comfortably.

"Yes? I told Mr. Falkenstein—"

"Sure. Few more questions. You and Miss Williams not together, you said. All the time. Quite a crowd of people there. Before the program started, people millin' around—runnin' into friends—movin' on again."

"That's right," she said. "You know how those affairs go. There were refreshments, and for a wonder quite good—it's difficult to serve such a crowd, even buffet. It was just coffee and tea and cake—Mrs. Foster and a woman I didn't know were pouring when I went in. The coffee and tea, I mean. Margaret was already there—"

"With some people you knew?"

She thought. "She was talking to Joan Pitt when I first saw her, I think. When I'd got a cup of coffee I went over to join them and we talked awhile—as well as you could in such a crowd, it was fairly noisy—and then I saw Estelle come in with a little group and went to speak to her, and she came over to us when she'd got coffee." She stopped.

"Fine. You with Margaret up to when the program started?"

"Oh, no. This was in the big reception room at the front, and the auditorium off it—they had the tables set up along one side of the auditorium, for the refreshments. No, somebody came up and said Margaret must come and meet Celia, and she went off —some woman I didn't know—and then Stella came in with her husband and came over— It was the usual jam. People—as you say—milling around. Balancing cups and plates and dropping cake crumbs all over. And the club officers spelled each other at pouring, I think, I know there was a different pair there when I took my cup back—" She was looking surprised at the close attention the old man paid to all that.

"What time was this, hey?"

"Well, the—what they call the get-together hour, for refreshments, was supposed to be seven-thirty to eight, but people came in late, and it was more like eight-thirty when the program started."

"Mmh. You with her then?"

"Margaret? No. No, I'd been talking to Stella, when the lights went down—to let us know to find seats—so we went in together. I don't know where Margaret was then. Stella and her husband and I sat in the right-hand section, on the aisle. I did notice Margaret later, she was a couple of rows ahead and across in the center section, with the Enrights."

"So. How long did this program last?"

"Too long," said Martha Weglund with dreary humor. "I don't really know why I've kept up membership in that— The usual preliminaries, pledge of allegiance, and an introducer who introduced somebody else who introduced the new president, and then there was a girl who sang—somebody's daughter, I suppose, pretty awful. Do you really want to hear all this?"

"You're doin' fine—go on," said Mr. Walters.

"Well—then somebody else introduced the speaker. This woman psychiatrist. And she talked. For quite a long time—it was fairly boring. That ended about—oh, ten-fifteen. And everybody thanked everybody else, and that was it."

"People start leavin' right away?"

"In the kind of way they do, a thing like that—you know,

drifting toward the door, saying good night to people they knew — Some of the women had checked their coats and there was a little crowd waiting at the—"

"You see Margaret again?"

She said, "Yes. She looked quite nice that night, she had on a plain black dress with just one big gold pin, and her real pearl earrings—well, cultured pearls. I'd got stuck with Ruby Redfern, she's such a bore, but I saw Margaret a little way off, she was going toward the checkroom."

"Getting her coat to leave."

"I suppose. She was talking to some woman I didn't know, and then she started on toward the— She saw me and just waved to me. Of course she wouldn't hang around longer than she had to, she had a regular working day coming up, and she'd have her mother to get to bed when she got home. She'd want—"

"She look just as usual then?"

"What? Why, of course. Just in a little hurry to get her coat and— I don't understand why you're interested in all this. I mean, I want to help you any way I—but the police—"

The old man sat back, frowning. "Apologies," said Jesse hastily. "Interrupting you at work—sorry. But thanks very much."

She shrugged. "I'm glad if I've helped," she said simply. "But I should get back—"

"Yes. We'll find our way out. . . . And just why were you interested in all that, maestro? Idea that she'd learned something Sunday night that created the urgent errand next morning?"

"You mind the Scripture," said Mr. Walters. *"Rise before the hoary head—"*

"Honor the face of the old man," said Jesse. "All right. But did that say anything to you?"

"Something I knew before. Deadly boring social events like that, lot of noise, idle chatter, no chance for private peaceful discussion. With anybody."

144

"Well, for God's sake, about what?"

"That's the question," said the old man abstractedly. "What?"

Clock was annoyed at the necessity of ignoring Gallagher and the art gallery. He still thought that Gallagher was a fairly hot suspect for Williams; if he was addicted to something, from the Mary Jane to H, all the likelier that he'd be hair-trigger. But pending Kelleher's bird singing, and a Narco raid on the Diadem Galleries, Homicide had to keep hands off.

It wasn't, of course, as if they hadn't other things to do.

Petrovsky and Keene, getting the preliminary paper work done on the wholesale slaughter, had gone back to hunting men from the list on the Masked Monster, and about four o'clock brought in another possible. This one, Richard Klein, had got on the list because he'd once been picked up as accessory to a heist job; otherwise, he had a pedigree of petty theft, D. and D., one assault which hadn't been very serious.

When they started to ask him questions about last Thursday night, he said, "Hey—hey, you tryina pin that Monster onto me? Connect me with that one? Oh, brother, but you are reachin' on that! That one's big-time, ain't he? Really big-time, man, killin' a dame?"

"I guess you could say so," said Petrovsky. "So?"

"Like me, I ain't big-time," said Klein. "I ain't got the guts for a thing like that. I dunno if I wish I had, man. But I ain't. Got the guts. Las' Thursday night, lessee—yeah, I was at my sis's place, she ast me for dinner— I give you the address—"

And the one fairly good lead, on the other mystery on hand, they couldn't follow up.

Fran told Jesse that one of the agencies had sent a girl over, but she was obviously impossible, not trained at all and had adenoids. "It'd be silly to hire somebody you'd just have to fire the next week. I called that agency and told them firmly you do not want a half-educated inexperienced twenty-year-old. I—"

"Great," said Jesse. "Offend them so now they won't even try to oblige me."

"Nonsense," said Fran. "Let them know where you stand, they'll knuckle down." She took herself off at five o'clock. But before that, there was another client making a will and one with a damage suit in mind. All the damn paper work, and he really couldn't expect Fran to go on obliging for weeks.

He didn't have anything to do at the office after she left, but delayed, leafing over *Official Detective*, because he was half afraid to go home: he admitted it. . . . Never looked at these true-police things before, but the old man was right, as he usually was: surprisingly, some quite good writing. And he knew from Clock just how simple and sordid the real-life crime could be, but this was very salutary reading for the general public, he thought, underlining just how difficult and dirty the cops' job was, and yet how fascinating in a sense—dealing with the perennial human nature. That was the trouble with people —human nature. . . .

When he did go home, it was to face an ultimatum. "Because Athelstane's gone on a hunger strike, Jesse," said Nell distractedly. "He hasn't eaten since breakfast yesterday, and not much then. If this creature's just out of the house awhile, and I can reassure him—"

Athelstane was sitting, huge and brindle and sad, behind Jesse's armchair. Sally had bounced to greet Jesse with her rasping bark, and he reached to pat her automatically. Athelstane turned his noble head sadly away from this spectacle. He had done his best, said his expression, to be a good and loyal servant to the Two Important Humans. If they now preferred this insignificant girl to a real dog, he could only resign himself to the fact that he was no longer loved, and pine away and die. His tail didn't thump once. He didn't come to wash Jesse's face, rising up on mastiff legs with accustomed joy and love.

"You *see*," said Nell almost tearfully. "My own darling monster—and she's a dear little thing, Jesse, if a terror in some ways

146

—but she's not *ours*. We've *got* a dog. You just take her with you tomorrow—"

Jesse regarded her in horror. "But I can't take a Pekingese dog to *the office*—"

"Oh, my heavens!" said Nell. "Fran can take her on walks around the block. You can ask every client who comes in if they wouldn't like— I wonder if Miss Williams had her pedigree somewhere. Just, if she's out of sight awhile, I might be able to reassure Athelstane that we still love him the most. Please, Jesse."

"Everything happens to me. My God, a Pekingese named Sally in a lawyer's office—"

Fran listened to Jesse's disjointed explanation unbelievingly. "But if the thing's upset Athelstane, of course you'll have to get rid of it. Well, of course, find a good home, even a silly toy like — You want me to take her for walks around the block. Really, Jesse."

"Asking clients if they'd like— For God's sake! Nell said— Look, I'm due in court, damn it, I can't— You just look after her. Sally, this is a nice lady, a friend, you be good now." Jesse dropped the leash and fled.

Fran looked at Sally. A Peke. Sally looked back interestedly. She had a tan face with black spectacle markings around her round bulging eyes, a pushed-in face, a wet black nose, and a bulging forehead. Her tail stood up hairily over her back. She was about nine inches high and bowlegged as a cowboy. The rest of her aside from paws and stomach was jet black. Having thoroughly investigated Fran's shoes and every square inch of the outer office, she made two tries at scrambling up on the waiting room couch and finally managed it. She began to lick her front paws. She was very, very hairy.

What next, thought Fran, and started to work on the will.

The electric typewriter she understood, but wills were something else again: in triplicate, the long legal pages, the Latin, the blue binders. She forgot Sally, struggling with the will. Nearly two hours later, with Jesse due back from court, she stopped for a breather—another page to go—and discovered that her cigarette case was empty. "Damn," she said aloud. There was a new pack in her handbag, but she didn't dare move. She was surrounded by pages and pages of the will, copied in triplicate, and how on earth Miss Williams had ever managed she couldn't imagine; this desk was not big enough to accommodate a six-page single-spaced draft and all the double-spaced triplicate pages of the fair copy. If she got up, pages would scatter out of order at random.

"Of all annoying things," said Fran. She looked across the room at a movement, and there was Sally, just waking up from a nap. "You," said Fran. "You—toy! Not that I'd claim Athelstane's trained, but if they tried he could be. A real dog. Say, Athelstane, fetch my handbag here, and he'd—"

Sally raised her head and looked at her thoughtfully. She got up and went down the couch to Fran's bag. She caught the handles and tugged it to the edge of the couch, tilted it to fall to the floor. She jumped down and took hold of the handles again and towed it over to rest at Fran's feet. She barked once.

Jesse came in a minute later. Fran was still staring at Sally. "But she understands English!" she said. "She— I just said it and she did it. And me saying brainless— She understands English as plain as—"

10

"SO YOU'RE beginning to get acquainted with Sally," said Jesse. "Find out there's a little bit more to her than it looks. I've got to call Andrew. I suppose it's time you took her out for lunch." And he added vaguely as he went into his office, "But it's not her brain that causes the trouble."

"Lunch," said Fran, still feeling rather dazed. She also supposed, on mature reflection, that Sally understood "fetch" and "handbag" only, but it had still been quite a performance. She found Sally's leash, collected her coat, and started for the drugstore on the corner.

At the lunch counter, surreptitiously she fed Sally all the roast beef out of a sandwich. Sally enjoyed it immensely, and sat licking her chops while Fran finished her own lunch. Possibly, thought Fran, take a walk around the block before it started to rain again.

She noticed that Sally, owing to the bowlegs, rolled like a mariner as she walked, but she got along quite fast for all her size. Fran, shivering a little even in her warm cloth coat, let her dawdle at an occasional tree on the side street, and Sally was investigating thoroughly the base of a bare-looking crepe myrtle when a man with a large Dalmatian on a lead came strolling by. The Dalmatian bent, friendly, to sniff Sally's tail; and Sally whirled, snarling, and launched herself at his throat.

The Dalmatian backed up in a hurry; Fran grabbed up Sally, and the man laughed. He was a nice-looking middle-aged man in a stained gabardine topcoat. He said, "Sorry, I shouldn't have let him get that close."

"I'm the one— For heaven's sake, I didn't know she'd— She's not my dog, and—"

"Oh," said the man. "You didn't— Well, friendly advice from a pro dog-handler, miss, you best keep an eye on her in the street. They're friendly as can be to people, Pekes, but they'll tackle anything up to a mountain lion with no provocation." He grinned at Sally and pulled her ears. "She's a cute one. Come on, Dick." He went on with the Dalmatian.

"Well!" said Fran, looking at Sally. "I guess I revise some ideas." They got back to the office just as it started to rain, and she told Jesse about the Dalmatian. "I hadn't an idea they were—"

"I said it's not her brain that makes trouble." Jesse, hat in hand, was buttoning his topcoat; he paused. "Fran, for the love of God, would you take her? I don't mean permanent, just till we can get things sorted out and come to some decision— It'd be a godsend."

Fran looked at Sally, who had scrambled up on the couch again and was washing mud off her paws. "How about it, Sally? You like to come home with me? There isn't any big clown of a mastiff to bully—and Andrew'll have to get to know you before he really appreciates you." Sally put her head on one side, listening.

"She's used to women—she'll settle down O.K.," said Jesse. "Thank God for sisters."

As he went out, Fran was saying again, "But I just can't get over it. About as big as a minute, and you—"

Jesse, sitting in divorce court waiting for the client's case to be called, had had a small brain wave. Mulling over every word that Miss Williams had said on the phone that morning, he had stuck at that half sentence "I had to look up the address, it's West—" What? West L.A., West Something Street? More important, had she written it down after she looked it up? In her address book?

She had an address book; it had been in her handbag, he thought Andrew had said. He fidgeted through the court session, and getting away by eleven, went back to the office. . . . That dog. Fran at least finding out something about Pekes. He called Clock's office, but the best Sergeant Pitman could offer him was Petrovsky; Clock was off somewhere.

"Do something for you, Mr. Falkenstein?" asked Petrovsky amiably.

"Margaret Williams' address book—you still got it there?"

"Should be on Andrew's desk somewhere—why?"

Jesse explained the brain wave. "Suppose you have a look—any addresses with a West in them."

"Idea," said Petrovsky laconically. "Hang on." Three minutes later he came back and said, "I've got it. Here's—wait a minute —Aldecott, Boynton, Con— Jeans— Here's a Pitt on West Wayne Drive, Hollywood. Somebody named Harris on Cynthia Avenue, West Hollywood. A Mrs. Severn on—what the hell— West Wanda Drive in Beverly Glen. And Westmoreland Avenue North in Hollywood, a Mrs. Anderson. That's it."

Jesse asked for the specifics and, after thanking Petrovsky, peered at them doubtfully. Looking up the address for her urgent errand, would she have stopped to write it into the address book? But she had been a very methodical person, of course.

He remembered Martha Weglund mentioning a Joan Pitt, so that address was probably n.g.—old acquaintance. Any of the others— He hadn't an appointment until two.

When he left the office he was feeling immensely relieved about Sally. If Fran would just take to her, now— Sally was quite a character, but she was also quite enough dog for one household.

He went to the nearest address first, Westmoreland Avenue North. It was one of the side streets near the Los Angeles City Junior College, and he went around three blocks twice before he found a place to park. Anderson, Petrovsky said. It was an old pseudo-Spanish stucco house; he ducked into the little square porch and pushed the bell. After a moment the door opened.

"Yes? I don't buy at the door." A woman about thirty-five, pleasant-faced, dark-haired, neat, in a blue cotton house dress.

"Not selling anything." He offered her a card. "Like to ask you if you knew Margaret Williams."

"Oh, yes," she said, looking at the card. "Come in. Oh, she worked for you, didn't she, I recognize your name. I'm Julia Anderson." He went in, to a comfortable if small living room, very orderly and clean. "Wasn't it terrible her getting murdered like that? Crime growing so all the time, but I said to my husband, it doesn't seem possible—I mean, a person you knew. I—"

"How did you know her, Mrs. Anderson? Mutual friends or—"

"Oh, no—she used to come to the beauty salon where I worked. She's been doing her own hair the last few years because of the prices going up, but it was when I was still working there I took on that job for her, and I'm still doing it—had been, I mean. Oh, Mr. Falkenstein, do you know how Mrs. Williams is?"

"Not too good—she's in a coma again." He had called the hospital yesterday.

"Oh, that's awful, I'm so sorry. She—"

"Just what—er—job did you mean, Mrs. Anderson? For Miss Williams?"

"That's right. I quit work when Bobby was born, of course, it isn't right to leave even older children unsupervised—he's eight now and Linda six, both in school, of course—but I kept on with that, it earned a little extra. I used to go to the apartment every Saturday to shampoo and set Mrs. Williams' hair, you see. She's such a nice old lady, and Miss Williams nice too — It doesn't bear thinking of, does it?"

So that explained away that address. Nobody newly known who posed an urgent errand. Jesse looked at his watch: a toss-up between West Hollywood and Beverly Glen. He chose West Hollywood at random and, slowed by rain, found the address on Cynthia Avenue. This was a cut above central Hollywood: newer, more spacious homes, upper-class residential area. The woman who came to the door was middle-aged, plump, very well dressed, and carrying a hat.

"Yes? I'm afraid I was just leaving—"

Jesse asked his question hastily. "Mrs. Harris? I think you knew Margaret Williams?"

"Oh," she said. "Yes, I did. Why? Are you a police officer? I couldn't believe it when I saw the papers—anybody you know, it's always a shock. I didn't know her very well, but—"

"Mutual friends, or were—"

"Well, we were both members of the Professional Women's Club. Why?" At Jesse's self-introduction she thawed. "Oh, I see, her employer. Of course you'd be concerned. My address in her — Well, as it happened we were both on the reception committee for the Silver Tea last spring, there was a certain amount of discussion and arrangement, I expect that was why she'd—"

And that explained that address. And if he was going to get any lunch at all— He drove back to Hollywood and had a sandwich at the drugstore on the corner before going back to his office. Sally was asleep on the couch and Fran just finishing the will.

"No potential secretaries?"

"Not so far."

The first afternoon client told him he certainly was an indulgent employer, letting his secretary bring her little dog to work.

"Such a cute little dog, isn't it? I hope you don't find some of your clients object— Personally I like dogs but some people—"

"Er—it's just for today," said Jesse.

Clock was swearing about the routine that went on forever. They hadn't located any more of the possibles from the computer's list, and he didn't feel they were going to drop on X that way. They now had a hit-run up on Spring, one D.O.A., and the usual crowd of witnesses all telling different stories. It was raining again.

What annoyed him most was that he was still thinking of Terry Gallagher as a fairly hot bet for the Williams case, and he had to keep hands off pending Kelleher's investigation. And how long that might be was anybody's guess.

When he came back from a hasty lunch Dale was typing a preliminary report on the hit-run. Petrovsky was out with Keene and Mantella, presumably looking for men from the list. And all the men on that list would tend to be loners, at least very transient, and if they were still anywhere in the county most of them would have moved from the last addresses R. and I. had.

However, there was a lab report in on Kane. He started to read it.

Lab analysis of the clothes she'd been wearing. Clock read the list absently. One pair white nylon panties. One black nylon lace garter belt. One blue nylon lace brassiere. One white nylon half-slip. One mismatched pair nylon stockings, one dark tan, one lighter tan. Double-knit synthetic one-piece dress, pink. All-wool lined coat, black, with fake fur collar, white. Navy-blue low-heeled pumps. Analysis of stains on clothing—

She hadn't, of course, expected to be going out anywhere. Home alone nursing the cold, sitting around in old clothes.

All the clothes except the panties were stained with rain and mud from the street. Stain of orange juice, recent, on the dress

154

near the hem. Face powder from collar of coat, analyzed as such-and-such a brand, translucent pink. Lipstick stain at neckline of brassiere, a different brand, rose coral. And so on and so on— Nothing in it. But, Clock suddenly wondered, why had Lucille Kane been tied up? Their X (Clock refused to think of him in the journalese, what a nickname) had done that only six times, to the four women who didn't know how to drive, and the two who made a mess of shifting gears. And the husband had said Lucille Kane drove her own car.

He picked up the phone absently and asked Sergeant Pitman to get him Stewart Kane, if he was home. . . . "Mr. Kane? Sergeant Clock. No, sir, I'm afraid nothing definite yet. What I—"

"I can understand a thing like that would be difficult, Sergeant. By what the papers say—"

"Yes, sir. What I'm wondering about right now is why your wife was bound and—well, immobilized. As the autopsy report told us."

"Oh. She was? You mean, tied up, before he—"

"Yes, sir. He's only done that in a few other cases, you see, usually where the woman didn't know how to drive a car—or where she didn't know how to shift. I think you said your wife had her own car?"

"Certainly," said Kane. "She'd driven for— Well, that's queer, isn't it? Wait a minute, you just said—about gears? Shifting gears?"

"That's right. The little we've got, his car has a stick shift." Both cars.

"Oh," said Kane. "Oh. Well, I expect that's the reason, Sergeant. Lucille had never driven anything but automatic transmission."

"I see," said Clock. Rather unusual? She had been fifty-two. But time got away—automatic transmissions had been around for some time. "I beg your pardon?"

"They couldn't afford a second car until her first husband's business was built up—she hadn't driven until then, and of course with a beginning driver—but she'd been driving for years, she was a good driver—"

"Only not knowing how to shift gears," said Clock. "I see. Thanks very much, Mr. Kane." He supposed Lucille had had a funeral yesterday. And so the lab report got them no further at all. Nothing new on that anonymous X.

He was still sitting there, telling himself there were things he could be doing, and watching the rain stream past the windows, and thinking of Fran, when his inside phone rang and he picked it up. "Clock, Homicide."

"Well, you pulled the plug, Andrew," said Kelleher resignedly. "I think it must have been you, my boys have been well concealed or so I thought. But by all indications they're getting ready to pull up stakes and run from the Diadem Art Galleries, and we've got no choice but to pull a raid and hope there's evidence on the premises. Would you like to join us in case there's some evidence on your homicide suspect?"

"Very neighborly of you," said Clock. "Now?"

"As fast as you can make it."

That turned out to be quite a donnybrook. Clock took Petrovsky with him, leaving Mantella and Keene starting to question another possible Keene had just brought in. When they got to the Diadem Galleries Kelleher's men were already in and swarming over the place hunting down the occupants.

By the time all the occupants had been rounded up and frisked and handcuffed, nearly everybody had sustained a few damages. Deacon and what would turn out to be his immediate henchmen had put up a fight: Kelleher was going to have a beautiful black eye, and one of his men was still laid out making crowing sounds from a low kick. Clock, diving after a man who'd slipped past a Narco officer and fallen down the front stairs, had just laid hold of him when the man swung at him backhanded and caught him a powerful blow on the nose. That let him out of the rest of it; he sat on the stairs dripping blood in a stream until fifteen minutes later Petrovsky brought him a towel saturated with ice water.

"Better lie down awhile," he advised. The ruction was still going on, in dying spasms; but by the time Clock's nose stopped bleeding they had twenty-one people lined up in custody in the main room of the gallery. Four of them were women—all young women, and Kelleher knew two of them.

"Both whores," he said, feeling his eye. "Do a little sideline in introducing sellers." Gallagher was among the men.

More to the point, from Kelleher's view, was the nice evidence they came across: nothing as big as they'd hoped, but quite sufficient. About ten thousand bucks' worth of Mary Jane and Methedrine, and nearly a pound of uncut heroin.

"Uncut," said Kelleher thoughtfully, eyeing that: it had been in a frozen-food container once holding fried chicken, in the freezer of an old refrigerator in one of the back rooms. "Now that's not far from the original importer. Interesting."

It was. The undiluted H was cut nearly as soon as it was brought in, as a rule: practically all of it coming in, by several routes, from China now. Via Mexico, San Francisco, Canada. And uncut heroin hadn't, probably, been here very long. But that wasn't Clock's job.

"Can I have Gallagher to question?" he asked.

Kelleher said, "Be my guest. Unless you can pin a homicide on him I want him back, of course. But he's small fry, I can guess. One of the boys paid to deliver to the suppliers or sellers. Take him."

Clock and Petrovsky took Terry Gallagher up to the Homicide office and sat him down in an interrogation room. Gallagher was certainly not the type to have joined in that melee voluntarily; he'd probably got in the way of some more warlike characters. He had a bloody bruise on one cheek and his pretty fawn-colored sports shirt was torn, one sleeve half out of it. His wavy blond hair was disordered and he looked ready to cry, his lower lip turning ominously.

"You bullies!" he said. "Big bullies, just c-coming in, beat everybody up! All the silly laws ab-about it, just like Prohibition, nobody thinks anything about that now— People want it, they'll get it some way, and what's it *matter?* Just for kicks, and it's just the silly laws— Lots of people like a drink now and then, it's just —" His voice trailed off breathlessly.

"Well, no, Gallagher, it's not the same," said Clock dispassionately, "but I won't waste time arguing about that with you." The brainwashing along that line most of them had fallen for, and you couldn't reason with them. Let it go. Not his business. "What I want to talk to you about is a homicide. A week ago Monday night."

"Oh, you're back to that again," said Gallagher petulantly. "Just silly. As if I—" He began to smooth his hair, felt in his pocket for a comb, looked ready to cry again when he couldn't find one. "I'm in such a *mess,* and I just paid seventeen bucks for this shirt— Can't I—"

"You'll be given some nice clean clothes at the jail," said Clock dryly. "About Miss Williams, Gallagher. Were you there, and did you see her when she came home that night?"

"No, I told you, no, no, no, no," said Gallagher childishly, beating one fist on his knee. "I told you where—"

"Now, Gallagher. The nice sober stag party at Bernie's? Uh-uh. That was just to get you off the hook— I made Bernie a little nervous, a cop dropping in unexpected, maybe? And maybe he gave you hell for bringing me down?"

"I *told* him how it was! How could I help it if you got this crazy idea about me? I didn't even *know* that woman, I've only lived there a little while— Her acting so mean about Tina, saying— And what's going to happen to Tina? You said jail—just for—"

"So let's have it, Gallagher. Where were you that night and can you prove it?"

"Oh, for *heaven's* sake," said Gallagher. "For *heaven's*— All these silly ideas about it, it's just like liquor, Bernie explained that and— Well, if you've got to know, I was delivering some stuff that night. That's all. To some sellers. Different places."

"Names and addresses," said Clock. Useful for Kelleher as well.

"Oh, heavens, I suppose Eddy or Bert or somebody'd tell you anyway. What's it matter? The Victorian Room on Vermont— the bartender there. The—"

Clock had been at Wilcox Street before coming down to Central. "That's a fag joint, Terry. Every now and then it gets closed up but before we can turn around it's open again. You run with that kind?"

"Don't you *dare* call me a fag!" shrieked Gallagher furiously. "I am not! I don't! But Bernie sells wherever there's customers, wouldn't he? I was other places that night—up to midnight. Another bar on Western, and this girl's apartment in West L.A., and—"

Clock looked at Petrovsky. Gallagher caught up with on this narco count, probably that was straight. And, usefully for the cops, there was small honor among thieves— With the whole bunch in custody, very likely they'd be falling over themselves to implicate all their erstwhile pals as deep as possible. Pass this on to Kelleher: in the course of chasing down the buyers he might come up with some corroboration on Gallagher's alibi.

But that was probably the truth, reflected Clock. And it was frustrating.

Margaret Williams still posed them a funny little mystery.

Coming home, Clock was somewhat surprised to be confronted by Sally, daring him to come one step further. Fran hastened to explain to her that Andrew lived here too. "Friend, Sally. He's all right, see?" She patted Clock's arm.

"Miss Williams' lapdog," said Clock. "Well, I can't say I care for the things—hardly what I'd call a dog—but if you want it, Frances—"

"Oh, my, you don't know Sally," said Fran. "Just wait. Well, we needn't keep her permanently, it's just to take her off Jesse and Nell's hands—she upset Athelstane."

"That?" said Clock.

"That. Well, I didn't know about Pekes either. Wait till you do. Tough day, darling? And *what* happened to your shirt?" as he took off his coat. *"Andrew—"*

"Just a nosebleed," said Clock. "Nothing to fuss about, Fran. I went out on a raid with Kelleher, damn fool that I am, and somebody banged me on the nose. I must have lost a pint of blood."

"I've got T-bone steaks," said Fran. "Build up some fresh. And you take that shirt off this minute so I can start it soaking in cold water, or I'll never get all that blood—"

"Think we'd been married twenty years," said Clock. "I haven't kissed you yet. . . ."

He called Jesse after dinner and told him about the raid, and Gallagher. "So that little ride on the merry-go-round was n.g. I really thought—"

"Did you?" said Jesse. "I didn't. Because that couldn't explain away where the hell she'd been all day, or why, or that very peculiar clue—if it is a clue—of the front cover of *Master Detective.*"

"Well, no," admitted Clock, "I'll give you that. I don't see that the first point is so important—"

"Because you don't realize how out of character it was."

"But the magazine cover— Well, if you have any bright ideas, or our old maestro, I'll be interested. And thank you so much for wishing that dog in name only on us."

"Just wait— And by God I do have a thought," said Jesse with a groan. "That Gallagher had a dog too, and— I'll be damned if I'll take responsibility for Tina, but I'd better call Shackleton, damn it."

Nell was feeding Athelstane by hand and calling him endearing names, encouragingly. After a day spent alone with Nell, suspiciously hunting for Sally and each time more pleased not to find her anywhere, Athelstane was showing signs of rising spirits and condescending to eat the best round steak cut into bite-size pieces. He had thumped his tail twice for Jesse, even if he hadn't left Nell to go and listen to the telephone.

Jesse reflected that Athelstane was the delicate plant, emotionally speaking. Sally was the tough one. Sally, taken to a new place and new people, putting up with them unruffled, even with spirit. Maybe Sally the Brain somehow understood that her old home was forever lost, and faced the future with her hairy tail up and her heart undaunted.

But the shivering whimpering Tina Jesse drew the line at. He called Shackleton and explained; belatedly he realized what a shock he was giving Shackleton, one of his tenants arrested in a raid on a dope supplier. Shackleton, incredulous and shaken, rallied and said that poor dog, he'd go get her right off, see she was taken care of. Jesse didn't think Mrs. de la Croix would be interested in Tina. Cravenly, he left Tina on Shackleton's hands.

"There, darling, you can see she's gone, and you're our only dog again. You don't have to worry, darling, she won't come back, it's all right." Nell stroked Athelstane's ears and he leaned against her lovingly and pushed her back into the sofa cushions.

And Jesse, regarding the pair of them absently, was again thinking round and round on it—just what in hell's name had Miss Williams' extremely urgent errand been?

Clock was, on Jesse's recommendation, looking at the current *Master Detective* and discovering that the old man was right as usual, and Fran was buried in the enormous tome of a cookbook Nell had given her, when the phone rang at nine-forty. Clock went to answer it.

"We've got a break," said Sergeant Raven on the night desk.

"You won't believe it, but the M.M., as Pete calls him, has struck again—and she got away from him. All safe and sound."

"Got away!" said Clock. "You don't— Who and what and how? Can we—"

"Talk to her now? Sure. She's down in First Aid right now, not much hurt. A Mrs. Rose Barry. The uniformed men spotted it right off when they heard her story, and relayed it to us and brought her down, quarter of an hour ago. We're anxious to hear about it too," and Raven chuckled. "Jumped out of the car and ran, middle of Sunset Boulevard—"

"My God!"

"Sounds like a spunky one, all right. You'll be coming in— I called Pete too."

"You bet your life I'm coming in," said Clock, and banged the phone down and went to find a clean shirt, stripping off his dressing gown. He told Fran about it.

"Well, good for her," said Fran. "I never could understand all those women just standing still for it, when they could guess what he'd do— I think I'd try to put up a fight, at least."

"With a loaded gun in your ribs? You ever find yourself in a position like that, you—but I suppose it's no use to tell you," said Clock. "And damn it, that reminds me about that damn lock." The first thing (and a typical thing for a cop to look for, said Fran) that he'd discovered about this apartment was that the lock on the door didn't possess a dead bolt; if they were going to stay here, he said, he'd have had a new lock installed at once.

"I've got a watchdog now," said Fran.

Clock looked at Sally, asleep beside her, and snorted. "Dog in name only," he said, and went out.

"Just wait till he gets to know you," said Fran to Sally.

"Well, of course I was frightened," said Rose Barry almost indignantly, as if they'd accused her of being mentally deficient. "I was terrified. All alone in the house—Bill's up in Fresno for the firm, he'll be home tomorrow—and the Duke not there.

He'd have *eaten* him, but now I think I'm thankful he wasn't, that man might have shot him."

"The Duke?" said Clock.

"Our German shepherd. Betty—that's my daughter Betty, they live in La Cañada—they'd been having prowlers around and we let her take the Duke for a while."

Mrs. Rose Barry was sitting in Clock's desk chair while they talked to her—the night-watch men Raven, Lindsay, Jacobs, and Clock and Petrovsky. Raven was taking notes. Mrs. Barry looked about forty and was probably older, a slight, slim woman once very pretty and still attractive, with pepper-and-salt hair in a severe cut, a fine white complexion, big brown eyes. She had a dark bruise on one cheek; she was flushed and talking animatedly.

"I was frightened to death," she told the Homicide men. "All I'd read about the man in the papers—all those other women, and killing one of them just last week! I was looking at TV when the bell went, and of course I didn't open the door right away —after dark, Bill always says— I turned on the porch light, and there's a peekhole thing in the door, I opened that and called who was it—I couldn't see much at that, that thing is too high —and when he said Western Union I was *absolutely terrified*— because of Jon, you see."

"Jon?" said Petrovsky.

"Our son Jonathan, he's in the Marines and— So I opened the door and there he was. That hideous ski mask right over his whole head, and before I could think he slashed the screen door and had it open. He poked the gun at me and said to give him my handbag, and about then I was realizing who he was. That Masked Monster. Killing that woman just last— And when he grabbed my arm and hit me in the face, after he'd taken all my money, and said we were going on a little drive, well, I just thought I wasn't *having* any." Mrs. Barry looked at them defiantly. "Personally I couldn't understand it, those women just meekly letting him march them off—"

163

"Well, with a gun—" said Petrovsky.

"The gun!" She laughed. "He wouldn't shoot, not in a crowd. On a crowded street. I knew that. He handed me the keys and shoved me into the car—and by the way, I can tell you what that is. It's a Chevy—a Nova II. There was adhesive tape over the name on the dash, but I drove one of those for five years up to when Bill got me the Gremlin six months ago, and do I know that car? It was a Nova. About six years old."

"The hell," said Petrovsky softly.

"Well, he said to turn on Crescent Heights Boulevard and go up to Laurel Canyon, but we're only a block up from Sunset—" The Barrys lived on Selma Avenue. "I just turned the opposite direction and barreled the thing down to Sunset, before he realized what I was doing—and by the grace of God the light was with me there so I turned left onto Sunset and gunned it down a block— I knew he'd be so taken by surprise, he wouldn't *do* anything—"

"Women," said Clock, awed. "Talk about taking chances—"

"And the light was red at Laurel Avenue, I just threw on the brake and *fell* out the door, and ran. I expect all those cars in the left-turn lane are still cussing me, but I made the sidewalk, and began yelling to people to call the police, that was the Masked Monster in that car—"

Of course, by what they had and were getting up in Hollywood, the citizenry had acted about as usual. Quite a lot of witnesses, middle of the evening on Sunset Boulevard, and they had just what they might have expected. The car had taken off into traffic, and there was no make on it at all—unless Rose Barry was right. And all she could add was just more of the same —ski mask, dark suit, dark sweater, medium-sized, no special accent.

"You took one almighty chance, Mrs. Barry," said Clock respectfully. "You couldn't know he wouldn't—"

"One like that?" she said scornfully. "Did they say you're Sergeant? Forcing women off with him to beat them up—he's a coward, and a bully. Stand up to him—I knew he wouldn't fire that gun. Oh, by the way, I think it was a Hi-Standard .22 revolver, Bill's got one like it."

Clock looked at Petrovsky, who appeared amused.

"After the *day* I'd had already," said Rose Barry. "Really. The washing machine going kaput, and all the wrong-number phone calls, and the soft-water serviceman coming just as I was doing my nails—we never use the back door on the drive except for the soft-water man, and three locks to undo—and just as I was about to start off to the market, that idiotic telephone salesman wanting us to buy a lot in Forest Lawn—"

And a little bell rang in Clock's head. He said, "Forest Lawn? A salesman—"

11

"BUT DOES it mean anything?" Clock asked Petrovsky again on Friday morning. "If it isn't just coincidence? Patricia Morgan had a solicitor trying to sell her a lot at Forest Lawn the day she was attacked. So even if we go and ask, and find that all or most of the other women did too, does it mean anything at all?"

"Well, a lead of sorts—"

"Is it? I don't know how they operate, but I assume that that's a job solely on commission, and the best salesman in the world'd have to hustle to earn much at it. I'd have a guess there's a fairly high turnover in salesmen. And then too, our X may just have used that excuse to get the women talking. He—"

"So all right," said Petrovsky, "it's still a lead—if the other women remember one like that."

"If you ask me, it's the hell of a useless lead," said Clock irritably. . . . He and Fran had spent some fruitless time last night trying to persuade Sally that dogs did not belong on beds. Sally had been polite, but unconvinced, and had indeed spent the night curled in a ball on the electric blanket.

If it was going to be any kind of lead, it had to be checked out first. Clock, Petrovsky, and Mantella split up the list of victims and got on the phones. An hour later they forgathered to compare notes.

166

It checked in a way. Of the thirteen living victims of the Masked Monster, ten definitely recalled, when specifically asked about it, that a salesman for Forest Lawn had called on the phone, either the day of the night they were attacked, or the day before. The others couldn't remember.

"So what the hell?" said Clock. "It's nothing—they never laid eyes on him."

"It's something," said Petrovsky. "Psychos, who knows what they'll do? This could be him. For some nutty reason wanting to talk to the women. It's more routine to do—that does break cases, Andrew. You'd better chase up to Forest Lawn, find out where they hire these people, and get a list of current salesmen on the job. Then we go looking for them and haul them in to question."

"It's a waste of time, Pete. Anybody could say he was working for Forest Lawn, for God's sake." But Clock had been a cop for a while too, and knew that the routine had to be followed up, however unprofitable it looked.

It had stopped raining about midnight, but looked as if it might start up again at any moment. Grumbling, Clock went down to the lot for the Pontiac and headed for Forest Lawn Memorial Park in Glendale. And another thing, he thought as he drove, he'd put his foot down presently if Jesse didn't find a new secretary; he'd had time enough to do that: monopolizing Frances. Wishing that dog in name only on them . . .

Jesse, with the morning free, went to look at the last remaining "West" in Miss Williams' address book: Mrs. George Severn, on West Wanda Drive in Beverly Glen. Mrs. Severn was, as he could have predicted, yet another member of the Professional Women's Club who had served on that tea committee with Miss Williams last April.

She hadn't written down the address of her urgent errand. Of course not, thought Jesse: it was too urgent. Shouldn't take more than an hour. It was useless to speculate on it: there was no way that he could see to deduce what it could have been, where, to whom, or why.

He had had to cancel a couple of appointments this afternoon: the bank had arranged with the local tax office to open Miss Williams' safety box all formally, evaluate the contents.

He was just back at the office when Fran appeared, late. "Thank heaven, the manageress likes dogs and part of the yard is fenced. She said she'd be glad to keep an eye on Sally, the dear little thing. Little does she know."

"Too true." The phone rang and Jesse shoved the office button. "Falkenstein speaking."

It was the hospital. They regretted to inform him that Mrs. Hortense Williams had just passed away, having never again regained consciousness. Would he care to speak with the doctor? If he would hold on a few—

"There are no relatives at all, you see," he told the doctor. "I suppose it's up to me, make the funeral arrangements. Suppose you want to do an autopsy?"

"We'd like to, yes, sir. You were her lawyer? Well, I see no reason why we shouldn't be able to release the body on Monday. Is that all right?"

"Fine. I'll check back with you to confirm that, Doctor. Thank you." He hung up. "Now that little job to do. Up to Forest Lawn again."

"Forest Lawn? You and Andrew," said Fran. "It now appears —though he doesn't think it'll give them anything—that the Masked Monster may be selling burial plots up there."

"And how very appropriate," said Jesse.

"But of course you do realize, Sergeant Clock," said Claude Devore, "that almost anybody could pose as one of our salesmen. That is, I should think that nearly any resident of the county would know we have salesmen out—soliciting by phone, calling to follow up—"

"I do realize it," said Clock. "But this has shown up, Mr.

Devore, and we like to be thorough. It's possible that this man is one of your legitimate salesmen, or once was." Devore looked shocked and incredulous; he was a tubby little man very neatly dressed, with a few strands of hair carefully pasted across a bald skull. "Do you have any particular requirements for the job?"

"Well, beyond requiring them to dress neatly, make a good appearance— For the most part, of course, it is telephone solicitation. When a phone call elicits some interest, it'll be followed up by an appointment to— But really, Sergeant, the type of people we get— For one thing, we really haven't many salesmen in the field that way."

"Oh?"

"Well," said Devore, deprecating, "I can't tell you that anybody'd get rich at that, Sergeant. We pay a fair commission. And it's more than the profit motive. I don't know whether you're aware of it but one of our founder's great ambitions was to educate the public to the need for being prepared. People have been educated into buying insurance, looking ahead in other ways—in fact, of course, it is now mandatory to carry automobile insurance—and we feel that it is one of our duties to impress upon the public what peace of mind can be achieved by — You take me. A funeral so often does—er—happen unexpectedly, that is, the necessity—"

"Yes, yes," said Clock. "You said not many men?"

"Well, in that part of the job, no. On duty here and in the office down the hill, to help people arrange suitable ceremonies as they come to us, yes. But the telephone solicitors are all women—as a rule, housewives working part-time to earn a little extra. If they find someone expressing interest, one of our salesmen will follow it up."

"But you do have a list of your salespeople?"

"Oh, yes, of course, but really, Sergeant—"

"Well, I'd like to see it, please. See the names of the men on it."

Mr. Devore pushed a button on his very modern desk; his

office in one wing of the old mausoleum, which also housed a valuable collection of bronzes and the stained-glass reproduction of Da Vinci's *Last Supper*, was not spacious but comfortable. "Miss Higgins, will you bring me a list of our current sales force, please. . . . But I feel sure, Sergeant, that you won't find this dreadful criminal among *our* people—what an idea! It seems more likely to me that this man simply used that as an excuse to get the women to talk to him. I'm sure—"

"Well, we have to look, sir," said Clock.

"Oh, yes, of course, I suppose so," said Devore mournfully.

When Clock examined the list, he thought, Waste of time to check them all out. Upwards of forty men—and a long list of phone solicitors, all female. This would be no use at all, of course; he wished he'd made a bet on that with Pete. But he thanked Devore, copied the names, and started out. As he rounded the last curve of the narrow road down the hill, where the big fountain played in the middle of a green lawn to one side, he was surprised to see Jesse's Ford just passing through the tall iron gates. He touched the horn and drew up, and the Ford stopped even with him. "What the hell are you doing here?" asked Clock. "Thinking of being prepared with the nice burial plot all paid for in advance?"

"I couldn't afford it till I get paid back from Margaret's bank account. Mrs. Williams died this morning. Hospital wants an autopsy, we can fix the funeral for Monday. Thought I'd get it off my mind."

"Well," said Clock. "You could say that X got two with one blow. Poor woman. And have you had any brain waves on that?"

"I have not. Going to open Margaret's lock box this afternoon, all official— Don't suppose any clues'll turn up, but you never know. And no, I haven't found a new one yet. And you're supposed to be the officer in charge of investigation."

"Things come along a little hot and heavy sometimes," said Clock.

170

Things continued to. When he got back to the office he asked Pitman, from force of habit, if anything new had gone down.

"Yep," said Pitman. "More rocks off freeways. No, nobody killed this time—for a wonder—but a mess, four cars involved —the Harbor Freeway again. Johnny went out to look. We had a tip called in on that Gerald Eboe—"

"Who? Oh, the A.P.B. from Denver, yes."

"That he's living with an old pal down in Huntington Park. Dale went out to look at that. That body in MacArthur got identified—old pensioner, his landlady missed him and came to us. More paper work."

"Glorified clerks, that's us," said Clock. He looked into the detective office: Keene was there typing a report. "So, more leg work," said Clock. "Here's a list of Forest Lawn's salesmen."

"And aren't we gluttons for punishment," said Keene. "You don't seriously suppose the boy we want is on that list, do you?"

"I don't know," said Clock. "There's a bare outside possibility that he could be. We'll have to look."

"I know, I know. The routine. Let me finish this report."

"What on?"

"Suicide. Hotel over on Olive. Nobody loves me, I'm broke, this'll show Joe how much I love him."

"One of those. I'll take half that list." Clock went into his office just in time to take an outside call. The General Hospital. Mr. Robert Felton was asking to see Sergeant Clock if it was possible. Mr. Felton seemed quite rational, if the sergeant—

"Hell," said Clock, and went out again. Robert Felton had been in protective custody in the guarded wing at the General; he ought to be dried out by now.

He was. He gave Clock a faint anxious smile when he came into the room; Felton was sitting on the bed, dressed in the hospital-white jumpsuit they had issued him. "Good of you to see me," he said. "I've got myself in a mess, haven't I, Sergeant?"

171

"I would say so, Mr. Felton. Nothing that can't be straightened out, if you stay on an even keel. Your business is still operating, your clerks seem steady fellows and concerned for you, what we heard from them."

"Yes," said Felton. "The money—well, I suppose it can all be straightened out in time. What I—why I wanted to see you, Sergeant, I—I guess I said some wild things—that night—but I'd like to say now, I guess I'm back in my right mind, and I don't —I really don't think I *could* have—have done that. To Miss Williams. I *wouldn't* have, even drunk. It—terrified me to think I might have, but now—"

"Well, I doubt it too," said Clock. "I'm glad to see you're back in control, hope you'll stay that way, Mr. Felton."

"Yes, I—mean to. I will. I—it was all too much, but I—want to get this mess cleared up. I wondered—I suppose it might be a help to have a lawyer—if her employer would be willing to — Do you think—?"

"You can always ask him," said Clock noncommittally. He didn't add that the lawyer seemed to be busy enough right now, the paper work piling up and no secretary to cope. And if he didn't find one soon—

He got back to the office again just in time to take another outside call.

"Andrew, can I get into the jail?" asked Jesse. He sounded harassed.

"Easily. Was it a misdemeanor or a felony you had in mind?"

"Such a funny man. This is turning out to be a busy day. I want to see Gallagher."

"What the hell for?"

"I've found a home for his dog. What'll he get?"

"His dog? Well, it's a second felony count for him, and the judge he'll probably get is death on the drug bit. I'd guess a three to five. I'll call the jailer and pass you in."

"Thanks very much," said Jesse.

When he had got back from Forest Lawn, Fran said another agency had sent a girl over, even worse than the last one. "Buck teeth and atrocious clothes. I—"

"I couldn't care less what she looks like, if she can type and take dictation and file."

"Well, that's unrealistic. You want someone to give a good impression, after all. And this one couldn't, anyway. I tried her on dictation and she was hopeless. You want somebody efficient, and I agree with you about two. I called that agency and told them—" The phone rang. "Mr. Falkenstein's office. Oh, yes, Mr. Shackleton—just a moment. . . . I'm going out to lunch now, Jesse," as he picked up the phone.

Jesse waved her out. Fran had been feeling slightly anxious about the apartment manageress, Mrs. Kressner, and after she'd ordered a sandwich at the drugstore she phoned her.

"Everything all right, Miss—I mean Mrs. Clock? My goodness. You should have warned me." Mrs. Kressner began to laugh. "Some people came to look at eight on the ground floor, and they asked about pets, and I said if they were quiet and all — They had this cute little poodle with them and I thought they'd like to see—a nice fenced yard if not very big—"

"Oh, dear," said Fran apprehensively. "What happened?"

"Oh, they were very nice about it, really. The man fell down and tore his trousers getting the poodle away from her, but they said they didn't mind at all, only they thought something nearer the suburbs— My goodness, you should have warned me," said Mrs. Kressner, still laughing. "She looks so innocent."

"Thank goodness you've got a sense of humor," said Fran. "That dear little thing— "

What Shackleton had to say was, "About that dog, Mr. Falkenstein. That miserable little thing of Mr. Gallagher's."

"What about her?"

"Well, she isn't my idea of a dog at all, but Brenda Lightner's taken a fancy to her and says she'll take care of her if it's all right

173

with Mr. Gallagher. I suppose he'll be going to prison— My God, one of my tenants murdered and another arrested for drug peddling, what the world's coming to I don't know— Do you suppose that'd be all right, Mr. Falkenstein? And what should I do about all of Mr. Gallagher's things? His clothes and all? The apartment's furnished, but he brought in a stereo, and there's all his clothes—"

"Well, damn it, I'm not his lawyer," said Jesse. "I'd advise you to pack everything up, you can always charge him storage when he gets out. I'll try to find out about the dog. And, Mr. Shackleton—" He told him about Mrs. Williams, the funeral. Shackleton was genuinely grieved, said he'd let everybody know. Also, thought Jesse, make a note to have Fran call Martha Weglund and tell her; she'd want to know.

Having called Clock, he went down to the jail and had a brief talk with Terry Gallagher, who was feeling sorry for himself. Gallagher, neat and clean again in the jail-issue tan shirt and pants, looked despondent. He said naturally he was just terribly, terribly relieved to know that Tina was being cared for, and Miss Lightner looked like a nice girl, and it was all right with him. Even when he got out, he supposed he wouldn't try to keep a dog again and Tina's pedigree was in the left top drawer of his bureau if Miss Lightner wanted it.

It was twelve forty-eight and Jesse was eight miles from a one-thirty appointment at the bank, and he hadn't had lunch. He swore as he climbed back into the Ford; it had started to rain again.

Dale, checking out the tip on Gerald Eboe, found him peacefully playing draw with the buddy he was staying with and a couple of others—there was a flyer out with his official mug shot now—and brought him in. They booked him in at the Alameda facility, and after a hasty lunch Clock went down to Communications and sent off a teletype to Denver: they could come get him anytime.

174

As Clock waited for the elevator, a couple of men came up talking: Sergeant Boyle of Vice, and the other one a stranger to Clock. "Well, Clock," said Boyle. "Keeping you busy? You got a smell of that Masked Monster yet? This is Quackenbush—Sergeant Clock."

"Not a smell," said Clock, nodding at the other man.

"The glamorous cases they get up in Homicide. Us, just the dirty little stuff at the bottom. Sometimes—"

"Glamorous, hah. Glorified clerks."

"—it gets a little dirtier than usual. Hell of a thing we're just getting cleared away now. These punks. Bunch of louts from Virgil High School grabbing the girls and feeding 'em barbs. Make 'em easier to rape, you take me. What gets into—"

"Now you don't tell me!" said Clock. "I will be damned. I think you'd both better come up to my office, I want to show you a couple of reports on a suicide." Reba Schultz, he thought. "She links up to that. And of course, hell take it, there'll be no possible charge—no evidence to say it was the same louts—unless we can break 'em down to confessing it. But I'd damn well like to rub their noses in it a little, and have the parents realize just what they've done, and— Don't you *dare* tell me that they're juveniles?"

Boyle looked interested. "A suicide? Nope, they're all eighteen."

"Praise heaven for small favors," said Clock. "Whatever a softheaded judge may hand them, maybe we can put a little fear of God into them at least."

"And you're just the boy to do it, all right," said Boyle amusedly. "I heard you just got married. Congratulations. You do your courting through a ski mask maybe, or over the phone? Wonder any pretty girl didn't feel nervous, you in ten feet of her."

"You go to hell," said Clock. And Pete was going to be interested in this one too. Lean on these punks some, see if they'd come apart. "How'd you get onto them?"

175

"One of the girls finally told Mama. By what we've got, they didn't try that very often, and probably the girls were leary of confessing what had happened. One of the punks said enough willing ones available, they didn't have to— In high school," said Boyle. "I swear, what's happening to people these days—"

Quackenbush spoke for the first time, in a surprising bass voice. "Sodom and Gomorrah," he said succinctly.

At the bank, the bank manager and the representative from the I.R.S. were tediously formal. The official order-to-examine was gone over, Jesse was asked to sign this and that; the other two men signed solemnly. Paper the curse of the twentieth century, thought Jesse.

Finally the bank manager decided that ritual had been satisfied; they all trooped down to the vault in the basement and sat at a long table in the center of the room where the little cubicles were built round the walls to ensure the box renters privacy. A Miss Snade was summoned, and they all went into the vault with her where she located Miss Williams' safety box, used the bank key, took Miss Williams' key from Jesse, slid the box out. They took it back to the long table.

"Mr. Falkenstein," said the manager formally. "I think you may—"

Jesse opened the box. It wasn't one of the vault's largest: about eighteen by six, four or five inches deep. The first thing he lifted out was something a little queer; he looked at it curiously, sliding it out of its protecting envelope. His dithery little Miss Williams, in private life the police buff, studying the police textbooks, reading all the real-life police magazines. And spotting the wanted man for J. Edgar— This had meant something to her, she'd been proud of it. It was the photostat of a check, made out to Margaret Williams for one hundred dollars, signed by the editor of *True Detective* magazine. The magazine that offered a reward to its readers for spotting the fugitives from

176

justice. He laid it down without comment; the manager and the I.R.S. man made surprised noises, looking at it.

The next thing was a will, in a manila envelope labeled in her neat writing. Inside, the familiar blue cover, the neat copy of an electric typewriter. He looked at the heading—an attorney whose name he vaguely recognized, address on Vermont. He'd never suspected Miss Williams of being secretive, and wondered why she'd gone to another lawyer.

"No point reading this aloud," he said.

"No, no, certainly not."

He glanced over the will. A rather detailed will; Miss Williams preparing for all contingencies. Everything of which she died possessed left to her mother, if the mother was still living. In the event that her mother predeceased her—Jesse stared—all the cash she owned, the common stock, bequeathed to the pension fund of the Los Angeles Police Department. Her personal library to the Los Angeles Public Library, including all bound volumes of periodicals. Her pearl earrings, the amethyst ring, her mother's engagement ring, and all other jewelry to Miss Martha Weglund, also any of her clothes Miss Weglund chose, and any of the furniture. Named executor of the will, with the attorney who had drawn it, Mr. Jesse Falkenstein. There were two codicils added to the last sheet. The first specified several pieces of garnet and ruby jewelry, sounding old-fashioned, evidently acquired since the will had been made, to go to Miss Martha Weglund. The second, made only seven months ago, entrusted her dog to the care of Mr. Falkenstein, if said dog should be in her possession at time of death.

"Well," said Jesse. He put down the will. "And damn it, for all her careful looking ahead, this is worth damn all—she predeceased her mother. Wonder if—" He dived into the box again and came up presently with an ordinary business-size envelope, sealed and labeled in a shaky hand, *Property Hortense Williams*. Sealed: had she simply asked Margaret to put it in the box, Margaret unaware of the contents? Probably. Curiously Jesse slit the envelope. A single sheet of stiff bond paper (borrowed from Margaret?)—a painfully scrawled single paragraph. It said baldly, *This is my last will and testament. In case my daughter Margaret should die before me, seeing that there are no relatives to either of us, I would like for all I possess at time of death to be given to Mr. Falkenstein my daughter's employer because he was kind to her and she thought very highly of him. This day March 19——(Signed) Hortense Mary Williams.*

"Well, I will be damned!" said Jesse. And talk about legal complications— He wondered if Mrs. Williams had had a premonition. But simple enough to tidy it up legally, at that: a holograph will was legal in California, and that will was the important one. The beautiful correct one all properly drawn up in technical language by the attorney wasn't worth the paper it was typed on. And after the holograph will was filed—he doubted very much that there'd be sufficient value here to have to go through probate—he and the other attorney could just quietly parcel out the odds and ends as Margaret had wanted them parceled out. And that would be that.

He handed the second will over and pulled the next thing out of the box. Stock certificates: common stock. Fifty shares, fifty shares, forty shares. Very probably held since the father's death: part of his savings. "Value?" he asked the I.R.S. man, who passed them on to the bank manager.

"Oh, dear me. I believe this company was merged with— You'll have to apply for new certificates— At a rough guess, four to five thousand."

Which still kept the estate small enough that the I.R.S. man was (pray heaven) wasting his time here, Jesse hoped. *Money answereth all things*, so said the Scripture, but—

A marriage certificate. Hortense Mary Kitchener, Donald Richard Williams. A birth certificate, Margaret Harriet Williams. A death certificate, Donald R. Williams. Jesse looked at the three pieces of paper on his long-fingered hand there—the sum of it all, and adding to what? And suddenly thought of Nell, the baby so imminently due, the new life surging as old life ebbed.

He wished more poignantly than ever that he had really known Margaret Williams. An interesting and unusual woman. Flitting around his office for nine years, and all silently engaged in her one-step-removed love affair with the stalwart police officers, trying so hard to write the publishable detective novels: getting flustered rather easily but unafraid to stand up with her opinions, even to the V.I.P.s, the published big-name writers and the august TV producers and the famous sponsoring firm.

"Well—" he said. "I'll be seeing this other lawyer. Don't think there's anything here for you," and he gave the I.R.S. man his one-sided smile.

"A list must be made," said the bank manager fussily, "but as it appears that you are the legatee—"

Jesse called Clock, just catching him at six o'clock as he was leaving the office, to tell him about that. "I will be damned," said Clock; and after a moment, "That's—that was nice of her, Jesse. The pension fund. Even if the will isn't—"

"Not all that mercenary, Andrew," said Jesse. " 'Nother proverb—no, it's Solomon—that says, *Treasures of wickedness profit nothing*. Legatee be damned, I figure the residue ought to be parceled out the way she wanted. And I owed her two weeks' salary. After the funerals get paid for, the pension fund can have what's left, and Miss Weglund her personal bits and pieces. And it appears I had legal right to give Sally—"

"Don't mention the name to me," said Clock. But he sounded rather pleased with himself.

Clock was feeling satisfied that he and Petrovsky had instilled a little fear of God into those damned punks. If no charge could be made, still the punks had been cowed, lectured about Reba Schultz.

And the hell of that was, the only legal charge was contributing to delinquency, and what would they get? Even from a reasonably intelligent judge, probably no more than a suspended sentence, probation to parents.

Sometimes Clock felt a little tired of the thankless job that was his job.

The start had been made on looking at salesmen employed by Forest Lawn, and so far they all looked upright and respectable, with clean backgrounds and no remotely suspicious traits.

He went home to Fran, and felt better, relaxing in the comfortable living room that was home now. He told her that when Jesse gave her the dog in name only, he was disposing of his own property. "Well, how funny," said Fran.

She had visited a petshop and bought a bed for Sally: a smart kapok-filled round dog bed, the small size, covered with bright blue canvas.

Sally sniffed at it politely and the minute lights were turned off made two scrambles at the big double bed before achieving the foot, and settled down on the electric blanket.

Jesse called their old maestro after dinner and brought him up to date. "Oh, you don't say. Well, all that doesn't matter, does it, Jesse? Nice touch, dispose of everything the way she wanted, but it doesn't take us any farther with what happened to her. Which I am very damn curious to know." There was an interval of silence broken only by a faint splash as their old reprobate renewed his drink. "You quoting the Talmud. So can I. *In the multitude of words there wanteth not sin.*"

"Meaning?"

"Well, I've been thinkin' about first causes. Sometimes things come along kind of fast, and—um—sort of obscure the original simple little facts. Make it look complicated when it isn't, necessarily, at all. You think slow and careful about actual facts in this thing, Jesse, and— Well, I just saw something I should've seen right off. Hope I'm not startin' to go senile, overlookin' that."

"That'll be the day. What?"

"The paper," said the old man. "The— Now, it's a thing you ought to see for yourself. I'm not about to do your thinking for you. Supposed to be a smart young fellow, and Andrew too— of course, he didn't hear the Weglund woman—"

"Only," said Jesse, "naturally we're not quite so smart as anybody your age who started out with any brains at all."

"That's right, as I've said before. You had that storage place come 'n' pack up everything in the Williams apartment."

"I did. Seemed the easiest thing to— And what's to be done with it all now—well, after we've parceled out all the bequests, I suppose donate what's left to the Goodwill or—"

"But you can get at it? Payin' the storage bill, you can go and take some of it away?"

"I suppose so. Why? What do you want from all that?" Jesse was surprised.

"Tosh," said the old man, annoyed at himself. "You confusin' my mind with all the damn odds and ends. That Gallagher, and Felton, and the fool dogs—have you got rid of that Peke yet?"

"Fran's got her. Andrew says dog in name only."

The old man laughed. "Wait till he finds out. . . . And all the other bits and pieces that showed up, to sort of obscure the simple facts. Of course, even when we look careful, just how the hell to tell *what*—but we'd better look. I'd better look."

"At what, for God's sake?"

"Well, if my brain's still workin' right," said old Mr. Walters, "which I got no reason to think it isn't except that I should've thought about this sooner than I did, there was what her mother said. Her sittin' up late, when she had to be at work the regular time next morning. And—yes, that's a thing I'd like to ask Andrew too, about that funny clue of the magazine cover. If what I'm thinkin' there could be—

Well, where's that warehouse? Vermont Avenue. Meet you there at nine A.M., all right? I suppose you'd have to be the one, get things out."

"But what—"

"You just be there," said Mr. Walters. "G'night."

Jesse wondered just what bee the old man had in his bonnet now. Simple first causes?

12

CLOCK LOOKED at the front page of the *Times* on Saturday morning with a little dissatisfied grunt. Fran, having put her lapdog out in the yard, was being domestic over eggs and bacon. "And I still think I was right, a fairly harebrained idea," said Clock. . . . It had been Petrovsky's idea, and both Clock and Mantella had argued against it, for different reasons.

"We know it's him, for ninety-nine-percent sure," Petrovsky had pointed out. "Calling the victims he's picked, posing as the Forest Lawn salesman. Don't ask me why psychos do things. But, so we give it to the press—"

"And have a spate of hysterical women calling in, 'He's after me,' " said Clock.

"I don't think we would, Andrew. Also tell the press, emphasize the fact that all the *bona fide* phone solicitors for Forest Lawn are female. And they won't have an army of 'em calling fifty thousand people a day, after all. It's something positive to do. If he does pick another—and when he missed one, the first one to get away from him, it could be he'll try for another one sooner than usual—and calls her first, we could—"

"Woolgathering," said Mantella. "Don't you think he can read?"

"Well, it just might break the case," said Petrovsky stubbornly.

"Look," said Mantella, "something was said—the Robbery men on it first—about how he always makes sure there's I.D. on them. Wants them known as more of his work. The egotist as well as the nut. You think he's not reading everything in the press about him? I think it might scare him off for good."

In the end, Petrovsky had argued Clock, halfway against his will, into trying it. He had given the story to the press in time for the various editions today, and the *Times* was the first out with it. The boxed story, five paragraphs on the front page, made all the points, and Clock just hoped that every female who read it would read as far as paragraph three where it was emphasized that all genuine telephone solicitors for Forest Lawn were women.

Finish taking a look at the Forest Lawn salesmen today, clear them out of the way—none of them so far remotely possible. And they still had a lot of men on the original computer list to locate: more likely X was there somewhere. . . .

"At least," he said, kissing Fran good-bye, "you can stay home where you belong today. Or is it house hunting?"

"After the week I've had with all those cursed wills," said Fran, "I'm staying home. Except for market later on. Have a good day, darling."

Jesse was waiting at the big warehouse on Vermont Avenue, when a checker cab pulled up and old Mr. Walters got out of it. "You just park and wait," he instructed the driver, and added automatically to Jesse, "Damn D.M.V. Just as good a driver as I ever was, think I'd gone senile just because I got to my eightieth birthday." It was still a grievance, three years later, that he didn't have a car any more.

"So what do you want in here, maestro?"

"I'd like, if possible, to see the fellows who cleared out that apartment. But let's find out what rigmarole we got to go through to lay hands on some of this stuff."

They went in and asked. The desk man they talked to was surprised and a little disapproving that anybody should want to get at possessions only stored away five days ago; but he said resignedly he'd get the papers to be signed and take them up to locate whatever they wanted. . . . The men who had actually packed it? Sighing, he looked up records and said, "Oh, that was Wenger and Brannigan. Last Monday—Berendo Street, that's the job. Well, you're lucky, they're here right now, I think, stacking up a load. Let me check." He picked up the phone and added, "But I hope you won't take up too much time, sir—we're busy, a place like this, we can't— Just what was it you wanted? No complaints, or—"

"No complaints. I just want to talk to 'em, and I'll be happy to pay for the privilege, you want."

"Oh, really, that isn't— Say, Mike. Are Wenger and Brannigan still here? Yep, that's what I figured. Third floor, eh? O.K., thanks. Now, sir, all this Williams storage is on the eighth floor, but—"

"Talk to the fellows first, hey?"

The man shrugged and led them to an elevator. Up on the third floor, they surveyed what looked like chaos: crates, cartons, wooden boxes, stacks and stacks of them, against the walls, and forming long aisles from wall to wall: furniture that wouldn't fit into boxes stacked, draped in huge plastic sheets to keep off the dust: dimly in one corner they could see the shape of a grand piano, something that might be a printing press—"My God," murmured Jesse, awed.

"Quite a lot of stuff to keep track of," said old Mr. Walters.

"Eight floors of it. But we got a system. Lay hands on anything people call for, ten minutes. Come on, they'll be over here."

They found Wenger (large, sandy, and growing a beer drinker's paunch) and Brannigan (smaller, dark, and muscled) sweating over stacking cartons neatly against one wall. Wenger and Brannigan were just as pleased to stop work for a while. "These men seem to have some questions to ask you, job you did Monday. I guess you can knock off to talk to 'em." Their guide went back to the elevator.

"What job was that, Mr.—"

Jesse introduced himself. "This is Mr. Walters. He's the one with the questions. Fire away, Edgar."

"The apartment on Berendo," said Mr. Walters promptly. "You cleared out everything but the stove."

"Oh, that place. Hell of a job," said Brannigan. "Look, we can smoke out on the fire escape." They all went out there. It was overcast and gray again today, but not raining. "Everything just lying around, we had to pack it all up, dishes, kitchen stuff, clothes in closets and drawers. Did somebody die? Usually it's that kind of job we get when somebody's died. People moving, wanting to store some things, usually it's all packed for us, we just got to move it."

"That's right," said Wenger. "All those books—my God." Jesse felt guilty.

"Well, now. Like you to think back—to the second bedroom there. A lot of bookcases, bed, desk, bureau—and I'd have a guess there were quite a few magazines lying around loose. You remember that?"

Brannigan drew on his cigarette, thinking back. "There were. Sure I remember that. No books or magazines in the other bedroom, but that one—piles of 'em. And in the bookcases, some big books, magazines all bound together."

"Fine. It's the loose ones I'm after. All of 'em. Every single last one. What'd you do with 'em?"

"Oh," said Brannigan. "Them. Seemed funny—women's clothes in that closet, but all those were the true police magazines. Sensational stuff, you know. Seemed funny that anybody'd pay to store things like that too—"

"Well, you didn't just throw 'em away, did you? Just because—"

"My God, mister," said Wenger, hurt, "acourse not! This place's got a reputation, we guard your goods. You leave an empty cigar box with us, labeled and all, you come back ten years later and it'll be right here waiting. No, we put all those in cartons, I remember that—must have been, gee, forty or fifty of 'em—"

"Hah," said the old man, sounding pleased. "Know where they are? Where you put 'em?"

They looked at each other. "All that went up to the eighth floor, sure. Jimmy had a spot cleared and we just dumped all of it there. Jimmy mighta stacked it different later, but it'll be there. You want to go look?"

"That's just what." They rode up further in the big rumbling freight elevator, and on the top floor were confronted with the same orderly chaos. Wenger and Brannigan led them across to the back wall, where a thin morose-looking Negro sat at a battered desk reading a paperback on astrology. "Say, Jimmy, all that stuff last Monday afternoon, all labeled Williams—it about where we dumped it?"

"Down in the corner there." The Negro didn't look up.

It occupied, somewhat to Jesse's dismay, a surprising amount of space: all the furniture, even neatly stacked and plastic-wrapped—well, five rooms of it after all. The refrigerator (and come to think they'd have had to clear that out too, the food in the cupboards: he should have thought of that, and he wasn't about to ask what had happened to it), the rugs, and all those damned books, now in cartons— "I labeled the cartons," said Brannigan. The cartons all stacked together, and of course they had packed the loose magazines lying around first, so those cartons were at the bottom of the dozen stacks. Half an hour later, sweating, Brannigan said shortly, "There you are." Three cardboard cartons, each one piled with magazines; the old man insisted on opening them to check.

"You absolutely sure this is all of 'em, every last one around that room?"

"Mister, I'm sure. I'm the one packed 'em all away, all the detective magazines, and I remember they filled three cartons."

"So thanks very much, boys." Mr. Walters solemnly fished out a bill for each of them.

"Say, you don't have to—"

"No, no, you been a big help. Now let's get these down to the cab, Jesse—"

"You'll have to sign all that out with Jimmy, sir—"

Eventually they got the three cartons down to the street and the cabdriver helped load them. "And just what the hell have you got in your head about all the old magazines?" asked Jesse.

The old man chuckled. "Operative point they aren't. They'll be, I think, all of last year's *Official Detective*, *Master Detective*, and *True Detective* she hadn't sent off to get bound yet, and all the issues out so far this year, lessee, up to March, I suppose. They get the March issue on the stands before we're into February."

"Well, and so?"

The old man shook his head at him. "I know you had things on your mind, Jesse. And all these—um—extraneous bits showing up to sort of cover up the basic facts. But you do remember what Mrs. Williams said?"

"She sat up late that Sunday night—Margaret."

"Rustlin' papers. That's so. We thought maybe she couldn't sleep, after the party. But there's all sorts of reasons for sittin' up late."

"And she didn't have the codeine, to put her to sleep," said Jesse. He'd almost forgotten that codeine. "What are you going to do with all those?"

"I'm goin' to look at 'em," said the old man. "Very thorough

and careful. Though I don't know exactly how we might spot—
Oh, well, have a look, and maybe have to hunt up every female
at that party who— I'll be in touch, boy. You take me down to
Mar Vista," he added to the cabdriver, and climbed into the
cab. He poked his head out the window to add, "Thanks very
much. Let you know if I come up with anything."

The cab shot off, and Jesse looked after it, exasperated. He
had the feeling that he ought to know what their old maestro
was talking about, but he didn't.

When Jesse got back from the bank the day before he had
called the lawyer who drew up Miss Williams' will—John Kirkbride. They set up an appointment for eleven at Kirkbride's
office. Jesse had been surprised, learning about the other lawyer, that Kirkbride hadn't contacted him; the homicide had
been reported by the press, if not in detail. But it transpired that
Kirkbride had been away on a contested will for an out-of-state
client: the estate consisted of land up near Bakersfield, the title
unclear, and it was, said Kirkbride, quite a mess.

"But you're not interested in that. I was never so surprised in
my life when I heard about that—that Williams woman. Ordinary sort of woman—but it was a queer will, wasn't it? And
worth nothing, if her mother— So what's the situation?"

Jesse explained it succinctly. "I see," said Kirkbride, and
added irrelevantly, "She came in to make that first codicil after
she inherited a little jewelry from an old aunt of her mother's
—last living relation they had, she said. And then afterward
about the dog— Well, it won't be much of an estate, of course,
but—"

"Don't know how you feel about it," said Jesse, "but like
Solomon said, *He that maketh haste to be rich shall not be
innocent.* And I could maybe use that cash for a new car and
so on, but I'm not going to. Think I'd feel better about it if I
parceled it out just the way she wanted."

"That's very generous, Mr. Falkenstein." Kirkbride looked at him curiously. "And up to you, of course. I see Mrs. Williams didn't think to name any executor." He looked at the shakily scrawled holograph will and smiled; he was a nice-looking middle-aged man with a crest of gray hair and a square jaw. "Laying up treasure where moth and rust do not corrupt, eh?"

Jesse laughed. "Well, something in that, we can suppose. Besides, you could say I've got a stake in the L.A.P.D. Recently acquired a brother-in-law down there at Central Division. The thankless job, you can say—and right now he's the fellow trying to catch this Masked Monster."

"Oh, you don't say? There was something in the paper yesterday, a Sergeant—"

"Clock. Altogether, you could say," said Jesse thoughtfully, "kind of a stormy send-off into matrimony, after they got back from Honolulu. Me monopolizing Fran and all—and the dog in name only— Mmh, yes. Mr. Kirkbride, you got an efficient secretary?"

"Two. Very efficient. Why?"

Jesse sighed. "I wish I had. And to think how I complained about our Margaret— Every girl any agency's sent me has been either half moronic or completely untrained, and even if my wife wasn't expecting so imminently, she can't type. And—"

Kirkbride laughed. "Oh, my God, do you tell me anything? I know. I had to get a new receptionist last year, Marge quit when she had the baby, and the types the agencies sent out— everything from tarts on the make with the miniskirts and false eyelashes to the morons who'd taken a year of filing in high school. You must be in a fix, Mr. Falkenstein, if you've got any kind of practice."

"I am feeling harried," said Jesse plaintively. "The only word. I've got three more wills to be copied, one of 'em kind of complicated, a business contract, and a couple of deeds of gift, and two damage suits coming up, and five divorces, and now this rigmarole about Margaret's stock certificates to see to—and God knows what next week's clients will hand me—"

190

"Listen," said Kirkbride, "let me ask Helena—my girl Friday. Been with me twelve years, I wouldn't know what to do without her. It could be she'll know somebody, you never can tell. Anyway, I'll ask her."

"Be very much obliged," said Jesse, and meant it.

"But you said—the murder—not just an ordinary mugging? Something personal? That ordinary woman—" Kirkbride looked incredulous.

"Something more. Looks like that, all right, and a couple of very funny little clues have showed up too, but none of 'em seems to add to anything."

Kirkbride looked at him quizzically. "I seem to recall seeing your name linked to a couple of other murders, Mr. Falkenstein. You'll have to turn Sherlock and solve the case yourself."

"Not my job. Accident I got into anything criminal—not a criminal lawyer," said Jesse, annoyed. "But with Andrew concentrated on his Masked Monster— Well, anyway, least said soonest mended. I'll file the will and let it go. Clear things up as we can. And thanks very much—"

"I haven't done a thing. But I'll ask Helena about a girl."

"And I'll keep my fingers crossed," said Jesse.

Clock and all his men were back at the routine. Dale had found and brought in a man off the first list, as a possible, and he had just the kind of pedigree to make him sound very possible indeed, so they were leaning on him heavily. His name was Clyde Heffner and he had a record back to age fifteen of attempted assault, one statutory rape, one rape-assault, assorted muggings, and one heist job. He was currently on parole from Folsom on that, and he was living in a rooming house on Seventeenth Street, and so they were questioning him sharp and hard.

It was going the usual way.

"So, last Thursday night, Clyde. Eight to nine o'clock. Where were you?"

"I don't remember. I don't hafta talk to you. I'm clean."

"So prove it, Clyde. Thursday night. Where?"

"I don't remember, damn it! One night's like another— You know I'm on P.A., so I ain't s'posed to go in bars, pick up a dame, do nothing but twiddle my thumbs! So—"

"All right, what do you usually do nights?"

"Nothing. I gotta job help this guy in this secondhand furniture store. Hard work, liftin' all that heavy stuff. I'm tired nights. Well, sometimes I go see a movie is all."

"Where?"

"Anyplace—places around. The cheap ones."

"Is that where you were last Thursday night?"

"I don't remember."

After a while they dropped that and started tackling him directly about the assaults. They didn't get any reactions to the victims' names, or the descriptions of the two cars, or anything else. When he grasped what they were talking about, he started cussing. He wouldn't do anything like that, like kidnapping those dames, he never did, and he didn't have a car, couldn't drive on P.A., and they were all nuts, try to pin that on him—

"Well, the cars," said Petrovsky. "There's nothing to say he has access to one, let alone two. I know he sounds right for it, but—"

"Does he?" said Clock. "On second thoughts, does he? Just for one thing—so we know now that X the psycho phones them, claiming to be selling for Forest Lawn. He'd have to sound—as those who remember say he sounded—polite and grammatical and so on. Do you think Heffner could?"

"Well, I don't know. Do we ask for a search warrant?"

Clock was hesitating, debating about that, when Sergeant Pitman came in a hurry up to where they stood talking outside the interrogation room. "Sniper over at the main library. Three cars on it now, they think at least one corpse—"

Clock and Petrovsky dove for the door, Clock detouring to grab a box of ammo from his desk. They collected Mantella, just bringing in another man, and Keene, and fell into the Pontiac downstairs.

When they got to the main branch of the Los Angeles Public Library on Fifth Street, they found a horde of uniformed men deployed about the building like guerrilla warriors, a uniformed sergeant with a bullhorn in one of the five squad cars, and the usual witless citizenry gathering to observe excitement. As the men from Homicide got out of the car, a shot was fired from inside the front door and one of the uniformed men staggered back against a car, feeling his arm. The crowd began to scream and run in all directions.

People! thought Clock disgustedly. You'd think they'd have more sense—

They made it to the shelter of the entrance porch. "What's up?" asked Clock.

The uniformed sergeant there, gun out, peering round the doorjamb cautiously, said, "We got a call from one of the librarians, man acting suspiciously. All she said. When a car got here and the men went in, he started shooting. Berserk. We don't know the situation in there—he may be holding hostages. I came down and got some more men up here pronto—Jim's just gone round to look for a rear entrance."

"There's got to be fire exits," said Clock. "We were told a possible corpse?"

The sergeant jerked his head. "Round that side of the building. Woman came running out the front door about as I got here, he shot at her four times and she got around to the side there before she— There's an ambulance on the way."

More shots came from inside the building. The man with the bullhorn was trying to talk him out, patient and promising. "Any idea who he is?" asked Petrovsky.

"Nope. Doubtless we'll find out," said the sergeant. More screams at the shots—the crowd just scattered, still there. A Traffic man came up and said there was a rear door, but it was locked. They all swore and went to look for fire exits.

But as Clock and the sergeant got round the back, the rear door burst open and a man came running out. Clock saw at a glance that the door was the type with heavy crossbars inside, to lock automatically on closing, and with instant presence of mind he dived at it, caught it when it was within two inches of closing, and fell heavily against it, stumbling. His four left fingers went numb, but he jerked the door back and held it.

"Man—gone wild!" panted the fellow who had dashed out. "Shot one o' the girls—got a big gun—you better be careful! I sneaked out past the stacks—"

The sergeant began calling up men. They left two at the rear door, stationed more at the front, and the rest of them went in quietly. After that it was all quite tame.

In the big main lobby of the library, up by the checkout and return desks, the sniper was standing facing the front door. Three women librarians behind the desks were frozen, staring at him, and four other women, presumably patrons, were huddled together against one of the desks. They could see a pair of feet protruding from behind a desk. The sniper hadn't any idea that there was a bunch of cops coming up behind him, and before the expressions on the women's faces told him, they rushed him and took the gun away.

The gun was a 30–30 hunting rifle. The librarian wasn't dead but had lost some blood. The Traffic man outside wasn't dead either but had a broken leg. The woman who had run out was in fair condition, would recover.

The sniper had no I.D. on him and refused to talk. They booked him in and took his prints. Twenty minutes later the computer told them he was Angelo Carezza, missing from Camarillo; he had a long history of violence and was diagnosed as a schizo.

It was one o'clock and none of them had eaten.

Over lunch, Clock and Petrovsky decided that it would be a waste of time to talk to Heffner any longer. They let him go. About then a man wandered into the Homicide office asking for

Clock, a middle-aged man with a tanned weatherbeaten face, and he wasted some more time for them. He was James Ratchett, and he was a cousin of Lucille Kane's, and her husband had written to the family, of course, they didn't know him but he seemed a very nice fellow, didn't he, and Ratchett had to be in town on business, he had a big farm up toward Fresno, sugar beets mostly, and thought he'd just— Knew Lucille well when they were kids, but since she married the first time and moved to the city— And the police didn't have a line yet on this killer? It did beat all, to think of poor Lucille getting killed like that—

They were polite, and Ratchett finally took himself off. "The citizens," said Petrovsky, lighting a cigarette. Clock's inside phone rang and he picked it up. It was the desk sergeant downstairs.

"Excuse me, Sergeant, you've got a caller, if it's all right to send him up. A Mr. Walters."

"Send him up!" said Clock. Some people had the common courtesy to ask, he thought. And what might their shrewd old maestro be after?

He introduced him to Petrovsky, who looked curiously at fat, untidy old Mr. Walters with his handlebar moustache and ashes on his vest. "Don't want to interrupt any important business, Andrew."

"We're taking a deserved breather. What can I do for you?"

Mr. Walters sat down. "I'd like a look, Andrew, if it's possible, at that magazine cover. 'Nother little bit of the thing just occurred to me, and in fact it'd sort of be a clincher to a little theory I've built up. Just before startin' to work my way through all those magazines, y' know, I thought I'd like a look at that, and I got just one little question for one of your lab men."

"Being mysterious as usual," said Clock. "Telling us young fellows we ought to see things for ourselves."

"Well, I kind of think Jesse should have. You've been bothered by these other cases I expect you've had too, as well—Jesse said—as this Masked Monster. Reasonable you might not think much about first causes, on Miss Williams. But d'you think I could have a look?"

"No reason why not. Come on, I'll take you up." At his gesture Petrovsky trailed along. "This, Pete, is the gifted amateur Sherlock who has built Jesse's reputation. And part of mine. We feed him the information, and he goes away and thinks about it and presently hands us the right answer and says we should have seen it for ourselves."

"Tosh," said the old man. "All you young men runnin' around harried these days, you got no time for contemplation, like they say. Me, I got nothin' to do since I retired—"

"Having made several million bucks, though why you have to rub our noses in your vulgar riches by giving us that damn set of sterling—"

"Humph. Same as that case we had a couple months back," said the old man seriously. "Like to give people things they can hock, comes the big bang and everything shot to hell. Besides, I'm happy to see young Fran settled down proper."

In the lab, Clock introduced Winter, who was pleased to show off his exhibit. "Just a few little bits we couldn't recover, but you can see the edges line up. Rough, but very definite. Now this upper section—"

"Um," said Mr. Walters thoughtfully, looking at it. "Yes, I see. This larger piece was the one they found in her mouth? All wadded up—"

"Possibly used as a gag—he may have just reached for the nearest thing, if it was on impulse he—"

"Impulse," said the old man, and smiled. "I got just one question for you, Mr. Winter."

Winter looked interrogatively at Clock, who was smiling too.

"Special consultant. Answer the man."

"Yes?"

"You looked at both these pieces of paper acourse—shiny, slick paper, magazine cover—and analyzed what was on 'em?

Sure. You set up this little exhibit—shows beyond all doubt piece of magazine cover in her mouth came off this same exact copy of *Master Detective* that was in the back seat of her car. You found saliva, mucus, as expectable, on piece in her mouth —and maybe lipstick?"

"Why, yes, just a trace—"

"So," said the old man gently, "did you find any lipstick on the other piece? The piece still attached to the magazine?"

Winter looked puzzled. "Why, yes, as a matter of fact we did, sir. In fact, a little more lipstick than on the other piece. Just a smear—just above the torn edge here, you can see it if you look close. We identified the brand," and he named it. "Pastel pink."

"And that does sort of clinch it," said the old man to himself. "And if that isn't the hell of the funniest clue—" He sighed a long sigh. "And I tell you something, Andrew, Jesse's goin' to look far and wide for a secretary as bright as Margaret Williams. She was quite a girl, our Margaret. With plenty of guts. When I think how it must've gone—"

"What? What inspiration's struck you? Lipstick?"

Mr. Walters shook his head. "I got a little homework to do before I explain that to you, Andrew. But I guess something'll show up to point a right direction, at least. I better get on home and start the homework."

That was all Clock could get out of him, and he felt unreasonably annoyed at their aged Sherlock.

Fran called Nell at four o'clock. Nell said crossly that her back was killing her, and she'd be damned relieved to have this project *over*. "Whichever—though it could be twins, as enormous as I am. I feel like a hippo. Will I ever get back to size twelve? What? Oh, yes, Athelstane's fine—since he's sure she won't be back—eating like a horse. But on top of everything else, I'm feeling annoyed at Edgar—"

"My darling lamb Edgar. Why?"

"Well, I don't know what he said to Jesse, but it is maddening,

Fran— Jesse came home at one o'clock and he's had *The Art of the Fugue* stacked on the phonograph ever since—it's the third time round for the Toccata in D minor—and I am going slowly mad."

"You know he always thinks better to Bach," said Fran. "Just as it's tinkering with clocks with Father. And you can always take some aspirin. I'm just going out to market, hope I get back before it starts raining again."

It was five-twenty when Fran ran the Dodge into the garage and collected the bag of groceries from the back seat. She caught Sally's leash between two fingers and trudged around to the front door of the apartment. She'd taken Sally along to give her a little exercise, after all the rainy days. She started up the stairs, Sally hopping energetically from tread to tread, rolling on her bowlegs.

The apartment was the front one on the left. And the door was ajar.

Fran stopped on the landing. She had, of course, locked the door when she left. The lock, her cop husband said, minus a dead bolt. Any lock without a dead bolt, the breaker-inner could use the little plastic card, depress the lock tongue, and be in with no trouble at all.

Goodness, said Fran to herself. The breaker-inner? The door was ajar a good six inches—

Common sense. Go down to Mrs. Kressner's apartment, summon the cops. From Wilcox Street, here.

Fran backed up a few steps, to start down the stairs again.

Sally, however, possessed no such innate caution. She pushed in the open door and, barking furiously, charged into the apartment. "Sally!" said Fran, and ran in after her.

She had got to the middle of the living room when a big man came stumbling out of the hall. He was kicking out savagely— Sally was firmly attached to his left ankle—and he swiped at Fran wildly, backhanded. A knife in his hand— She felt the blade just graze her cheek, and then he hit her hard on the shoulder and she fell, dropping the groceries she still clutched. Sally yelped sharp and high. Fran scrambled up dizzily—was that blood on her face? She staggered to the door—the living room empty. The man was at the top of the stairs, still trying to kick Sally, who had let go of his ankle and was making savage rushes at him, nipping where she could reach. He had, Fran suddenly noticed, her jewelry case in one hand. He kicked at Sally, overbalanced, fell down with a crash, and started to roll down the stairs. He was cursing at the top of his voice.

Sally hopped down after him, and as he lay half-stunned on his back at the bottom, she pounced for his throat, a small black avenging fury.

Doors opened and people came out. "Police," said Fran. "Call the—" And that was blood streaming down her face, a scar, what would Andrew—

She sank down on the top step.

The next thing she was clearly aware of, besides the uniformed men down there, was someone. Saying, "Hey, that's an artery, better get him in fast—somebody get this damn dog off him—"

"Sally," said Fran faintly.

"Bleeding like a stuck pig—artery, all right—"

Sally came hopping up the stairs to Fran, who gathered her up. And for the first time Sally licked her hand. Her pushed-in black nose was cold, and slightly bloody from the burglar.

13

"Now this," said Clock, "is quite a dog we've got here. In capitals. My God, this little scrap of a— She half killed him! Quite the hell of a watchdog this is, Frances." He still sounded surprised. He had just finished talking to Wilcox Street station, and sat down in the big armchair with Fran across his lap. He looked down at Sally. "Come on, you too, girl." Sally made two scrambles before she achieved the seat, with a little help. "My God, you. Looking so birdbrained and frivolous. I can't get over it." He stroked Sally's head.

"Edgar says," said Fran, "that pound for pound they're the most dog there is. Tackle anything."

"I believe it. Quite a girl, our Sally, aren't you? I'll be damned, she would have killed him if the ambulance had been slower— and good riddance."

"No," said Fran. "Sally'd have been in trouble."

"My God, yes. Just as well. Not that he'd've been any loss." The burglar had turned out to be one Douglas Hume, with a long and bad record of violence and larceny; he'd served two terms for manslaughter. "My God," said Clock, tracing the strip of bandage on her left cheek where Hume's knife had grazed. "This hell of a watchdog saving you from maybe— Well, I guess I've got two girls now, hah?" He looked down at Sally, who was listening intently, and laughed. "I can't get over you. You look so innocent. Tell you something. I bet that big lummox Athelstane would have run and hid. They do say it's the little ones are the scrappers." He stroked Sally.

"And I haven't found all the jewelry yet," murmured Fran. The jewelry case, abandoned in midair, had scattered its contents down the stairs and over the entrance hall—fortunately it was all costume jewelry. "But I said you'd find out about her. Dog in name only—hah."

"I apologized, didn't I, girl? All intents and purposes, when it comes to guts and brains, she's bigger than Athelstane. A good girl. You can sleep on the bed if you want."

Sally uttered a little sigh. She reached out and licked his hand, and then curled herself down beside him and shut her eyes. After a few anxious days, Sally seemed to realize that she had won a new permanent place for herself: she was home again.

"My two good girls," said Clock fondly.

He was still talking about the hell of a watchdog on Sunday morning. "I didn't know about Pekes—what Fran heard from everybody who does—well, by God, they're dynamite. I can't get over it. Nine inches high and twelve pounds, and she nearly killed the guy. Quite a lot of dog she is. Enough guts for a—a mastiff. Never saw anything like that. Right at his throat, Fran said, when the squad car— The guy had to have a transfusion."

"I'll be damned," said Petrovsky. "They do say the little ones make better watchdogs."

"I believe it. You take that great big mutt of Jesse's, hell, he thinks everybody alive is his friend. Probably lead a burglar straight to the silver. But our Sally— And Hume was carrying that knife, God knows what he'd have done if Sally hadn't been there. Well, I told Fran, she's our dog from now on. That little scrap can sleep on the bed and have filet mignon every day, she wants it. She's quite a dog, in capitals."

They had some time on Sunday to talk—about Sally and other

things; it was a slow quiet day. There were no new calls. The boys out on the leg work, still hunting men on the list of possibles, didn't find any of them to bring in and question.

About three o'clock they had a queer one: the squad car called in, holding a man on the Harbor Freeway, a possible felonious accident, and a corpse. Clock and Petrovsky went out to look at it, and got there as the ambulance pulled up.

The corpse was that of a young woman, early twenties, dark hair, dirty jeans and a sleeveless black pullover, thong sandals, no sign of a handbag or coat. The corpse looked rather battered, but if she'd been hit at high speed—

"I couldn't stop," said the civilian. He was shocked and frightened, a well-dressed young fellow. "I saw her there, just lying in the road—the far right lane—but I couldn't stop. I tried to swerve, but—my God, I went right over— But I did stop, and I didn't know how to call the police, but then the squad car—"

Looking closer at the corpse, they could see what the attendant was telling them; they'd both seen a lot of bodies. This one hadn't bled for a while: not when the car struck her. "My guess," said the ambulance attendant, and looked up to where the overpass loomed, the Santa Monica freeway up there, "she jumped or fell. Dead about forty minutes, an hour."

By what the civilian told them, the body had been just in the road, to the extreme right, and on a Sunday there wouldn't be as much traffic along here as usual, a lot of it in the fast lanes: it wasn't surprising she hadn't been spotted before. They took a statement from the civilian and sent the body to the morgue. No I.D. on her; they passed a description on to Missing Persons.

In contrast to the day before, Sunday was rather boring; and Clock, thinking that, smiled ruefully. Never satisfied; they complained about the routine, the new ones coming along to work one on top of another: and also about the days when there wasn't much to do.

On Sunday evening the Clocks went to see the Falkensteins,

leaving Sally home in deference to Athelstane's nervous system. Clock regarded Athelstane with some scorn and said, "The big lummox. I'd like to see him tackle a burglar. Probably hide behind the davenport if one came."

"He would not!" said Nell. "You know how he tried to protect me that time that woman with a gun—"

"Hah," said Clock. "Came when you called him was all. Didn't know what he was getting into."

"Of course, he'd only have to lean on a burglar," said Jesse.

"That's what I say. Sally's just a scrap of a thing, but she's got twice as much guts—didn't let that stop her. She's quite a—"

"I've got some competition," said Fran amusedly, "as you see."

Athelstane visited everybody in turn and had his stomach massaged. He was feeling quite himself again, now he was the only dog around.

And Jesse, handing Clock a drink, asked, "No more leads on Margaret?"

"I'm bound to say I think it's dead, Jesse. I don't think we'll ever know. Unless our old maestro comes up with a brainstorm." Clock rattled ice cubes. "It was also the anonymous one. If you press me, I'm inclined to think that TV deal was the motive, it was one of those chancy characters. But we'll never get any evidence."

"I wonder. Edgar said—about that—after the fact. If it was, it was the childish, spiteful revenge."

"And if you ask me," said Clock, "any one of those people could be one like that. And forget it the next day, go on to something new. What I saw of 'em."

Jesse sighed; his lank length was stretched out in the armchair, long legs in front of him. "Like to get whoever did it," he said. "My funny Miss Williams, turning out to be—quite a gutsy, boldhearted female. Even as her dog."

"Our dog," said Clock. "That's right. So would I, boy. But tell me where to look. The evidence we had leads nowhere. I asked the lab about her hat yesterday—they got nothing from it except another trace of moth crystals. Well, I ask you. It suggests no place to look."

"No," agreed Jesse absently. "The old man seemed to have some definite idea. You heard from him? . . . Neither have I. I wonder—"

On Monday morning business picked up again for Homicide. A new body was reported in an alley off Fourth. Petrovsky came back from looking at it and said this one would probably end up in Pending too, it looked like a drunk slipped a Mickey and rolled. "Little overdose of the chloral or his heart was shaky." He started to type a report on it.

At least it wasn't raining again. There were men out hunting for the possibles from that list.

At eleven o'clock Sergeant Pitman buzzed Clock. "I've got a Mrs. Burt on the line. The desk transferred the call—I think you'll want to talk to her. She says somebody called her about burial lots at Forest Lawn."

"Hell," said Clock. Imaginative woman, seeing that article in the papers? He picked up the phone as the light flashed at him. "Mrs. Burt? Sergeant Clock, Homicide. Would you mind repeating what you told the desk sergeant, please?"

Her voice was mild and rather slow. She didn't sound upset, just concerned. "I saw what it said in the *Herald* on Saturday, about this man they called the Masked Monster. That he's called the women before—the ones he's going to kidnap like that—and pretended to be selling lots in Forest Lawn. The paper said the only ones really representing Forest Lawn would be women. Well, when this man phoned and said— I thought about it, but better safe than sorry, and the *Herald* said— I didn't want to bother the police for nothing."

"Yes, ma'am. When did he call?"

"About forty minutes ago. It wasn't until I hung up that I remembered what the paper said. I wasn't interested, I told him so and hung up—and then I thought about that. It was definitely a man's voice, yes. No, sir, he didn't give me any name, just said he represented Forest Lawn."

If you wanted to get psychological, thought Clock, and probably the head doctors would seize on that, all very darkly symbolical. Considering Lucille Kane.

And they had to go through the motions. She didn't sound like a nervous woman. He asked for her address and shrugged at it: Oxford Avenue below Los Feliz. Within the area, admittedly a very large one, in which X had been operating. "Would it be all right if we came out and talked to you now, Mrs. Burt?"

"Oh, certainly. If I can help you any way—"

Clock called Petrovsky away from another report. "I don't think it's anything, Pete. I always had reservations about giving that to the press. As Johnny said, he can read, can't he? Psycho he may be but he's played it all very cunning up to now. I'm inclined to think this is somebody playing a silly practical joke, having also read the story in the paper."

"And there we part company," said Petrovsky. "I think it could be him, Andrew. It damn well could. He *is* a psycho. The phone calls could be a compulsion of some kind. Anyway, we can't just ignore it, can we?"

"Obviously not." Clock was annoyed, because he didn't think this was a lead to their boy, but they had to treat it as if it was.

They went to see Mrs. Ruth Burt. She was a widow, about fifty-five, living in a small apartment house, six units, just off Los Feliz. She looked like an eminently sensible woman, and she was a registered nurse, taking the special private jobs, usually the morning shift, she said, but she wasn't on a case right now.

"Well, Mrs. Burt, we don't know that your caller was the man we're after," said Clock, "who's attacked all these women—"

"And killed one of them. That was dreadful."

"Yes. But we have to act as if it was, because you'd better have some protection. I'm sure you'll cooperate with us—"

"I'll be glad to, Sergeant. If there's any chance of catching him— What do you want me to do?"

"Not a thing. Just behave as you normally would. But we'd like to have one officer inside the apartment here—concealed, of course—and we'll have others outside. Just in case this is our boy. Don't worry—if it is, we'll have him before he could harm you."

"I see." She flushed pinkly, and her eyes were bright. "It sounds quite exciting, Sergeant. My, I hope it is him and we can get him!"

"And you know," said Clock to Petrovsky on the way back downtown, "that nothing will happen."

"I don't know that at all," said Petrovsky. "And I'll remind you of one thing. Of the ten women who definitely remembered the phone call from the Forest Lawn salesman, seven said he'd phoned that day—of the night he assaulted them. The other three say he called the day before. So if our boy doesn't show tonight to try for Mrs. Burt, he just may show up tomorrow night and we'd better stake it out then too."

"Well, I suppose it's a possibility. We'll have to do that, all right. Protecting the citizens. But I'm not holding my breath, Pete."

"Like to make a bet? Maybe I'll win this one."

"I won't take a chance," said Clock prudently. "I may not think much of this, but you just never know what a psycho might do."

Fran was back at Jesse's office, vainly cursing wills to be copied in triplicate. How Miss Williams had ever managed, on this desk—the long legal size sheets flapping all over, the outsize carbon— When she took a break at ten-thirty and went down the hall to the rest room, she caught sight of herself in the glass and scrabbled for Kleenex. Her hair was on end, she had a long streak of carbon ink down one cheek, and the bandage on the other didn't contribute to the general effect, she thought crossly. If those agencies didn't come up with an efficient girl soon—

Jesse was in court; he had an appointment for one-thirty. Fran phoned the drugstore and had them send up coffee. She took a breather from the will, luxuriously, over the coffee and a couple of cigarettes. It was just past eleven and she was thinking she ought to get back to work again—between the outsize carbon and the technical language she wasn't making much speed —when the phone rang.

"Mr. Falkenstein's office."

"Oh—has Mr. Falkenstein found a new secretary?" A pleasant contralto voice.

"No, he certainly hasn't. I'm just filling in, and he's very anxious to—" One of the agencies?

"This is Helena Cummings, I'm Mr. Kirkbride's secretary, perhaps Mr. Falkenstein mentioned—"

"Oh, yes, he did. I'm his sister, Miss Cummings. He's really frantic to get somebody, I'm not trained, I can type and answer the phone, but I'm going mad over these wills, and if you know someone—someone reasonably efficient—"

"Well, I do. That is—well, they—she's just come down to L.A. from Fresno. She's had experience, yes, working as her uncle's secretary. He was a very well-known attorney there, he just died a couple of months ago, and they—she wants to work in the city. I can certainly recommend her efficiency, she takes dictation at speed, she's a good typist, and very reliable."

"Praise heaven!" said Fran. "How soon can she come?"

"Well—" Miss Cummings hesitated and said, "If you'd like to try her out, I could phone her to go right over. Let me have the address again—er—Miss—"

"Mrs. Clock. Just," said Fran, "five weeks Mrs. Clock, we were just back from the honeymoon when—and Jesse roping me in to do all these wills— What's her name?"

"Oh, dear!" Miss Cummings laughed. "Well, I do hope Mr. Falkenstein will like her. Her name's Jean Gordon."

"Fine. If you would tell her to come—we can arrange about the salary and— Thank you *very* much, we do appreciate—"

"Oh, I'm only glad to have helped Jean out. I'm sure Mr. Falkenstein will find her satisfactory."

Fran thanked her again and lit another cigarette. Jean Gordon could finish copying the will. And she could start house hunting again.

Twenty minutes later the outer door opened and a girl came in. "Helena told me to come right over. I'm Jean Gordon." She looked at Fran anxiously, and Fran surveyed her approvingly. About twenty-seven, nice figure, dressed well but not flamboyantly, skirt a decent length, not too much makeup. A natural blonde, hair in a short feathery cut, and she had big brown eyes —an unusual combination.

"I hope I'll do," she said. "Really, w—I'm quite experienced at legal work, but the places w—I've tried, they all seemed to think it didn't count because it wasn't here. Fresno isn't a village, you know, and w—I may have worked for my uncle but he was a regular martinet, you had to be on your toes."

"Well, Miss Cummings gave you a high mark," said Fran, friendly.

"Oh, dear," said Jean Gordon unhappily. "She's my first cousin. I'd better say. But she wouldn't have recommended me if she didn't know I am efficient. I—"

"Well, you look fine to me," said Fran. "Now, about the salary —" She told Jean about that, the hours.

"That's just fine. The only thing is—" Jean hesitated. "We were rather hoping—that is, I know Mr. Falkenstein said a secretary, singular, but— Oh, well, we'd just better *ask*." She turned back to the door and opened it. "Jimmy?"

Fran blinked. Suddenly there were two of them—two pretty middle-sized natural blondes with big brown eyes. Double exposure. "Twins," said the new one. "I'm Jamesina, Jimmy for short. We're both trained legal secretaries, we both worked for

Uncle, and really we're both quite efficient, and we'd hoped to get in the same office—sharing an apartment and—"

Fran began to laugh. "But you're the answer to a prayer! Jesse's been saying two— You both look just fine, and thank heaven"—she got up—"one of you can finish this damned will."

"Hallelujah!" said Jimmy. "We're *in*!"

Jesse walked in muttering to himself about Justice Botts, and stopped short, blinking at the double exposure. "Meet your two new secretaries," said Fran. "Jimmy and Jean Gordon. I'm going home, thank goodness. Home to Sally."

They set up the stakeout at Mrs. Burt's apartment at six-thirty on Monday night, with Lindsay inside, Clock and Petrovsky under what cover there was outside, behind a lopsided but thick oleander hedge at one side of the apartment building. At least, in February, it was dark by five, and it was doubtful whether their quarry would hang around in his ski mask for several hours. If the caller had been X, and Mrs. Burt marked as a new victim, he wouldn't have spotted the watchers.

They waited until midnight, and nothing happened. Only a few cars passed down this short side street; all was quiet. At midnight they called it off, Clock swearing and Petrovsky complaining about a stiff neck. It had been a long cold wait. Lindsay at least had been warm, inside.

"And we'll have to do it again tomorrow night," said Petrovsky, yawning. "Be on the safe side."

"I know, I know," said Clock. They explained that to Mrs. Burt. "Occasionally he's made it the next night, you see, and just to cover all bets—"

"Surely. I do hope you catch him, Sergeant. I hope he does come."

"I'm bound to say, that phone call could have been just a hoax. Somebody seeing that article in the paper—"

She looked at him, head on one side. "You said that before.

209

I can't imagine what sort of person—but of course you get all sorts of people, don't you? I just hope you're wrong, Sergeant. I hope it's him, and he comes tomorrow night."

So did they. Clock went home and told Fran he was half paralyzed. "It's cold as hell and we had to stay put behind that damn hedge. And with this damn hand—" The four fingers of his left hand, where he'd caught the heavy library door, had swelled and turned light purple, and his hand was stiff. "Well, we've both been in the wars this week—how's your scar?"

"Thank heaven it won't be." Sally had come trotting in and Clock picked her up and stroked her. "A nice hot bath and some warm milk, you'll be as good as new."

"The bath, yes. The milk, no—make it a double Scotch. And I'm really taking no bets—"

Henry Nadinger was up for arraignment on Tuesday morning. Clock would waste the necessary time in court.

Overnight, Homicide had a new one to do the routine on: a heist job at a liquor store on Wilshire, the owner shot dead, at provisionally about eleven o'clock last night. His wife, alarmed when he hadn't come home after the normal midnight closing hour, had called Central and a car had been sent around. Alfred Calhoun, dead across the sill of the front door, had a gun still in his right hand, but unfired.

So on Tuesday, they had a new list to work on from the computer, which had been fed the M.O.: experienced heist man, record of violence, use of firearms. That turned up quite a long list of men from Records.

At times the Homicide office was a little pressed for time. The Williams case had died a natural death on them: it was very unlikely that anything like evidence would ever turn up on that now. Temporarily they abandoned the list of possibles for the Masked Monster to start hunting for the possibles on Calhoun.

The drunk probably rolled for his cash got identified on Tuesday: on welfare, with a record of petty theft, D. and D., shoplifting. He was no loss, but the city would have to pay for his funeral.

And at three o'clock they had a new flyer from the Feds—wanted man thought to be heading for California, fugitive from a murder-first charge in Pittsburgh. There was an official mug shot, prints, description.

"As if we hadn't enough—" Clock left that unfinished, expressively.

Jesse thought he could rephrase a couple of proverbs. Peace of mind was having two reliable secretaries. Just part of yesterday and today, he had found his double-exposure Gordons to be quietly efficient and nice girls into the bargain. The twins got along together just fine, no bickering, dividing the jobs between them amicably, and they seemed to like him all right too.

And bless John Kirkbride's secretary.

But he sat there over the notes for the damage suit, with the typewriter clicking steadily away in the outer office, and he thought of Clock saying the case was dead—they'd never get more evidence on it. The case Margaret Williams, who had been something more than he'd ever thought, a woman to admire. Why had she died, for what?

Damn it, thought Jesse, it said *Vengeance belongs to the Lord.* But he would damned well like to see Miss Williams' killer brought to justice in this world. That he would like to see happen. He wondered if the old man really had seen something more on that—

And of course, as old Jeshu put it, *Many have sinned for a small matter. . . .*

They set up the stakeout on Mrs. Burt's apartment at six-thirty on Tuesday night—Clock inside tonight, Petrovsky and Jacobs out behind the oleander hedge. It was a boring job, sitting on a stakeout. At least tonight Clock wasn't freezing to death, and Mrs. Burt made good strong coffee. But by seven o'clock he was lurking well out of sight of any curtain chinks, in the darkened bedroom off a short hall.

Mrs. Burt was in the living room, placidly knitting. Her son's wife was expecting a baby, she had told Clock; they lived in San Diego.

He was feeling sleepy and bored, in the dark there, when he glanced at the luminous dial of his watch for the tenth time. Only eight-fifty. He yawned.

And the doorbell chimed gently.

Clock was on his feet at once. By God, was this it? He went out quietly to the hall. The bell chimed again. Mrs. Burt had got up; she looked excited and queerly pleased. Clock nodded at her, gestured at the door, and moved into the living room, his gun out. He just hoped there wouldn't be any gunplay here, and unexpectedly thought of Rose Barry saying scornfully, "I knew he wouldn't shoot, a coward and bully—"

No screen door, of course, an apartment; and the apartment was on the ground floor. Only two other units on this floor, and she'd said one was occupied by a night-shift worker, a young bachelor, the other by a quiet elderly couple.

She opened the door. And—to Clock's split-second astonishment, even when he had known it was possible if only just— there he was. A middle-height black figure, ski mask over entire head, dark clothes, and the gun. The voice muffled by the mask. "All right, lady, give me all your money—quick!"

"Hold it right there!" barked Clock, surging forward. "Freeze!" He had about ten feet to cover, and he wasn't quite fast enough. The dark figure whirled and ran. Clock plunged after him out to the hall. Ten feet to the front door of the building—the Masked Monster was wrenching it open as Clock came up, and wriggling out.

"Pete—Lou!" yelled Clock.

They had, of course, seen him go in, and they were waiting. In case Clock missed him inside. They were on either side of the entrance, and converged on him as he came rushing out; and neatly as a pro football sprinter, the dark figure squirmed past and was gone, running down the front walk. They ran after him, Petrovsky swearing, and Clock fired a warning shot in the air.

He had no more than a twenty-foot lead, but he was a smaller, lighter man than any of the detectives, and ran faster. He fled straight toward a dark car at the curb, dived into it, and the motor caught— And died.

(One of the women had said the engine needed a tune-up, running rough and noisy.)

Clock yanked the door open, reached in, and hauled him out. He felt thin and bony.

"So let's have a look at what we've caught," said Clock with savage satisfaction; and as Petrovsky switched on his flashlight, he reached to pull the all-concealing ski mask off.

In the narrow beam of light, they looked at him. He was at least five inches under Clock's six feet two, and he looked up at the bigger men, motionless in crisis as a cornered rabbit. He had a thin face with a narrow tight mouth and a pointed chin, sandy blond hair drooping over his forehead, china-blue eyes, a prominent Adam's apple.

He just swallowed and shook his head to Clock's request for his name.

And Mrs. Burt came tripping down the front walk. "Have you got him? Oh, thank goodness! I'm just so excited, helping you get him— I'm going to call Bill in San Diego to tell— Goodness, I'm so glad you've *got* him!"

They had him: for a little while they didn't know who. He hadn't anything on him at all but the keys to the car, which was a Chevy Nova II, dark green, with a broken speedometer and the adhesive tape in indicated places. But the Chevy was registered to a Mrs. Norma Trent at an address on Fountain Avenue in Hollywood, and when Clock phoned, Mrs. Trent said in alarm that her son had her car—had there been an accident, why

213

were *police*—her son Rodney, he'd never had an accident, was a good driver—

"You're Rodney Trent?" said Clock. They had taken him into an interrogation room, and punctiliously read him the piece about his rights; asked if he understood that, he nodded once. Now he just nodded again. He looked very harmless sitting there, a weedy fellow about thirty.

"So all right, would you like to tell us about it, Rodney?" asked Petrovsky mildly.

He blinked at them. "I didn't really need the money," he said in a thin voice. "I've got a job. I used to work for Forest Lawn once, selling the burial lots and helping arrange funerals, but it was depressing. Awful depressing." They waited and he went on. "I got a job in a men's store now, selling. But my mother isn't going to like this, you know. She won't like it at all."

"You're the one got yourself in trouble, Rodney," said Clock. "Beating up the women. Didn't you?"

"I'm not sure why I did, but I guess that's so. Yes, I did. I don't have any friends, you know. I don't have a very interesting life. I never have had. You know, Mother's going to feel awful bad about this. I never thought you'd catch me."

"Would you like to tell us why you beat the women, Rodney?" One like this, legally speaking, was very chancy; they didn't want to lead him, give a defense lawyer any grounds for later on claiming duress; and there'd be a psychiatric evaluation, for what it was worth.

He shook his head. "I don't know, it was just a thing to do," he said vaguely. "I think—it all started with the ski mask. I can't ski, you know, I'm no good at sports—or anything much. But these ski masks came into the store where I work, and they looked funny—I'd never seen any before. I tried one on, just to see—and you know, it wasn't *me* any more! In the mask. It was just—nobody—in that mask. Anybody. I wasn't a—a nobody, like Rodney Trent was, at all. Nobody'd know *who* I was. Or what. And I stole that ski mask from the stock. Mr. Acker never knew, but I did. That was how it started."

"Andrew," said Petrovsky. They moved away from him. "A real psycho. We better not give 'em loopholes for later on."

And Clock was just as conscious of that danger. "You are so right," he said. Book him; they had nice solid evidence, the ski mask, the car, the M.O.

But he'd started talking now. "Sometimes I used my car," he said. "I've got a Study Silver Hawk—they don't make those any more—and then sometimes I used Mother's. I wasn't going to do it again, you know. I wasn't. Because you—somebody—somebody told lies about me. I didn't *kill* any of them. Those women. It was wrong to do—I knew it was a wrong thing, but it was like I couldn't help it, because with that mask on I wasn't *me* at all—but I knew it was me underneath the mask, and it was wrong—"

Which was interesting and useful, some judges still going by the McNaghten rules, knowledge of right from wrong: and good witnesses.

"But I was going to stop. When you told lies about me in the paper. I didn't kill anybody. Ever. I wouldn't do a thing like that."

They booked him into the Alameda facility. They felt pleased with themselves, dropping on their Masked Monster, the media harping on incompetent cops lately. There'd probably be a legal hassle over the homicide, the M.O. the only solid evidence. Right now, somebody would have to go and see Mrs. Norma Trent. Break the news to her.

Jacobs and Petrovsky tossed a quarter for that unenviable job. Petrovsky lost the throw and cussed.

Clock went home to his two girls.

14

THEY WOULD be busy awhile clearing up all the details on Rodney Trent, and the media would make headlines with that. When they came to look at Trent's background, he'd never even had a parking ticket—it had been a waste of time hunting him in Records; but of course he was the exception that proved the rule. Most of his kind had given the warning rattle before they got into big trouble.

Mrs. Norma Trent was merely bewildered and, later, grieved. She'd never had any worry about Rodney, she told them, a good boy, and it hadn't been easy for her, his father dying when he was only ten. He was a loner, she admitted, didn't go out with girls, hadn't any pals; he liked to read, mostly sat in his room reading when he wasn't at work. But people all couldn't be alike.

The gun was a Hi-Standard .22 revolver she'd got "for protection" all of fifteen years ago. It had never been fired.

She had her own business, a little dress shop on Fairfax.

Rodney went on saying he hadn't killed anybody. He wouldn't do that. Which was just what he would say. And Mrs. Trent, who said so too, backed him up that he'd been home—which was an apartment on Fountain Avenue—that Thursday night Lucille Kane had been killed. Clock read her as an honest woman, and it could be that she didn't clearly remember, was just taking Rodney's word, or was honestly mistaken. She said she thought he'd been out the next night; she could just be confused.

And there would be all the labor of getting the statements down on paper, the triplicate copies, the paper work for the D.A.—a lot of work, and with what result in the end?

Clock had called Jesse when he got home that Tuesday night, at eleven o'clock. Jesse offered congratulations. "Premature," said Clock. "It's all too likely the D.A.'ll decide not to charge him with the homicide. Of course he's denying that, what else? It's the same exact M.O. except that Lucille Kane's dead, but barring that, no tangible evidence. And in any case the head doctors'll say he's sick sick sick, and he'll probably get stashed away at Atascadero. At least they don't get let out of there so easy. . . . I hear you've got some office help at last."

"Thank God, yes. You're not going back to work on Margaret?"

"Jesse, it's dead. There's no lead at all. I told you what I thought about it."

"So you did. Been ruminating on Edgar's cryptic hints, and I see a glimmer of what direction he's going, but that's all. Damn it, Andrew, in this materialistic culture the money had to be the trigger, didn't it? The TV thing? Only—"

"And if it was one of those characters we'll never prove it."

"And if so, that still doesn't tell us where she'd been that day. As I've been saying all along, that's really the wildest thing about it, her simply vanishing away on a workday."

"Well, I haven't even a glimmer," said Clock. "And tomorrow being a workday too, I'll say good night. My God, it'll take us a week to get all the paper work done on Rodney—a bunch of glorified clerks, all we are."

They got Rodney to make a statement, and he signed it willingly. They would get the formal statements from everybody who knew about any part of the case, maybe thirty all told. They would show the Nova to the women who'd had a ride in it, hope for positive identification. Clock would be having some tedious discussions with the D.A.'s office, and as he'd said to Jesse, and didn't have to say to Petrovsky or any of the others, the outcome he could foresee: Rodney wouldn't be charged with the homicide, just quietly tucked away after a formal hearing.

And of course all Homicide's regular daily business didn't obligingly come to a halt until they'd finished with Rodney. On Wednesday morning Dr. Van Vogt sent up the autopsy report on that corpse from the freeway; Clock skimmed over it between interviewing witnesses. It said succinctly that whoever the girl had been, she'd been so full of heroin that, as the doctor put it, "she would not have known as you say which was up and up," and by the state of the body she had probably fallen or jumped from the overpass above, been killed instantly.

They still had, of course, the liquor store owner shot on that heist job, and the list of possibles to find and bring in. Quite unexpectedly, on Wednesday afternoon, Dale dropped on that X, just out hunting the next name off the list. He found Gus Prado in his shabby single room playing solitaire, and spotted the gun in his hip pocket. Prado was on parole, so Dale brought him in pronto, and legally they could and did confiscate the gun, which was an ancient Combat Masterpiece. Automatically it was sent to Ballistics for test firing, and Dale and Keene were still questioning Prado on the Calhoun shooting and getting the usual sullen answers when Ballistics called and told them it was the Combat Masterpiece had killed Calhoun: the surgeon had sent up the slugs from the body and they matched the test slugs.

"Well, they do say," said Clock when he heard that, "never two without three." And he hardly had the words out of his mouth when Lieutenant Fordyce of Missing Persons came in with a distraught weeping woman.

"Mrs. Alice Fisher. She's just identified one of your bodies as her daughter Wanda. The one that fell off the overpass or whatever."

"Oh, great," said Clock. Now they'd have to talk to her, get all the details about Wanda down on paper, and it would add to nothing: if some pal, also high on something, had pushed Wanda off the overpass while she was full of H, they'd never find out or be able to do anything about it. "I tell you," said Clock. "All those busy-busy lawmakers back in Washington. If they really wanted to be constructive, they might pass a law adding about twelve hours to the day."

"Now that's an idea," said Fordyce. "They've done a lot crazier things than that."

Clock, eyeing the weeping Mrs. Fisher, asked for a policewoman to sit in on the questioning.

And there was really no point in working themselves to death at the overtime; all this had to get done, would get done eventually, but it didn't have to get done all at once. Just before Clock left the office on Wednesday, Sergeant Pitman got a tip from one of their pigeons: that boy from Pittsburgh the Feds wanted was here. Clock said, "Tell the night watch."

When he got home (to his two girls) and finished kissing Fran, she said, "I'm sorry to talk shop, darling—you look tired to death—but Edgar called. He'll be here at seven-thirty. And Jesse. Edgar says he wants to meet Sally, and he's got a story to tell you."

"Oh?" said Clock. "By God, I wonder if the old boy's ruminated straight to the point and rung the bell again. I wonder—"

"Sure you'll be O.K.?" said Jesse.

"You run along and hear what Edgar's deduced—I'll be interested," said Nell. "Only my back is killing me and I'll be very happy to have this project over. In fact, I'm counting the days. I don't care which it is, or twins or triplets. You run along, darling, I'll just relax and listen to soothing music for a while. And you needn't look so contemptuous at the Viennese waltzes. I like waltzes."

"Froth," said Jesse, and kissed her and went to get his coat. It had started to rain again, late this afternoon.

"So this is Sally," said Mr. Walters, and sat down beside her on the couch. "A cute one, aren't you? And kind of like your late mistress, somethin' more than you look on the outside."

"You can say that again," said Clock. The old man smiled, but his eyes were serious. He'd brought along a lot of magazines, fifteen or sixteen of them, and stacked them neatly on the floor at his feet.

"Don't tell me," said Jesse, "that you've come up with the X on Margaret, Edgar. You said you had a story to tell us."

"That I do." Mr. Walters sat back and stroked Sally's head, and Clock said he'd want a drink, departed kitchenward to bring back three highballs and a crème de menthe for Fran. "Thankee, Andrew. Now"—he took a swallow of the highball and set it on the coffee table—"let's take all this neat 'n' orderly, hey? Because there were a lot of outside things come along to kind of make the wood invisible for the trees, if I got that quote right. So, that Monday Miss Williams phoned you, Jesse, and said she had an extremely urgent matter to tend to. Shouldn't take more than an hour. Only she never showed up all day, and that night she got herself murdered, sometime after midnight, and it was set up to look like the random mugging."

"All right, we remember," said Jesse. "And there showed up the very funny clue, part of the magazine cover in her mouth, and the—my God, I'd nearly forgotten the codeine—"

"Yep. And as you looked, Andrew, you found she'd been an unusual sort of female—like I said then, the one-tenth showin' above the surface. The detective stories and the MWI thing and the reward from *True Detective*. And then things started showin' up fast and furious, and you both went round chasin' your own tails on Margaret."

"How d'you mean?" asked Clock.

"Well, all the extraneous bits," said the old man, swallowing bourbon and water thirstily. "There was that Felton, f'r instance. It could've been Felton, drunk, you said. Mad about the car accident—"

"I'm taking it, by the way," said Jesse absently. "The damage was all to the body, engine's good as new—it's a two-year-old Dodge. The payments—"

"That's extraneous too," said Mr. Walters. "So, Felton. You thought about that Brenda girl's recent boyfriend till you found out he wasn't all that concerned. And then, hey presto, that TV business appeared, and that looked like a very hot bet for the motive, didn't it? All that money? Margaret interferin', alertin' the sponsor, getting that series of TV programs canceled? Couple of big names involved, and the hell of a lot of money. It looked—can we sort of put it that way—like the biggest thing she'd done to make enemies?"

"That's so," agreed Clock. "I still think—"

"Only, as I said at the time, the damage had been done. It'd do nobody any good to kill her, when the rug was already yanked out from under 'em. And you know, Andrew, show business people—most of 'em—they don't go very deep. They're—on-the-surface people, they tend to concentrate on the present moment, see what I mean. I got no doubt that they were all mad as hell about that cancellation, but I don't get the impression that any of 'em realized just so definite that it was her started the ball rolling."

"That writer Toomey—he wrote her a nasty letter—"

"Sure, he knew she'd meddled. Maybe didn't realize just so clear she'd been the prime motivatin' force in getting the sponsor taking action. As we said then, I don't think she realized it.

It hadn't been made public, that that series was canceled, before she died."

"Well?" said Jesse impatiently.

"Then, that Gallagher. With a little reason for not liking Margaret. Silly little reason, but there it was. And even—just on the edge of the thing—that writer she insulted, that Henry told you about. Piddling little things, but sometimes murders get committed over nothin' at all, don't they, Andrew?"

"They do, God knows."

"So. There were some funny little clues, but they didn't seem to tell us much. The magazine cover in her mouth. The codeine. The sequins and the moth crystals. Little bits and pieces, hey? And I couldn't see my way through it to any solid conclusion, boys, until—" Mr. Walters brought out his private bottle, offered it politely around, splashed bourbon into his glass and looked at it contemplatively—"until I said to myself, Now slow down here, 'n' stop thinkin' about nine things at once. It's easy to make guesses and build up theories. What, I said to myself, do we know—cold and hard—facts, that happened? The basic simple facts?"

"She'd found out something," said Jesse tentatively, "that made the urgent—"

"Now don't jump too fast, Jesse. What did we know? She'd been to a party the night before—call it a party. A lot of people there. We got from Martha Weglund that she was probably introduced to at least one stranger—could've been three dozen, was probably more 'n one. She came home, and her mother told us she sat up late rustlin' papers. And next morning she didn't say anything about not going to work, but then she called you with the excuse. We don't know where she was all day, but sometime that day she got the codeine. And at about midnight or just after, she got murdered—skull fractured with the blunt instrument."

"All according to Hoyle, maestro. You going somewhere?"

Mr. Walters swallowed bourbon and picked up the top maga-

222

zine from his pile. It was a copy of *True Detective*. "These magazines," he said, "very much on the side of law 'n' order. Most of 'em run the mug shots of wanted men now and then—this one does it regular. And vary the stories for readers, every once in a while they'll run a rehash of some old crime, a crime that never got solved, one of the historic criminals. It's not unusual, find some current case written up in these where the cops never got anybody. And you know, boys," said Mr. Walters with suspicious meekness, "Margaret sittin' up rustlin' papers—she wouldn't have made that kind of noise readin' a book, and I don't think she was readin' over one of her ambitious manuscripts. And these were the only magazines in her room."

"By *damn!*" said Clock, startled. "But we should have seen that—"

"I said you were bothered by all the outside things that didn't matter. All right. She—"

"You aren't going to say," said Jesse, "that she spotted a fellow off the Ten Most Wanted list at the Professional Women's party? Because I doubt—"

"Don't interrupt, Jesse," said Fran. "I'm dying to hear who she did spot."

Their old maestro cocked his head at her. "Well, now, I can't tell you that for sure 'n' certain, Fran. I can have a guess, but we don't really know—reason I brought along all these magazines, there's a possible X in all of 'em. But when I got that far, somethin' else came to me. She didn't tell her mother about it, probably for two reasons. She didn't want to upset her, and there wasn't time. She was reliable—she wouldn't want to be away from the office longer than she could help. But she 'had to tell her'—that what she said? Sure. Who? Now, let's backtrack some. Let's say she was introduced to—or just noticed—somebody, that Sunday night, who looked familiar to her, and she connected it up with one of these magazines. Somebody whose picture she'd seen—and not just an innocent bystander but, we can deduce, somebody wanted. A fugitive? And she didn't, can't we also say, remember just which magazine she'd seen it in, so it could've been one months old—from last year, the copies still waitin' to get bound up. Hey? She came home, and she spent a while hunting for it, and we can deduce she found it. Whatever it was." He opened *True Detective*. "Mug shots, men off the Most Wanted list. Doubtful, those. So I started goin' through all these magazines, hunting, and I collected— count 'em—nineteen cases, from articles in forty-six magazines, which could've been what she was lookin' for. Cases where— just listen to this—*(a)* the cops had a pretty good idea who X was but no evidence—or *(b)* they had somebody charged on evidence but he got away and is still loose—and *(c)* where a known criminal was under lock 'n' key for somethin' and got over the wall and's never been caught. Just seemed to me that kind a lot more probable—as bein' at that party—than the louts off the Ten Most Wanted."

"That many?" said Fran, surprised.

"Out of forty-six magazines. All last year's *Master Detectives*, *True Detectives*, *Official Detectives*, and up to this March's issues. And that was just the ones like that where there was a photograph. Now I'm not goin' to bore you with recitin' all these stories," said the old man, adding bourbon to his glass. "Because I don't think it's necessary. I don't *know* that I've picked the right one, it could be it was one of the others in this pile—" He sorted out one magazine and held it. "But I kind of think this might ring the bell. This bein' an imperfect world and men the sinners they are, I didn't come across this until just this afternoon. *Official Detective* for last April. And there's a very interestin' article in it about this fellow they never brought to trial. They were goin' to charge him with murdering his wife, back in Tarrytown, New York, but he got away before they served the warrant—smelled trouble, just slid out from under. But the sheriff there seems to've been a pretty shrewd old boy, Reardon his name was—this is six, seven years ago—and he went to work 'n' traced this Allen—that was what he called himself, David Allen—back. He had a little lead to Carbondale, Pennsylvania, from an old bankbook he found in the Allen house, and he placed Allen in Carbondale by his description. Callin' himself Greene then, and he had his wife killed by a burglar breakin' in while he was away from home. Nobody there suspected a thing—just a terrible tragedy. He came in for what she had to leave, which might not sound like much but added up—paid-for house, a little land, came to around forty thousand. Nobody thought anything about it when he left town. They'd only been married about a year, she'd been the village old maid. And, boys, in Tarrytown he'd done it over again. Married a respectable grass widow with a substantial, snug little income, nothin' big, and settled down all quiet. And that wife got killed about the same way—while he was out of town on business. They'd had a burglar around—only as it happened Sheriff Reardon caught him and he had an alibi for that night. The Feds took it up then and they traced him right back as far as they could. They've got his prints. His right name's Eugene Horvath, and the only thing he ever got picked up for was petty theft, thirty years back in Reading, Pennsylvania—that's when they got his prints. There's been a federal warrant out on him for five years, and not a smell. And"—Mr. Walters drank and at last opened the magazine—"the only known photograph of him is this kind of fuzzy snapshot the Tarrytown wife took of him when he wasn't noticing. One of her girl friends just remembered she had it, when this reporter came round gatherin' background for this story, so the Feds haven't had it before and it's published here for the first time anywhere. And"—he sighed —"there it was waitin' for us, I think. Because Margaret's marked it with a whole row of X's. I think this is the fellow."

"But—who connected with her could—" began Clock.

"*I* dunno who he is, here 'n' now," said Mr. Walters. "Do you, Andrew?" He held out the magazine.

Clock looked at the slightly blurred blown-up snapshot of a tall thin man with gray or blond hair, a long nose and jaw, and in naked absolute astonishment he said, "But that's—*but that's*—"

"I wondered if maybe you'd recognize him," said their old maestro interestedly.

"For heaven's sake, Andrew, *who is it?*" demanded Fran excitedly.

Clock looked up at them, still incredulous. "It's Stewart Kane," he said numbly. "Lucille Kane's husband."

Jesse slid down further in his chair. "So," he said gently, "your Masked Monster has been telling you the truth. He never killed anybody."

"Just like Margaret said," said the old man, swallowing bourbon. "Anybody can be anything in a city. You never know who."

"But my God—I see it, but—"

"You know all about this Kane woman. I don't. Didn't know who this Horvath might be, here 'n' now. But seeing as Margaret marked this photograph—probably that Sunday night—I could make a few guesses about how that went. Now we know where he's been here, build it up some more. Where did the Kanes live, Andrew?"

"West Drive, just above Hollywood B—"

"Sure," said the old man, nodding. "She met 'em at the party Sunday night. Maybe she knew Lucille, hadn't met the husband before. . . . Y' know, Andrew, there's no guessing how many he's accounted for. Seems to've made a career of it, the little they got on him. And there've been enough other cases like that too —the Smith fellow and so on. Marry a woman with a little property, nothing big but substantial, year or so later she had the sad accident. Him ostensibly off somewhere. And once before at least he made use of another criminal bein' around, put the blame on him. Fairly canny fellow—"

"Dear Edgar, *what* do you deduce about Miss Williams? What *happened?*" asked Fran.

"Well, easy enough to read it now we know who. She thought

226

it was extremely urgent to warn Mrs. Kane who her husband was—after she'd definitely identified him with this photograph. Margaret with the logical mind maybe didn't foresee it wasn't goin' to be so easy to make Mrs. Kane believe her. And I reckon that was our biggest stroke of luck," added Mr. Walters suddenly, thoughtfully. "If she hadn't been so logical—and I think pretty much flustered too—she'd have taken this magazine right with her that morning, to show Mrs. Kane and, later, the police—and we'd never have laid eyes on it, of course. But she didn't. . . . I think they were probably still arguing, Mrs. Kane sayin' she must be crazy, Stewart a nice kind husband, when he walked in. And—all speculation, but we could guess near enough—he saw right off that desperate situations demand— Margaret'd have gone straight to the police, if she could've got away—whether she'd convinced Mrs. Kane or not. I think he must've got the jump on her before she could scream, knocked her out or got her tied up, while his wife just stood there—"

"Trying to realize that what Margaret had said was true. I can see that." Fran nodded.

"Maybe. And then he dealt with her, y' know."

And Fran, leaping to what he meant before Jesse or Clock, said, "You don't mean— for *four days*, Edgar? Monday to Thursday night?"

"He couldn't have 'em killed too close together. Even the busy cops might smell a rat. He's a clever one, shrewd as they come. We don't know if he'd maybe planned to kill the wife right off. But he seized on this Masked Monster shrewd as be damned. Margaret—with her he had to do the best he could."

"My God—the codeine," said Jesse. "He fed her the codeine—"

"He didn't dare risk too much, it'd show at the autopsy. Just enough to keep her a little groggy, I'd guess." The old man poured bourbon, drank. "And tied up, and gagged. Can we guess where? Wife tied up, maybe on the bed in her room— Margaret maybe in the closet. Where her clothes collected the little sequins, off somethin' of Mrs. Kane's there—and the moth crystals. And, at a minute's notice off he sets to build an alibi. Where, Andrew?"

"The cabin up at Crystal Lake," said Clock, mesmerized. "My God, and he must have *gone* there—"

"Sure. So that's where. You look, I bet you'll find he stopped somewhere up there, some store—Big Bear Village, wherever —'n' established he was there. Opened his cabin, lit a fire. Only after dark he drove right back down again. He could make it in four hours, if he knows the road. To deal with Margaret."

"But, Edgar, that magazine cover—" said Fran. "He wouldn't—"

The old man held up his glass and looked at it. "You got to admire that woman's guts," he said. "It'd be about, I figure, eleven-thirty or so when he got back. She'd been doped with the codeine, and tied up, all that time—but I think she must've come to, maybe when he put her in her own car. Not strong enough to scream or struggle, even try to get out of the car— but conscious. And he wouldn't've wanted to waste much time there, you know, risk bein' seen or heard, as he set up his mugging. He'd want to get there, dump her, bludgeon her enough to kill, and get away. So I don't think she was tied up then. She was limp, he figured she was still unconscious."

"*She*—" Jesse sat up. "You mean—"

"Guts she had, and a logical mind, Jesse. She was lyin' in the back of her own car—car she'd been drivin'—and she was stiff and dopey and feelin' too weak to do much moving around— but she knew the danger she was in, and why. Hey? She tried," said the old man, "to leave us a clue. A big fat clue. Only she kind of overestimated the—um—mental resources of the L.A.P.D." He drank.

"For God's sake!" said Clock. "She deliberately—"

"Think that magazine'd fallen off the seat. She saw it close to her face there—and she used what strength she had to leave us the clue. She managed to bite off that piece of cover—lipstick on the piece still attached told me that—and half swallowed it. If she couldn't get away from him, if she was for the long jump, it—"

"—would show at the autopsy," said Clock. "My God. My God. She—"

"She had guts," said the old man simply. "That's the size of it."

Jesse drew a long breath. "Well, I can boast she thought highly of me. So her mother said. What a—"

"But do you mean to say he kept his wife tied up for four days afterward?" said Fran. "It's impossible—"

"Needs must when the devil drives," said Clock. "I see that, sure. I think he was right there, from Monday night on. . . . Those resorts up in the Angeles Forest'll be crowded, the winter sports fans, and Crystal Lake is fairly isolated. Nobody could say he wasn't there all the while, if the rangers found him there when we asked them, my God, to break the news—"

"Sure," said Mr. Walters. "Let the neighbors here see him drive off, Monday around noon. After he'd dealt with Margaret he walked up to where he could get a bus—even a cab, buses maybe not running that time o' night—get back to West Drive. And he stayed right with his wife the next three days, inside. His car left somewhere, few streets over—he'd move it every so often. Maybe he kept her doped with something so he didn't have to keep her tied—"

"The autopsy said traces of barbiturates—but he said she'd been nursing a cold. I never thought—"

"Uh-huh. And/or tied up, and he'd feed her a bit because otherwise—"

"Orange juice and beef broth," said Clock, "and I thought—nursing the cold, liquids and— And goddamn it, goddamn the press," he added suddenly. "They printed nearly every detail of those assaults, and we didn't think it mattered—just help to alert possible victims—but *I* helped him explain the one little slip he made! Those women he tied up—the Masked Monster

—they couldn't drive, and two of them didn't know how to shift. And when I asked him about that, I made him a present of the fact and he promptly said Lucille couldn't shift gears either. Of course— And the stains on her clothes, and now I think—" He looked at Fran. "Damn it, I thought she'd been wearing old clothes, just sitting around the house, but now— Her stockings didn't match. Different colors. And different colors in her underwear. I don't claim to know much about female clothes, but she had, I seem to recall, a lot of different colors on, navy-blue shoes and a black—"

"Well, of course no woman at all conscious of clothes would wear those together," said Fran.

"Interesting," said the old man dryly. "One thing they do know about Horvath, he's color-blind."

"Oh!" said Fran. "Oh, I see. He picked out the clothes and—"

"I'd have a guess," said Clock, "he'd stopped giving her dope the last day or so. He wouldn't want it to show at the autopsy. Just had her tied up. But that poor damned woman—four days —you'd have thought she'd have tried, but of course between him and the barbiturates, she wouldn't have a chance—"

"I tell you, he's a canny one," said the old man. "He had to take a chance with Margaret, smudge the steering wheel— probably wearing gloves—take the chance she drove in gloves. He didn't spot those shoes in her car, realize she usually changed shoes to drive. He didn't dare to stay too long there— probably fetched along the blunt instrument, hammer from the house or something. But with his wife—"

"He knew the vicinity to leave her, damn it, because that was in all the papers. Somewhere near the Stack. And goddamn it, we swallowed it without batting an eye—it never crossed my mind that—"

"Never would have," said Jesse in awe, "if Margaret hadn't taken a hand—and our Sherlock got the message."

"We weren't quite as smart as she thought we'd be, hey? It

was the best she could do—groggy as she was—hoping *Master Detective*'d point us in the right direction."

"What a woman," said Jesse reverently. *"A woman of valor who can find? Her price is far above rubies."*

"Amen," said the old man, and drained his glass. "Now you go get him, Andrew. The Feds'll help you."

And Martha Weglund said, "Lucille? Celia? Some name like that—I think it was Mrs. Klein, or was it Mrs. Adams, came and spoke to Margaret, said she must come and meet— No, I didn't know Mrs. Kane."

Mrs. Rathbone said, "Lucille Kane? Why yes, she was at the reception with her husband—nice-looking man, I hadn't met him before— A terrible tragedy that was, her getting killed just a few days later by that— What? A cold? Why, no, she said she was feeling better than she had in years, poor woman—"

The man who owned a little grocery store in the small community of Crystal Lake, in the Angeles Forest, said sure, Mr. Kane had been at his cabin from that Monday to Friday. He'd stopped by to stock up on groceries about four o'clock that Monday, they'd had a little argument about the date, reason he remembered. Mr. Kane had been coming up to his cabin, on and off for a few days, for a couple of years. And on Friday these rangers had come by, asked where to find him. Well, he hadn't *seen* Mr. Kane since Monday, but the rangers found him right there at his cabin, so—

They never got a confession out of Eugene Horvath. They picked him up, living quietly at Lucille Kane's house on West Drive: just waiting until her orthodox will got out of probate and he could legally claim her substantial property. (Nobody would be surprised when he sold the house and moved away.) And they would never, probably, know just how many legal wives Horvath had accounted for—the small snug substantial properties, the sad accidents or simulated burglaries, and the

231

bereft widower drifting away from the scene of sorrow. In the three cases they knew of, husband and wife had made wills in each other's favor, and what more natural?

And Tarrytown had priority on Horvath; probably he'd never come to trial for Margaret Williams and Lucille at all.

The sole comment the local cops and the Feds heard from Horvath was, "That goddamned meddling old maid! By God, if she fingered me, I did for her good! But just how the hell *did* she finger me, for God's sake?"

Horvath, thinking he was safe—he had shut up the meddling old maid. He hadn't reckoned on Margaret's last-ditch desperate wit—or their aged Sherlock.

"All that stuff in the warehouse," said Jesse. "The Goodwill, I said. Furniture, clothes—parcel it out the way she wanted, sure. But you know something? I think I'd like to have something—chair or bookcase or whatever—as a keepsake for our Margaret. Quite a female, Nell."

"She was," agreed Nell soberly, pulling Athelstane's ears. "What Edgar said, Jesse. You never know what a person is, in themselves—until the chips are down."

"Moment of truth," said Jesse. "At that, I guess we don't need anything tangible to remember her, do we?"

Clock came home late, frustrated and tired. The extradition papers had come through on Horvath. Horvath had posed quite a lot of work for L.A., and all to help out New York. Occasionally they got the offbeat things like Horvath; inevitably they also got the day-to-day crime that led only to the leg work, the tedious routine.

"Tough day?" he repeated to Fran's question. "The usual unidentified body. New York cops in with the extradition papers on Horvath. Another suicide. A knifing on the Row—"

"Darling Andrew, forget the office. I want you to look at this

232

house on Hillcrest, only about six blocks from Jesse and Nell—on account of—"

"Baby-sitting. Being forehanded, my God."

"Well, it's a nice house. Four bedrooms and den, Spanish—"

"*Four*— What are you plotting? Two is quite enough, one of each, and—"

"Darling Andrew—"

"Damn it," said Clock, "I wish we could have had him to try. Horvath. That damn— And if he gets some smart shyster back there to look for the loopholes—"

"At least," said Fran, "we got something out of it, didn't we? Legacy from Miss Williams."

Sally trotted in, rolling bowlegged, from her dinner in the kitchen. "And dinner in two shakes," added Fran. Sally bounced at Clock and he picked her up. "She needs combing," he said. "Her coat's all—"

"Competition," said Fran, amused. "I'll brush her after dinner."

"Don't be silly, Frances, competition be—" But Clock stroked Sally fondly. She curled herself round on his lap in the armchair, gave his hand an absent lick, and drifted to sleep contentedly.